BERTIE
AND THE
SEVEN BODIES

BY THE SAME AUTHOR

On the Edge
Bertie and the Tinman
Butchers and Other Stories of Crime
Rough Cider
Keystone
The False Inspector Dew
Waxwork
Swing, Swing Together
A Case of Spirits
Invitation to a Dynamite Party
Mad Hatter's Holiday
Abracadaver
The Detective Wore Silk Drawers
Wobble to Death

PETER LOVESEY

THE MYSTERIOUS PRESS

New York • London
Tokyo • Sweden • Milan

The Mysterious Press, 129 West 56th Street, New York, N.Y. 10019

Printed in the United States of America
First Printing: January 1990
10 9 8 7 6 5 4 3 2 1

Library of Congress Cataloging-in-Publication Data

Lovesey, Peter.
Bertie and the seven bodies / Peter Lovesey.
p. cm.
ISBN 0-89296-399-9
I. Title.
PR6062.O86B46 1990 89-12405
823′.914—dc20 CIP

A Note to the Reader

In the first volume of the so-called *Detective Memoirs of King Edward VII*, entitled *Bertie and the Tinman*, the reader was cautioned that it was extremely doubtful whether "Bertie," either as Prince of Wales or King, ever found the time or inclination to write a book. It follows that it is even less likely that he wrote a second volume.

Unless one believes in automatic writing, everything in these pages should be taken as fiction.

BERTIE
AND THE
SEVEN BODIES

1

Splendid! You have opened my book.

You are curious about the mystery of the seven bodies and my part in it. If I am mistaken, forgive me. I bid you good day. Kindly close the book and turn to some memoirs of a less sensational character. I recommend *Leaves from the Journal of Our Life in the Highlands*, by my dear mother, Her Majesty, Queen Victoria.

If I am correct in my deduction, bravo! Let us plunge together into the plot. It began innocently enough one spring morning in the year 1890.

"So! You have resolved to go back to nature, Alix," I announced with the air of one who has uncovered an intimate secret.

My pretty wife, the Princess of Wales, shot me a startled look. She was seated at the window in her sitting room at Sandringham. "What did you say, Bertie?"

"You are going back to nature. I perceive that you have finally decided to shed your steel appendage."

She frowned. "Is this a riddle?"

"I mean your bustle, of course."

"Bertie!"

"You can't deny it. This afternoon you wrote to your dressmaker informing her that you propose to wear the new narrow skirts in future."

She was open-mouthed with amazement.

Not without satisfaction, I said, "If you want to know how I made this discovery, I deduced it."

"*Deduced* it?"

"I observed what I saw before me and applied the scientific principles of . . . deduction." I paused, to let the word linger in the air for a moment. Then I directed my gaze across the room. "Upon your writing desk is a candle. The wick is blackened, but the candle is not much used. On a bright afternoon such as this, why should anyone light a candle except to melt sealing wax? I deduce that you wrote a letter. How simple when it is explained!"

Alix said, "There is more to explain than that."

"Quite so. On the floor to your left is an open copy of yesterday's *Illustrated London News* from which you have removed a page. The torn edge is clearly visible and so are the words 'Opposite: the new straight skirt as designed by Monsieur Worth.' So the chain of reasoning is complete. You saw the picture of the latest fashion from Paris and resolved forthwith to tear it from the magazine and send it to your dressmaker."

She rocked with laughter. "Oh, Bertie!"

"Do my methods amuse you?"

"You couldn't be more mistaken. I haven't the slightest desire to wear straight skirts. They make me look like a beanpole. And I haven't written a single letter all day. I was sewing. At some stage I dropped my thimble. I couldn't see it anywhere on the floor so I lit the candle to look under the writing desk. Some candle grease unfortunately dripped onto the carpet, so I ripped a sheet from the magazine to clean it up before it hardened."

"Alexandra, are you poking fun at me?"

"If you don't believe me, look in the wastepaper basket."

I looked, saw that she was right and emitted a bellow of annoyance.

Alix contemplated her fingernails. "Bertie dear, do you think it is wise to persist in this notion that you can be a detective?"

The question nettled me, I admit. I responded sharply, "Damnit, one small oversight and I'm branded as a failure. If I'd looked in the wretched wastepaper basket my chain of reasoning would have been different, altogether different. I'm forever being told to find intelligent pursuits and when I do I can't rely on my own wife for encouragement." I turned on my heel and marched out.

Alix knows that my temper is short and so is its duration.

By the next post I received an invitation that altogether restored my humor. A grand *battue* at Desborough in October. Desborough—what a prospect! After Sandringham and Holkham, there's no better shooting in the kingdom. Nine hundred acres in Buckinghamshire. Moreover Desborough Hall is one of the great houses of England, with Tudor banqueting hall, ballroom, gun room, chapel and ninety-odd bedrooms.

"I can't resist it," I told Alix over dinner. "I shall accept."

"Who does the invitation come from?" she enquired.

"Lady Amelia Drummond."

She shifted her head to see around the floral arrangement. "An invitation to shoot from a lady?"

"The widow of Freddie Drummond. Haven't you met her?" I heaved a long sigh to signal sympathy for our prospective hostess. "Perhaps you don't recall? She's easily forgotten, poor soul, rather plain in looks, but making superhuman efforts to keep Desborough on the social map. One feels obliged to show support."

"When did Lord Drummond pass away?"

"Last winter, in tragic circumstances. He was gored by a bull."

"How horrid!"

"Yes, he was a frightful mess, they said. He lingered for six weeks, covered in bandages. Then one morning he sat up, uttered something rather vulgar and breathed his last."

"I didn't catch that. What did he mutter?" Sometimes dear Alix trades on her deafness.

"I think it was 'Oh, bother.'"

"I don't call *that* vulgar. I've heard far worse from Cocky." Cocky is Alix's pet cockatoo. She gave me a searching look and then took a spoonful of Scotch broth. In a few moments she casually enquired, "About what age would Lady Drummond be, Bertie?"

I hedged. "You could look her up in Debrett. I'm not much of a judge."

"Younger than me?"

"Possibly."

"Under thirty-five?"

"Alix, I haven't the faintest idea. Is it important?"

"Conceivably."

Later that afternoon she cornered me at my writing desk. From somewhere in the clutter of her rooms she had unearthed a copy of *The Tatler* with a studio portrait of Lady Amelia, a ravishing dark-haired beauty in a ball gown cut perilously low. "Bertie, I don't know how you could describe her as plain."

I replied somewhat obliquely, "Where do you keep these old magazines? It smells so musty it must be ten years old at least."

"I looked her up in Debrett, as you suggested. She is still only twenty-seven."

I shut the magazine and handed it back to her. "I suppose you're going to try and stop my sport—just because the invitation comes from a young widow of tolerably good looks."

My dear wife gave me an indulgent smile. "Not at all. When have I ever stood in your way? Of course you shall have your shoot. And I shall come too and offer some sisterly sympathy to Lady Drummond."

"*You* intend to come?"

She smiled faintly this time. "One feels obliged to show support."

And so the visit was set in motion. Francis Knollys, my private secretary, wrote to advise our hostess of my requirements: a suite comprising bedrooms for each of us, dressing rooms and sitting room. Also accommodation for our retinue of equerries, ladies-in-waiting, footmen, valets, loaders, coachmen, grooms and a member of the Household Police, whose duty it is to guard us from anarchists. Then the guest list had to be approved, a crucial matter as it ultimately turned out. Of sixteen names submitted, I struck out three immediately. If one is planning an agreeable week in the country, one doesn't want to rub shoulders with people who have given offense in the past. Nor, if one wishes to shoot, is one obliged to stand comparison with *all* the best guns in the country.

We were left with thirteen names.

"Would you like me to join the party, sir?" Knollys knows my superstitious nature and volunteered at once.

"No," I informed him. "We have more than enough men in this party. We must cross out someone else. Who have we got? Eight gentlemen and five ladies. The balance is fraught with disaster. Who is this reverend fellow, Humphrey Paget? He doesn't sound like a shooting man."

"The family chaplain, sir."

"Ah."

"He buried the late Lord Drummond."

"The best day's work he ever did, from what I remember of Freddie. Better not object to a man of the cloth, I suppose. Who else have we got?"

"Marcus Pelham, Lady Drummond's brother. I presume he's there to perform the duties of host."

"That's as may be, but is he safe?"

"Safe, sir?"

"I wouldn't care to stand with a man who isn't safe."

"I understand he's an expert marksman, sir." Knollys glanced at the list again. “Then there’s His Grace the Duke of Bournemouth, who lives on the neighboring estate.”

“Dear old Jerry. Good man. Hopeless shot.”

“Not safe, sir?”

“Not in the least.”

“Shall I strike him out?”

“Better not. The list is pretty undistinguished without him. I’ll make sure he’s well down the line from me.”

“Claude Bullivant. He’s a commoner.”

“Ah, but he’s a card. I like his sense of humor. This is getting damnably difficult.”

“There’s Colonel C.D. Roberts, V.C.”

“A V.C., do you say? That’s our man. Blackball him. We can do without a hero turning the ladies’ heads, eh, Francis?”

So the number was painlessly reduced to twelve. I had already run through the ladies’ names. Two I hadn’t previously met, which lent a certain relish to the week in prospect.

The summer ran its all-too-familiar course: Ascot, Epsom, Goodwood, Cowes. I anticipated the shoot in Buckinghamshire as a change from my customary October *battue* at Sandringham or Balmoral. And a change is what I got. A never-to-be-forgotten week.

2

Those of my readers who haven't seen Desborough for themselves may care to be informed that it is approached by a mile-long avenue of beeches. It is an extremely large, moated, brick-built Elizabethan mansion much extended by its eighteenth century owners, who added a monstrous Palladian portico at the front and two extra wings. They also coated the Tudor brickwork in stucco, something I find as incomprehensible as putting a pretty face behind a *yashmak*.

We were graciously received. As custom decrees, our host and hostess, Lady Drummond and her brother Marcus, stood at the entrance flanked by their principal servants. Then in a charming, youthful manner Lady Amelia came running down the stone steps to greet us, bunching her skirt for ease of movement and affording glimpses of slender, white-stockinged ankles.

Beside me, Alix murmured, "No longer in mourning, it appears."

The young widow curtsied and gave us her well-rehearsed greeting. She had a most engaging voice, with what I can only describe as a gurgle when she spoke certain sounds. "Welcome to Desborough, Your Royal Highnesses. I hope your journey was agreeable."

"It is becoming so by the minute," I said.

"Your suite is ready, sir, and your servants are installed."

"Capital, my dear. What are the rules of the house?"

She looked uncertain how to respond, so I jocularly explained, "For example, my mother, the Queen, has a horror of smoking, and prohibits it absolutely indoors. At Windsor one evening, the German Ambassador, Count Hatzfeldt-Wildenburg, who cannot live without a cigarette, poor fellow, was discovered in his bedroom lying on the hearth rug in his pajamas, blowing smoke up the chimney. I hope I may light up an occasional cigar in your house without performing gymnastics."

I had brought the dimples briefly to her cheeks and now she found that winsome voice again. "No, sir, there are no rules."

"No rules at all?" I arched an eyebrow. "Isn't that rather reckless?"

She colored charmingly.

Then Alix remarked, "Rules are unnecessary when people know how to behave. Shall we allow Lady Drummond to show us to our rooms?"

Our hostess had spared nothing in making us welcome. Each suite was newly decorated, Alix's in cornflower blue, mine in green and white stripes. Log fires were blazing merrily and producing pretty effects on the crystal decanters.

"When is dinner?" I asked Lady Amelia.

"At half past eight, sir. I would like to present my other guests at eight, if it pleases you."

"I am sure it will please us enormously."

When we were alone, Alix asked what time we were wanted.

"Seven," I said firmly. It's a constant battle with Alix. At Sandringham I have all the clocks permanently put forward half an hour.

She gave me a suspicious look. "That seems rather early."

"It's the country life. Everyone eats early and retires before midnight."

The result was that we got downstairs at twenty past eight. I spotted a few familiar faces in the anteroom: Sir George Holdfast, of Holdfast Assurance, and Lady Moira, his wife (good people, supporters of many charitable causes, but *so* staid); Claude Bullivant, once the most eligible bachelor in London; and dear old Jerry Gribble, the Duke of Bournemouth, hand on the shoulder of a suit of armor, chatting noisily to a pretty young woman in black velvet. Trust Jerry to lose no time, I thought.

Our hostess made a deep curtsey that Alix later described as theatrical. It didn't offend me in the least. I seem to remember that Lady Amelia's dinner gown was apple green, or it might have been pink. I retain a very clear picture of the corsage, which I am certain was of cream satin, cut distractingly low and decorated with pearl beads. She had her hair bunched high and adorned with a posy of white blossoms. I do like to see a lady's neck and shoulders unadorned except for a few pearls.

Alix said pointedly that we ought to meet the Chaplain.

The Reverend Humphrey Paget demonstrably wasn't one of those clerics who practice fasting as religious observance. He was "Broad" Church, if ever a man was. And we had more in common than that, for he claimed to be a sportsman, in spite of his girth.

"An angler, if I am not mistaken," said I at once. "Did you land many trout today, Padre?"

His face was a study.

"Forgive me," I said. "I have recently interested myself in the science of deduction."

"Deduction, sir?"

"Yes. That distinct and even discoloration around the base of your heels suggests that you recently stood for some time in soft mud. Moreover, your toe caps, although splendidly polished, have several dull patches that could only have been made by splashes of water, say when a catch is landed. These indications, taken together with the knowledge that the River Ouse nearby is well stocked with trout, and the season ends on Saturday next, compel me irresistibly to the conclusion that you are a trout fisherman."

He glanced down at the telltale shoes. Then cleared his throat. "Your acuteness of observation is truly remarkable, Your Royal Highness."

"Anyone could do as well if he applied the method," I modestly remarked, passing on to another guest, a tall, pasty-faced young fellow with eyes like rock oysters. I should explain that the ordeal of meeting me has curious effects on some people. He was introduced as Mr. Wilfred Osgot-Edge, a poet.

"What's a poet doing at a shooting party—writing elegies on pheasants?" I jested.

He was tongue-tied, so Lady Amelia sprang to his assistance. "Wilfred also has the reputation of being the best shot in Buckinghamshire, sir."

"Good for you," I said generously. "A shooting poet."

"It is n-not so uncommon," he stuttered, then seemed unable to expand on the statement.

"Who else is there?" I asked. "I wouldn't care to hand dear old Tennyson a shotgun and stand nearby."

My wife, ever sympathetic towards the nervously inclined, said, "Lord Byron was a sportsman."

"And much else besides." I tried to animate Osgot-Edge with a nudge from my elbow. "Have you noticed how the ladies go pink at the mention of Byron? I really ought to read him."

The poet wound himself up. "I m-must say I like By- By-"

"Bicycling? You *are* an all-rounder."

The poet had no more to contribute. Casting about for deliverance, I caught the eye of Jerry Gribble, the Duke of Bournemouth, still in close proximity to his companion in velvet. "Jerry, you old bore," I shouted across the room. "The lady and I have been winking at each other for the past ten minutes and I still don't know her name."

She was brought to meet me, and I saw at once that this was no shrinking violet. The walk, the shining eyes, the knowing smile, the curtsey—all sang out "actress." Now I'm not one of those who regard treading the boards as the next thing to streetwalking. I pride myself on my encouragement of the dramatic arts.

"May I present Miss Queenie Chimes, sir?"

"Miss *what*?"

The lady giggled. "Queenie, sir. Queenie Chimes."

I said, "Queenie? Queenie? What sort of name is that? I didn't see it on the guest list."

Jerry coughed nervously. "My mistake, sir. I should have said Victoria."

I frowned.

Miss Chimes explained. "Girls who are called Victoria are nicknamed Queenie, sir, after her Majesty."

"Thank you," I told her formally. "The connection is clear to me."

She said, "Do you think it common?"

I stared at her. I am not used to people addressing me so directly. I said, "As a matter of fact, I have a daughter of my own called Victoria"—I paused—"but we don't call her Queenie." And then I smiled.

Everyone smiled.

I resumed, "You're quite right, my dear. Victoria is a common name. I also have a sister Vicky, and a niece Vicky. Very common. Very confusing. I shall be happy to call you Queenie. Altogether more distinguished."

Quick to sense my approval of the lady, Jerry Gribble took care to say, "Queenie and I are well acquainted. I would go so far as to describe myself as one of her patrons. She's with Irving at the Lyceum, you know. The great man personally thought of her stage name, didn't he, my dear? She was born Victoria Bell."

The lady gave me an endearing smile. "Bell . . . Chimes."

I chuckled. "I like it! Clever man, Irving. He obviously sees a fine future for you in his company."

"Oh, I don't know if I shall be good enough, Your Royal Highness," Queenie spoke up. She had an alluring, husky voice, as if she spent her mornings drilling the Irish Guards.

"I'm all for modesty," said I. "Are you currently in a production, Miss Chimes?"

"I am preparing a part, sir." Her eyelashes fluttered.

I glanced behind me to make sure Alix was still busy with the poet and said, "Would you care to read it to me?"

At which Jerry said, "It's a non-speaking role, sir. Have you met Miss Dundas yet?"

"Miss Dundas?"

"The Amazon explorer, Isabella Dundas, a most remarkable person."

At that point the announcement was made that dinner was served. Hastily the remaining guests, including Miss Dundas the Amazon explorer, were presented to me without time to discuss their remarkable attributes. We formed the procession, Alix, the lady of highest rank, on the right arm of young Pelham, leading us in, the rest following, and Lady Amelia and I last.

The banqueting hall is one of the notable features of Desborough, having somehow escaped three centuries of so-called improvements to the rest of the house. The only embellishments to the original oak and plaster are the escutcheons displayed high on the walls, the heraldic bearings of the Drummonds and their ancestors. Amelia (we agreed to be informal) pointed out her own. As a Pelham, she had a most exotic coat of arms with griffins and birds that I didn't recognize. Alix tried to convince me later that they were harpies.

The hall was such a barn of a place that Amelia had thoughtfully located the dinner table at the far end, where a grand fire was blazing and screens were strategically placed to keep out drafts. A small string orchestra played zestfully as we stepped between the ranks of liveried servants to take our places at the oval table.

The Chaplain said the grace and we were seated. Amelia was to my left, Alix to my right and Queenie the actress directly opposite me, too far off, I estimated, for our feet to make contact unless we sank down in our chairs with our chins resting on the table.

Queenie was flanked by Jerry Gribble and Claude Bullivant, and it was Bullivant, a delightful, black-haired rogue with a moustache as curly as a candelabra who opened the conversation. "If I were a padre, I think I should object to saying grace on a Monday."

"Why is that?" someone asked.

"Monday, surely, is a padre's day off. He's busy all weekend, marrying people on Saturday and taking services on the Sabbath. He's entitled to a rest."

The Reverend Paget gave a half smile and said nothing, so Jerry Gribble took up the running. "The Church is a calling, not a profession. A churchman can never have a day off like the rest of us."

"Oh, he *needs* a day to himself," piped up Lady Holdfast from one end of the table. She was desperately dull, poor old thing.

"I'm sure our friend the Chaplain isn't deprived of recreation," said I, mindful of the trout fishing.

"Perhaps he would care to enlighten us as to how he amuses himself when he is not at his devotions," suggested Bullivant and all eyes turned on the Reverend Paget.

"I, em, fit in a few private pastimes when time permits," he said. He seemed not to want to own up to the angling.

"Yes, but do you ever get a day off?" persisted Bullivant, wicked fellow, unwilling to let the Chaplain off the hook, so to speak. "How did you pass your time today, for example?"

"Today?" The Chaplain wiped his mouth with the edge of his table napkin. "I was, em, outdoors this morning."

"Fishing for trout?" said Alexandra.

He went extremely pink and twisted the napkin as if he were wringing out washing.

"Out with it, Padre," said Bullivant. "A man of God has a perfect right to fish. St. Peter was a fisherman. Is that what you do?"

"I may have given that impression. Inadvertently." The Chaplain now had his fist wound up in the napkin. "To be truthful, I was officiating at a funeral."

"A *funeral*?" said I.

"And this afternoon?" Alix asked the Chaplain after a pause.

"A baptism."

Mud on his heels and drops of water on his toe caps. I was forced to conclude that I hadn't altogether mastered the science of deduction. To avoid one of Alix's looks, I turned to our hostess and congratulated her on the soup.

This markedly relaxed the atmosphere. The diners turned as one to their neighbors and struck up conversations. I learned from our dear little hostess that she expected a record bag from the week's shooting. The woods were said to be better stocked than the head gamekeeper could remember for years and it appeared that most of Buckinghamshire would be beating for us.

"Curiously enough, I have never shot here in October," I told Amelia. "I once had a day's cock-shooting after Christmas. That must have been when your father-in-law was alive. So you see, most of these guns around the table have the advantage of me. Your brother Marcus, Jerry Gribble, Claude Bullivant, they're all regulars. I don't know about the poet."

"Wilfred? He was at last year's shoot," she said. "He's quick and accurate. But you're wrong about my brother. Marcus was never welcomed here while Freddie was alive."

"They fell out?"

She hesitated. "There was some jealousy between them."

"Over you?"

"Marcus and I were very close as children, sir. Don't misunderstand me, but I think he felt that Freddie broke up the family when he married me."

I glanced at the others along the table. Couldn't see much family resemblance when I studied Marcus Pelham. He had straight, straw-colored hair and one of those pink faces that turn bright red in the sun, or under scrutiny from the Prince of Wales. "And now that you're alone in the world, he's supporting you on occasions such as this. Good man," I said, privately thinking he ought to be tarred and feathered.

I refused to let it spoil my appetite. After the *consommé* came Dover sole poached in Chablis, followed by the dish that never fails to please me: ptarmigan pie. Presently something was said across the table about sleeping in strange houses. It's curious, isn't it, how even when half a dozen conversations are in progress around the table one intriguing remark secures everybody's attention? We all stopped talking except Jerry Gribble.

"Personally," he said, "I never have any trouble. I'm used to sleeping in strange beds."

"Ladies, take note," murmured Bullivant.

"That isn't what I meant. I've slept under canvas, on a train, aboard a steamship, under the stars—"

"In a haunted house?" put in Queenie the actress.

"Not to my knowledge—until tonight," said Jerry.

"Good God—this house doesn't have a ghost, does it?" said Sir George Holdfast in some alarm. His wife gave a horrified squeak.

"Oh, it must have," said Jerry, straight-faced. "In three hundred years it must have acquired one."

"A resident spook!" said Bullivant with relish.

Around me the unease was palpable. It was all very well joking about ghosties over dinner, but before long we'd be shown to our bedrooms by candlelight along dark corridors.

Osgot-Edge the poet spoke up. "I don't believe in gho- gho-"

"Going to bed in haunted houses?" said Bullivant. "Nor I, old man. I shall sleep in an armchair by the fire. You're welcome to join me."

Beside me, Lady Amelia drew herself up to speak. "I know you only say it to amuse, gentlemen, but there's something I would like to say in all seriousness. There is no ghost of Desborough Hall. If there was, I should have heard of it—and I wouldn't have remained here, least of all invited my dearest friends to stay."

"Well said, my dear," I told her and clapped my hands. Everyone did likewise—even Bullivant, looking sheepish—and the congenial atmosphere was quite restored.

Over the roast lamb I surveyed the party and amused myself pairing them off. Queenie of the Lyceum had, regrettably, to be linked with Jerry Gribble; it was perfectly obvious that she had been invited at his request. The Holdfasts looked likely to live up to their name, and they were such a dreary pair that none of us would object. Claude Bullivant was resolutely hacking a path to Miss Dundas, the Amazon explorer, though it was far from clear how she would receive him. The set of her mouth was daunting and her eyes glittered ominously. It crossed my mind that she might be stalking bigger game than Bullivant; once or twice she had looked my way and smiled.

As for the rest, I absolved the Chaplain and Osgot-Edge the nervous poet from any amorous intent and I could see that Marcus Pelham had eyes only for his sister.

What of the winsome Amelia herself, then? Up to now, she'd been scrupulously charming to everyone, as a hostess should. If you want to know whether I bedded her before the end of the week you had better read on. But one thing you must have gathered: noctambulations would be infernally difficult under Alix's nose and with a jealous brother roaming the house.

I was inquiring from Miss Chimes about Irving's latest production when there was an alarming cry from Lady Holdfast: "A bomb!"

Fortunately, Inspector Sweeney, my bodyguard, wasn't in the

room looking for anarchists, or the cook's *pièce de résistance* might have been grabbed and flung out of the nearest window. It was a *bombe glacée Dame Blanche*, a veritable monument of ice cream and fruit carried high on a silver charger by the cook himself in his tall hat to the strains of "See the Conquering Hero Comes."

I am at pains to describe faithfully what happened. The mood around the table, as I recall it, was high-spirited. We shouted, "Bravo!" and the cook warmed his knife over a flame before making the first cut. Then the portions were served. Jerry Gribble joked that this was obviously the ghost of Desborough Hall, the *Dame Blanche* herself. Alix asked for a portion with a cherry. Osgot-Edge knocked over his wine in the excitement.

Then Queenie Chimes pitched forward and collapsed—without a murmur—facedown in the *bombe*.

3

Such was the shock around the table that several of us cried out, "Good Lord!" in chorus.

Jerry was the first to come to the aid of Miss Chimes. He placed his hand under her forehead and raised her head.

I had the front view from across the table. The lady's face was thickly coated with white ice cream. Chunks were dropping grotesquely onto the black velvet of her dress. I may say that I've seen the fair sex in disarray of one sort and another on a number of occasions. A lady marked with mud or worse is a not uncommon sight in the hunting field. But one doesn't expect such mishaps at the dinner table. The effect upon me—and I am sure upon us all—was profoundly disturbing.

Jerry's levelheadedness in the emergency was admirable, if unexpected. He was putting his napkin to good use. As he wiped away the ice cream he disturbed one of Miss Chimes's eyelids, and I was alarmed to see almost nothing but white, the eye having rolled upwards. Most of us were on our feet, wanting to assist in some way. "Dead to the world," Jerry said. "Does anyone have smelling salts?"

Lady Holdfast produced a bottle of sal volatile from her handbag and Jerry removed the stopper and waved it under Queenie Chimes's nose. Without result.

There was no shortage of suggestions.

"Her nostrils must be blocked."

"We can't stand on ceremony—loosen her stays."

"See if her pulse is beating."

"She ought to lie flat."

"Better s-send for a d-d-"

"There's a sofa through there."

Claude Bullivant scooped the insensible young lady up in his arms and carried her into the anteroom where the sofa was. Amelia unbuttoned the dress at the back, and Miss Dundas the explorer showed how resourceful her Amazon experience had made her. She had fetched the chef's knife from the banqueting hall and she now proceeded to cut the laces of Miss Chimes's stays.

However there was still no apparent response from the patient. It seemed to me that her skin was too rosy for this to be a simple case of swooning, but the almost pure white of the ice cream still remaining on her hair and clothes may have overemphasized her color.

Then Jerry announced, "Her pulse is beating quite fast."

Everyone voiced their relief.

"Fast—is that a good sign?" I put in as a caution, and no one seemed to know the answer.

"Better send for a d-d-"

"He's right," said Bullivant. "She doesn't seem to be coming round. Suppose it's her heart?"

"God, no!" said Jerry. "She's far too young for that."

"You can't be certain," Bullivant pointed out. "I knew a fellow who rowed at stroke for Oxford in the boat race and collapsed on Paddington Station six months later. Twenty-two years old. His heart gave out."

Holdfast said, "But she hasn't rowed the boat race. All she did was sit down to dinner."

"I was simply making the point that youth is no proof against a dicky heart."

Jerry looked up in alarm. "Do you really think so?"

Amelia said, "I'm going to send for the doctor."

"No." Jerry got up from his kneeling position beside the sofa. "There's a quicker way. I'll take her there myself. We can make her comfortable in the carriage."

Servants were sent to alert the grooms and the coachman and fetch blankets and pillows.

Amelia turned to her brother. "Marcus, you'd better go with His Grace."

"He's got the coachman to help him," Marcus pointed out, rudely, I thought.

"Absolutely right," insisted Jerry, a gentleman through and through. "Don't break up the party. I'll manage perfectly well."

In commendably short time, Jerry's landau was brought to the front of the building. A footman carried Miss Chimes down the steps and lifted her inside and Jerry climbed in. We all watched in tight-lipped concern until the coach lamp had disappeared from sight.

"Wretched luck!" said Holdfast.

"Dr. Perkins will know exactly what to do," Amelia endeavored to reassure us. "He's terribly nice."

"Whatever it is, I hope it isn't contagious like the cholera," said Lady Holdfast.

Her husband said, "Moira, you've never seen a case of cholera in your life."

Distinctly subdued, we trooped back to the banqueting hall, where the servants had cleaned up the mess and rearranged the table, removing the places occupied by Miss Chimes and Jerry, and also our plates. Our portions of the *bombe*, of course, had long since melted. However, the chef, stout fellow, sent up a delicious-looking chocolate balthazar in its place.

"I'm in such a state of nerves," Lady Holdfast ungratefully declared, "that I couldn't possibly face food."

"Well, I can," I informed her. There are times when a firm declaration from me has a good effect on people, and this was one. We all cleared our plates, including Moira Holdfast, and some of us had second helpings.

It was during that polite interval between the finish of dessert and the withdrawal of the ladies that the house steward stepped forward and spoke confidentially to Amelia. I assumed at the time that it had something to do with the serving of coffee.

Thinking of my cigar, I eased back in my chair to afford Amelia a sight of Alix. The nod was given and the four ladies rose, drew on their gloves and removed to the drawing room.

Once we men had closed ranks and lit up, I remarked, "Pity this happened. I thought the young lady looked perfectly bonny when we were introduced. Has anyone met her before?"

The response was negative all round.

"I gather she's an actress, sir," said Holdfast.

"Presumably invited at Jerry Gribble's suggestion," added Bullivant.

"I doubt it," said Marcus Pelham. "My sister is perfectly capable of drawing up a guest list that pleases all concerned. She takes a particular pride in keeping *au fait* with the latest liaisons."

There were some raised eyebrows at that last comment.

Bullivant fingered the tip of his moustache. "*There's* food for thought, gentlemen." His brown eyes glittered. "I wonder . . ."

"You wonder what?" said Holdfast.

"I wonder which of us has prior claim on our lady of the Amazon."

"Who is that?"

"You know who I mean—the intrepid explorer, Miss Dundas. Which of us is to be the lucky man? What's the matter—are we all too shy to speak up? Well, in the absence of any other offer she's welcome to beat a path to my . . ." Bullivant's words trailed away as some awful possibility occurred to him. He coughed, glanced towards me and said, "Joking, of course, sir."

I let him squirm for a moment. Then I said, "If it makes any difference whatsoever, Claude, Miss Dundas is completely unknown to me. I never met her before this evening."

He gave a high-pitched giggle of relief.

Young Pelham told us, "The lady is a guest in her own right."

I turned back to Bullivant. "There's a thought to conjure with, Claude: Are *you* a guest in your own right?"

Even the Chaplain joined in the laughter.

Considerately, we got up to join the ladies after one cigar and a glass of port. Left to their own devices after some upsetting occurrence, the fair sex can easily work themselves up into a lather.

Oddly enough, they appeared unruffled. I won't say that anyone made light of what had happened to Miss Chimes, but between us we kept the conversation flowing agreeably. Indeed, I'm sure it would have flowed all evening if only Lady Holdfast had not come up with her paralyzingly stupid suggestion.

"Why don't we have a recitation?"

"Do you mean *poetry*?" I asked, trying to make clear my distaste for such things.

"Certainly, Your Royal Highness. After all, we are fortunate in having a published poet among us. I'm sure we're all dying to hear Mr. Osgot-Edge's work," she plowed on. "I must admit, to my shame, that I, for one, haven't read a line that he's written, and I want to remedy the deficiency at the first opportunity."

Osgot-Edge was even more alarmed than I at this development. He turned crimson and started making incoherent noises.

"It seems he didn't bring his poems with him," I said thankfully.

"That's all right, sir. I have a copy," said Amelia, making her first gaffe of the week. She was disastrously eager to please. "I'll fetch it."

"Before you do . . ." I tossed in another difficulty. "Who will read them?"

Osgot-Edge, poor fellow, said, "I f-fear I c- c-"

I was just beginning to think I'd scuppered the suggestion when Amelia spoke up again.

"Humphrey, *you* can read beautifully."

"Who the deuce is Humphrey?" was on the tip of my tongue. In time, I observed the Chaplain beaming like a lighthouse. The Church and two determined ladies are more than a match for me. I capitulated.

"This one is called 'To an Obstinate Boy,'" the Reverend Humphrey Paget announced when the book had been fetched and we were settled.

> *"He fidgets when the grace is said,*
> *Wicked child.*
> *He should be fed his daily bread,*
> *In the wild,*
> *Where hungrily the king of beasts,*
> *Day by day,*
> *Is heard to roar before he feasts,*
> *'Let us prey.'"*

"Oh, my word," said Lady Holdfast.

"Ha, not bad," said Bullivant. "It's a pun. 'Let us prey.' How about that, Padre?"

"One applauds the intention of the poem without altogether approving of its phrasing," said the Chaplain guardedly.

I glanced across at Osgot-Edge to see how he took the criticism. He was sitting with his head back, staring at the ceiling.

Lady Holdfast said, "If you want the truth, I didn't really like it."

"What are you objecting to?" Bullivant asked her.

"It was too outspoken for me."

"Outspoken? I don't call that outspoken."

"Possibly not, but I think I shall retire before the next one is read out." Which was inexcusable, considering that she was chiefly responsible for inflicting the poetry on us.

"You can't go to bed, Moira," said her husband, quite properly alert to the discourtesy involved.

"Well, I shall retire to another room."

"The poems can't all be as strong meat as that, my dear. I'm sure the Chaplain can find one more suitable to read out."

"Why don't we ask Mr. Osgot-Edge to suggest one?" said Miss Dundas.

"That should see us through till bedtime," murmured Bullivant.

Whereupon I decided to speak up. "Better still, why don't we ask Mr. Osgot-Edge to make a selection of five or six poems that the Chaplain, if he is willing, can prepare, rehearse and read to us another evening?"

"Oh, splendid!" cried Sir George. "I second your suggestion, sir."

I gave a nod and pointed out that the suggestion originated with Miss Dundas. She rewarded me with a tilt of the eyebrow. Peculiar woman, I thought. Not unattractive, however.

The Chaplain and the poet seemed amenable, so we were spared more poetry, at least for the present evening. Instead I regaled the company with my experiences hunting tigers in India and, though I say it myself, it was a damn sight more entertaining.

We called a halt this side of midnight, needing to be up and about quite early next day for the shoot. After the good nights had been said and Amelia had escorted us to our suite I passed a short time gossiping with Alix before retiring to my bedchamber. In view of what follows I had better explain that we have slept in separate rooms for years.

Having confirmed what I would wear next day, I dismissed my valet, washed, prayed for my mother the Queen and good shooting in the morning and got into bed. A comfortable bed it was, too, a spacious four-poster evidently reupholstered for my visit. I do like a well-sprung mattress. My feet found the spot where the warming pan had been, and I believe I was asleep in ten minutes.

TUESDAY

4

The next thing I knew a voice close to my ear, a lady's voice, was whispering, "Are you awake?"

Woolly-minded from sleep, I struggled to make sense of it. I had difficulty remembering where I was, let alone whether I'd started the night with a companion. It was too dark to see much. Some hours to go until dawn. Was she a dream? I kept very still and listened.

She repeated, "Are you awake, sir?"

I said, "If we're on sufficiently intimate terms for you to visit me in bed, you'd better call me Bertie. Who are you?"

"Amelia Drummond . . . Bertie."

"Amelia." My brain stopped being bleary at once. I knew precisely what was happening. And on the first night! So bold! I wasn't sure whether to be flattered or alarmed. She was taking an appalling risk with Alix's bedroom just across the corridor.

She said, "I do apologize for disturbing you. I knocked twice, and I thought you must have heard."

She'd *knocked* on my door!

She asked, "May I light a candle, sir?"

"Bertie—and keep your voice down."

She whispered, "Bertie."

She said it rather fetchingly with that gurgling note in her voice. I responded in a tone equally warm, "Well, Amelia, do we really require a light?"

"I think we do." Amelia cleared her throat. "I regret to say that I am the bearer of bad news." She struck a match and I saw that she was standing beside the bed fully dressed. Bad news indeed.

"What is it?"

"Jerry Gribble has just returned. I sat up to wait for him." Her chin trembled. "Miss Chimes is dead."

"Dead?" I sat up straight.

"She failed to recover consciousness."

"Oh, my hat! That's dreadful. What was it—her heart?"

"I don't know. Jerry thought you should be told at once. He's outside."

"Call him in. You did the proper thing, my dear. Absolutely the proper thing. Forgive me for appearing so confused. Would you hand me my dressing gown?"

Jerry entered the room looking grim. He stood at the foot of my bed with hunched shoulders, taking long, heavy breaths.

I told him to sit on the bed. "My dear fellow, this is too appalling . . . ghastly. When exactly did it happen?"

"Before I reached the doctor's," he told me. "She died in my arms, poor child. Some popping sounds came from her mouth. Like turning off the gas. I knew she was going. I don't think she was in pain. I hope to God she wasn't."

"What a tragedy," I said. "Did the doctor give an opinion?"

"He said it was too early to be sure, but he suspected from my description that she had been in a state of coma, of uncertain origin."

"Coma?"

"She could have suffered a hemorrhage of the brain. I had to take her to the hospital. They'll carry out a postmortem later in the week." He covered his face. "I can't believe this has happened."

The poor fellow was ready to weep, so I did my best to keep him from breaking down by saying gently, "How long had you known her, Jerry?"

"Six months, I think, sir." He was having difficulty in speaking. "We met down in Kent at a cricket match."

"Ah, cricket." A less harrowing topic. "Was that Canterbury, by any chance?"

"No, Gravesend."

We couldn't get away from death. "Gravesend? I know the ground. I know Canterbury better."

"This was definitely Gravesend. The Thespians were playing a team got up by my former brother-in-law, Lord Peterkin. I didn't see much of the game once I got talking to Queenie. She came around the ground selling tickets for the Actors' Retirement Home—the tombola, I mean—and that was how we met. It's such a treat talking to a pretty young girl when you live alone in the world."

"It's a treat in any case, Jerry."

"I'm glad you understand, sir. And she didn't have designs on becoming a duchess. I made it abundantly clear that after two marriages gone to pot I wouldn't consider a third. She understood that."

Amelia spoke. "Jerry, her people will have to be told. Do you know who they are?"

Jerry made a dismissive gesture. "It's all right. She had no living relatives. She told me that herself. I'll arrange everything. I'll give her a decent funeral. Lord, to be talking about a funeral when a few hours ago she was sitting at dinner with us!"

I reached out and put a hand on his shoulder. "Jerry, I think you should have a stiff brandy and get to bed. There's nothing else you can do tonight."

He glanced towards Amelia. She cleared her throat, took a step closer to the bed and said, "With respect, sir, the reason we took the liberty of waking you was to find out your wishes."

"My wishes?"

"This tragic event casts a shadow over the party."

"Without a doubt," I agreed.

There was a moment's silence.

Amelia resumed, "We thought it proper to enquire whether you wished to call off the shoot."

"I see. Out of respect, do you mean?" It hadn't occurred to me. I pondered the matter. My first thought was to soldier on. That's the way of the Prince of Wales, even in adversity. Besides, my charming hostess had gone to no end of trouble and expense to arrange the *battue*. Eighteen months and more of preparation goes into any shoot worthy of the name.

Then I remembered how easily things can be misconstrued. I once got into no end of trouble with my dear mother the Queen for omitting to postpone the Marlborough House Ball when Arthur Stanley, the Dean of Westminster, died. Mama was very attached to the good Dean. What really put the lid on it was when I had the funeral brought forward to avoid a clash with the first day's racing at Goodwood.

Yes, this had to be thought about. On the other hand, the death of an unknown actress couldn't be compared with the passing of Dean Stanley. "What do you think, Jerry?" I asked.

After a moment's reflection he said, "I think Queenie would have wished for a quiet funeral, sir. If it gets out that she died at a house party at which you were present, all of Fleet Street will be there."

"By George, you're right! We don't want to give the press a field day. If I return home tomorrow, they'll want to know the reason why. Those blighters can make a scandal out of anything." I turned to Amelia. "My dear Lady Drummond, with your permission we'll proceed with the arrangements as planned."

"Certainly, sir, if that is your wish."

"I shall explain everything to your other guests in the morning. And Jerry . . ."

"Sir?"

"I shan't expect you to join the guns."

"Thank you, sir. I'll go into town and see the undertaker."

"Good man." I gave him a sympathetic smile. "These things happen. It was the hand of fate."

He got up and left the room. I put my hand to my mouth and yawned, ready for sleep again, and then realized that the candle was still alight on the chest of drawers. Amelia was about to follow Jerry through the door.

"Would you mind?" I asked. "The candle."

Somewhat to my surprise she shook her head and then put her finger to her lips like a conspirator. She meant to return after showing Jerry to his room.

Frisky young filly, I mused. After the distressing scene just enacted I can't imagine how she can be so—what is the word I'm groping for?—singleminded.

And you, dear reader, could be forgiven, nay, applauded, if you expected me to close the chapter here for reasons of good taste. However, I must continue, and insist that you read on. What transpired is not what either of us expected.

She returned, yes, after a short interval. I, meantime, had settled down in the bed, making extra room on the side nearest the door. She had left the door ajar and she crept in, closing it silently behind her, and then paused.

I said whimsically, "This is a little unfair, my dear. I'm in my nightshirt and there you are already dressed for breakfast."

She said nervously, "Your Royal Highness—"

"Come now—it's Bertie between you and me."

"B-Bertie."

"Now you sound like the blessed poet."

"There's something else. It may not be important." Her tone of voice was anything but frolicsome.

I sat up in bed. "What is it? What else happened tonight?"

"After Miss Chimes collapsed, the servants cleared her place at the table."

"I noticed, yes."

"I don't know what to think. I didn't want to mention it in front of Jerry. He was so upset. My butler found something. A small piece of paper cut from a newspaper. The *Times*, I believe. It had been tucked into the frame containing Miss Chimes's name."

"Her place setting?"

"Yes."

"A piece of newspaper? What did it say? Anything significant?"

"It just said 'Monday.'"

5

"She was poisoned," said Alix flatly.

We were in her dressing room the next morning and I had just given her the news of the sad business, breaking it to her with particular care. I could well foresee my dear impetuous wife insisting upon our leaving the house forthwith, regardless of my high-minded decision to continue with the shoot. However, she remained calm. I'm afraid it was I who became excitable.

"Poisoned?"

"It was something in the food," said Alix. "That is obvious."

"Oh, Alix, I can't believe that!"

She was intractable. "Where did she collapse? At the dinner table. She was perfectly well until then."

"My dear, that's absurd. People don't murder each other at dinner parties."

"Bertie, you never listen properly to what I say. I didn't say it was murder. I said she was poisoned."

"Isn't that the same?"

"Food poisoning."

"That's equally absurd."

"Not in this house," said Alix in a voice suddenly as prim as a Mother Superior. "I should like to know when Lady Drummond last inspected her kitchen." She paused and eyed me unadmiringly through the mirror on the dressing table. "I have the impression that she would rather visit bedrooms."

"Now that's unfair, Alix. It was quite proper that she knocked on my door last night. I had to be told the bad news, for heaven's sake. And as for your food poisoning, why should it have killed Queenie Chimes and left the rest of us as fit as fleas?"

This time she gave me a look that would have toasted a crumpet. "I shall count the guests at breakfast. And I shall avoid cooked food of any sort. I advise you to do the same."

"I shan't be so ill-mannered."

"You mean you can't make do with a bowl of prunes."

"I mean, my dear, that I have the fullest confidence in the catering arrangements."

When we got downstairs I was told that Jerry had been up before six, had eaten an early breakfast and gone out. He had very decently asked Colwell, the house steward, to pass on his regret at not joining us, either for breakfast or the shoot. It was clear to me that this was a typically considerate act on Jerry's part; he had felt that his presence at breakfast would have put a blight on the party.

The Reverend Humphrey Paget hovered, Bible in hand, at the door of the breakfast room, wanting to know if I would be gracious enough to give the first reading. I rather shocked the fellow by saying that one or two simple prayers from him ought to be sufficient on this and other mornings. He wasn't to know it, but at home I always take breakfast privately, in my rooms, where my morning readings are taken invariably from the *Sporting Life*.

We followed the Chaplain in. It looked a full muster to me, including the house steward, the groom of chambers, butlers and housekeeper, but I was conscious of Alix taking a mental register. I must admit to a tremor of unease when I noticed that Bullivant wasn't present; however, he burst in shortly after, blaming a lost collar stud. I turned to Alix and asked in a whisper if she would now risk a kipper.

After prayers, I thought it fitting to say a few words, firstly of regret at the tragic news of Miss Chimes, then to suggest how best to conduct ourselves in the light of what had happened. I said I had thought hard and long whether to cancel the shoot. The decision had had to be taken early, for the beaters had been called for eight o'clock to start driving in the birds from the fields and hedgerows. The planning for this week of sport had begun more than a year ago and the arrangements couldn't be altered at the drop of a hat. What with loaders, beaters, stops, pickers-up, drivers and catering staff, we would be using some two hundred personnel. It was the climax of the year for our hostess, dear Lady Drummond, and her gamekeepers. So I ventured to suggest that if any one of us had been called suddenly, like poor Miss Chimes, to our Maker, we would have wished the week's sport to continue regardless, and this was agreed to a man. I added that Jerry would be making arrangements for her to be given a decent, dignified burial in private, which would be impossible if I returned suddenly to Sandringham and the press got to hear of the tragedy. I'm sure that the point was well taken.

The servants withdrew and breakfast was served. Notwithstanding Alix's fears about the cooking, I ate as heartily as I always do before a shoot. It seemed crystal clear to me that the unfortunate Miss Chimes had been afflicted by some seizure of the brain or heart quite unrelated to anything she had eaten.

An hour later, about half past nine, I mounted the dog cart with the other guns, Bullivant, Holdfast, Pelham and Osgot-Edge, and we were driven at a canter to the first stand.

The lofty beech trees of Buckinghamshire are a handsome sight at any season. On this October morning, shafts of strong sunlight imprinted fiery red and gold upon the autumn foliage, and if that sounds poetical, I wonder what Osgot-Edge made of it. He was seated back-to-back with me, spared the agonies of small talk.

Instead I palavered cheerfully with Holdfast, who sat beside me in his deerstalker and tweeds, stout, apple-cheeked and bright-eyed with anticipation of good shooting. Away from his insufferable wife he was not bad company at all, and I respected him for his charity towards dumb animals. I'll say this for Sir George: his name is on more horse troughs than any other man of my acquaintance. There's scarcely a cab horse in the kingdom without reason to be grateful to him. Of course, he married an old nag as well.

I remarked, "I suppose you've been shooting here for years like most of the others, George?"

"That's true, sir, except for last year, when I was down with shingles. The coverts are as good as any I could name."

"Sandringham included?"

"Sandringham slipped my mind, sir."

I laughed. "Did you hear the latest story about Harty-Tarty? He made a record bag at Chatsworth."

(Harty-Tarty, readers, is the affectionate name by which my friend the Marquess of Hartington is known. A charming fellow, he is indisputably the worst shot in England.)

"A record bag? Lord Hartington?" Sir George sounded incredulous.

"Yes, he took aim at a wounded cock pheasant which was limping in front of a gate. He bagged it."

"My word!"

"Yes, and with the same shot he hit the retriever which was chasing it."

"Killed it?"

"Oh, yes. And what's more, he hit the retriever's handler in the leg."

"No, that's too much!" said Sir George, doubled up with mirth.

"It wasn't. He shot the Chatsworth chef, who'd just arrived with the lunch."

Ahead was a clearing where two shooting brakes had already transported our loaders and the pickers-up and their animals. The dog cart came to a halt and I stepped down first. As we walked the short distance to the stand, I made a point of giving specific instructions to young Marcus Pelham, "You're our host, so you're the captain of guns today. Treat me exactly as you do the others."

He wetted his lips and ran his fingers nervously through his pale hair. He hadn't expected this. "In that case, sir," he said after a moment's hesitation, "let's make the draw." He beckoned to his head keeper, a short, silver-haired fellow I remembered from my previous shoot at Desborough.

The keeper invited me to pick a disk from his leather pouch. I drew number three. Holdfast was two, Bullivant and Osgot-Edge were four and five, which left one for Pelham.

I marched to my peg, sank the point of my shooting stick into the turf and signaled to my loaders.

"And was the shooting to your satisfaction, Your Royal Highness?" Amelia asked me anxiously when the ladies joined us for luncheon after three stands. A marquee had been erected beside the tributary of the Ouse that runs through the Desborough estate. We were enjoying our preprandial champagne whilst the morning's bag was being laid out for counting. It was a scene fit for a Christmas card: well over five hundred pheasants, twenty or more wild ducks, five or six woodcocks and sundry partridges, hares and rabbits.

"Your head gamekeeper is a miracle worker, my dear," I answered. "If I were you, I'd double his wage and recommend him for a knighthood."

"And the beaters?"

"Performed splendidly. The birds were beautifully presented, as fast and high as one could wish."

"That *is* a relief. Some of the men have never beaten before."

"It's always so. If they are well supervised, you get no trouble."

A suitable distance from us, the smocked army of about a

hundred and fifty estate workers and farm laborers recruited for the week had grouped around several grand log fires, cooking sausages and onions, or some humble fodder with a smell just as appetizing. I can tell you that I was in grave danger of being lured away from the inevitable quails in aspic and game pie that awaited me in the luncheon tent.

I shall cleave to the memory of that scene by the river, refusing to have it taken from me by what happened after. Thirsty dogs lapping in the shallows; the smoke of the fires curling upwards; loaders at work cleaning the guns; and best of all, the ladies in their elegant walking costumes, looking like birds of paradise, so brilliant were the plumes and feathers in their bonnets. Our hostess, I recall, wore a stunning blue jacket and a jay's feathers in her hatband. "After yourself, sir, who was the most successful?" she asked me with an impish look.

"My dear Amelia, it's not meant to be a competition," I told her, though of course she knew, "but I can tell you in confidence that the poet hardly missed a thing."

"He surprises everyone year after year," she said. "People underestimate Wilfred."

"Is that so?"

"Oh, assuredly so." Something in the way she answered made me prick up my ears.

"It sounds to me as if you know of other talents in his repertoire."

She flushed and laughed. "Sir, I thought we were discussing his sporting prowess."

I changed the subject. "Has Jerry Gribble returned?"

"He hadn't by the time we left the house, sir. There's a lot to attend to, I think."

"Of course."

Presently luncheon was announced and we went into the marquee and took our places at the trestle table. This time I was seated opposite Miss Dundas, who surprised me by straight away asking the name of my gunsmith.

Talking guns with a lady was a novel experience. I suppose I should have realized that she was likely to own a weapon of some sort for use in the jungle. It turned out that she knew my gunsmith, Mr. Purdey of Oxford Street, tolerably well.

"My dear Miss Dundas, we ought to have invited you to shoot with us," I said affably.

Without batting an eyelid she said, "I don't kill for sport, sir. If

I am obliged to shoot, so be it. There's no pleasure in the slaughter."

"Do I sense, Miss Dundas, that you don't altogether approve of shooting game?"

Her cool smile told me I hadn't flustered her. "Oh, I'm willing to shoot in self-defense, but I've never yet been threatened by a pheasant."

"You'd eat one, I dare say," I riposted.

"Yes, but I wouldn't stuff my larder with several thousand. There isn't room."

I laughed and so did she. It was the first time I'd noticed how small, even and immaculately white were her teeth. Her complexion, tanned by the tropical sun, certainly showed them to advantage. With the dark brown eyes, she had something of the Celt in her background, if not the Latin. I've always found women of that coloring difficult to resist for long. A whimsical thought occurred to me. Whilst Alix stood guard against the alluring Amelia, perhaps I might manage a discreet adventure with Miss Dundas.

The tiresome Lady Holdfast, seated on my right, broke into my reverie by lightly tapping my knee with her finger.

You're an optimist, I thought, and then I glanced along the table and observed that nobody had yet picked up a spoon. "Heavens above!" I cried, snatching up mine and scooping up a chunk of the fruit. "You needn't have waited for me. Damn it all, this is a picnic."

Somebody gave a nervous cough. They still hadn't gone for their spoons.

"Dear Father in Heaven . . ." came the Chaplain's voice from along the table, and I knew that I had made a *faux pas*.

"Didn't notice he was with us," I confided to Amelia after the amen was said.

"Humphrey? He likes to join in the meals," she told me. "He goes about his parochial duties at other times. He looks after the village church as well as our own, you know."

"He must be worn to a frazzle."

She smiled at the notion. "It doesn't show."

The ladies stayed to watch the first drive of the afternoon, in the part known as Roebuck Wood. Folding chairs were put out for them where the pickers-up waited at a safe distance behind the gun stands. I'm never sure whether the fair sex take much pleasure in watching a shoot. Some, I am told, pass the time with their hands over their ears, but I've always had my sights on the birds overhead.

We were rotating positions at each stand so that each gun had a fair day's sport, and I found myself between Holdfast and Bullivant. Young Pelham blew the horn to start the drive and we heard the tapping begin deep in the wood.

How stirring is the rattle of sticks on trees and the screech and churr of startled wildlife—music more thrilling than any I can recall in a concert hall. I waited, flanked by my loaders, picturing the activity in the coverts as the fugitive birds scampered ahead of the beaters. A pheasant has a natural reluctance to take to its wings and it requires a well-managed beat to put it up precisely over the guns without flushing too many others at once.

This *battue* was faultless. They presented the birds in a long, soaring sequence almost vertically above us. I worked with three guns, receiving from the loader on my right, firing and passing it empty to the other man, never shifting my eyes from the sky. Barrel after barrel the fusillade went on as we picked our targets, swung and fired, dropping the pheasants with steady precision until the cry, "All out, gentlemen." The beaters were at the hedge and the horn was blown a second time to signal the end of the drive.

Ears ringing, I thanked my loaders, took out a cigar and strolled across to the ladies while the dogs were doing their work. The smell of cordite was all about us.

"I never saw such marvelous shooting, sir!" cried Amelia, and I saw Alix give her a sidelong glance.

"What was that, my dear?" I said out of mischief, cupping my ear and drawing closer to Amelia.

"Your shooting is incomparable!"

"Oh, I wouldn't say that. One or two in Europe are at least my equal. We'll see what the bag amounts to."

Alix had turned her back.

The other guns joined us and I noticed Bullivant walk straight up to Isabella Dundas and present her with a long russet tail feather he'd picked up. She fitted it under her hatband and twirled about like a dancer to display it, incidentally affording us all a sight of her ankles. Then she gave him an amused look that I didn't know how to interpret. Claude, I decided, would have to be watched.

Amelia was still at my elbow singing the praises of my marksmanship. The other guns, notably Osgot-Edge, had not been so well positioned to impress the ladies. Even so, I suspected that she was overdoing the tribute, and so, evidently, did her brother

Marcus, for as he was passing he prodded her thigh with the blunt end of his shooting stick and said, "Sis, you're making a nuisance of yourself." Addressing me, he said, "Would you care for a nip, sir?"

He held out his brandy flask.

"Not now," I said. "I shoot better with my head clear. Which way is the next stand?"

He pointed. "Beyond the ridge. It should be the best of the day, sir. The birds have already been driven out of their roosting ground into a smaller covert, so when they're flushed out, they fly towards home."

I nodded my approval. A pheasant will always fly better towards home than away from it. "How long will it take us? Shouldn't we start, or the light will go?"

A wagonette had been brought up in case we cared to ride, but I suggested legging it through the wood, and no one demurred. We said our farewell to the ladies, who were being conveyed back to the house to change into tea gowns. I generally find that I have a splitting headache by teatime after a shoot and don't much care what anyone is wearing, but that doesn't stop the ladies, bless them, from parading.

The dead birds were tidily lined up for counting, almost two hundred pheasants, one of the gamekeepers said, bringing our day's bag past seven hundred.

"Somebody missed a few this time," I jested. "I picked off sixty for certain. Seventy, I'd say."

Bullivant asked Marcus, "Do you think we'll take a thousand today?"

"Easily."

I said, "I trust we can improve on that as the week goes on, gentlemen."

Holdfast remarked, "With Jerry Gribble in the party we should."

"I wouldn't count on it," said Bullivant, grinning. "Have you ever seen Jerry shoot?"

"That's enough about Jerry," I told him curtly. Jerry *is* hopeless with a gun, but I won't have my friends ridiculed behind their backs at any time, let alone when they are making funeral arrangements.

With Marcus Pelham leading, we started along a bridle path towards the ridge. Osgot-Edge fell in behind young Pelham and Bullivant joined him, evidently willing to try for some kind of intelligible conversation. I forgave him a little for his crass remark about Jerry.

I brought up the rear with Holdfast and discussed insurance. I know as little about insurance as I do about poetry, so it was pleasing to discover that according to actuarial tables I can look forward confidently to attaining my sixty-ninth birthday, whereas young Pelham who is half my age will be lucky to get to sixty-one. Don't ask me how it works.

The top of the ridge afforded a fine view of beech woods and bracken. We were almost at the limit of the Desborough land. It was bordered by a road, just visible in stretches between the autumn foliage. Everything across the road and as far as the eye could see belonged to Amelia's neighbor, Jerry Gribble. Closer to us, Marcus Pelham pointed out the tower of the family chapel and beyond it the gamekeeper's lodge and some of the tied cottages.

A short distance below us on the slope was the small covert where the pheasants had been driven in readiness to be put up for the last stand of the day. The army of beaters, conspicuous in their long white smocks, was making its well-disciplined way in silence up the incline and around the covert to begin the drive.

I complimented Pelham on their performance and enquired whether they would get a decent supper at the day's end. Rabbit stew awaited them. My juices stirred and sang a short cantata at the thought.

To cover the sound I said, "I fear we mustn't linger, gentlemen. Let's go down to our positions."

We set off again, skirting the covert.

The last stand of the day was cleverly sited in a hollow with good cover, far enough from the covert for the birds to fan out and reach a challenging height. Our loaders and the dog handlers, who were being conveyed there by horsepower, had not yet put in an appearance, which irked me slightly at the time, but was to prove fortuitous.

Discussing the wind and its possible effect on the flight path of the birds, we continued for some time down the slope before anyone thought to mention an object lying on the open ground selected for the stand. Brownish in color, it might have been a blanket thoughtfully provided in case any of us needed extra warmth at the end of the day: that was my first assumption. Farther down the hill I formed the view that it was a recumbent man, perhaps an assistant gamekeeper sent ahead to meet us. If so, he was in for a surprise when we woke him from his slumbers.

"Is he one of your men?" Holdfast asked Pelham.

"If he is, he won't remain one," said our host through gritted teeth. "Excuse me, while I deal with it." He quickened his step.

Tactfully the rest of us slackened our pace.

Pelham approached the motionless figure, leaned over, grasped the shoulder roughly and attempted to rouse the man. Without success.

Pelham looked up at us. "I think he's dead."

"What?"

"Look."

We gathered around. He was indisputably dead. He had a revolver beside him and there was a hole in his head.

6

Things spoken in moments of extreme shock tend to look rather puerile when written down, so I don't propose to repeat what was said over the corpse. Rest assured that my companions and I were made aghast by our discovery. It was Jerry Gribble.

Young Pelham was the first to make a pertinent suggestion. "I'd better call off the drive, sir."

"The drive? Good God, yes."

"Shall I tell the keepers what has happened?"

"No, no. Can't do that." I gave the matter some rapid thought. "Say that His Royal Highness was called away on an urgent matter of State, so shooting is abandoned for the day."

He set off at a run.

I picked up the fatal weapon and turned it over carefully in my hands. It was a revolver made by my own gunsmith, Mr. Purdey of Oxford Street. There were five more bullets in the chambers. Poor old Jerry, I reflected ruefully: didn't trust his aim even at that range.

Then Claude Bullivant reminded me that our loaders and the dogs would arrive at any minute.

"Head them off, then," I told him. "Which way are they coming? By the road? Get down there and stop them." I waved the gun in that direction, giving Bullivant a moment of unease. "And one more thing, Claude."

"Yes, sir?"

"You'd better return to the house with the loaders. Inform the ladies that we expect to be late for tea." The commands sprang unbidden to my lips. I say it myself, I'm a first-class man in a crisis. I would have made a very good general on the battlefield. I suppose it's in the blood.

Bullivant lingered. "Is that all, sir?"

"Give them our apologies, of course."

"But they'll want to know why."

"We don't want them to panic. Oh, for pity's sake, Claude, you can keep a crowd of females in suspense, can't you?"

I was left with Wilfred Osgot-Edge and Sir George Holdfast for company. I pocketed the revolver and we sat on our shooting sticks and stared at each other.

Holdfast rubbed at his face as if the gnats were troubling him and said through his fingers, "I'm sure you're right to send the loaders away, sir, but it does leave us with a difficulty. What are we going to do with the body? The wagonette would have come in useful."

"Good point." I wished he'd mentioned it before. "How far are we from the house?"

Osgot-Edge almost fell off his stick trying to tell us it was a mile away.

Holdfast said, without, I'm sure, grasping the significance of the remark, "Jerry's own house is closer."

I seized on it at once. "That's where I intend to take him. Let the poor fellow be laid out on his own bed." I didn't say so, but I instantly foresaw several advantages in the plan. For one thing, it would spare the ladies—and our hostess in particular—some distress. A dead body on the premises is no help at all to a house party. And without wishing to mislead the authorities, we would save them hours of work by letting it appear that Jerry had died on his own side of the fence. You see, when a man puts a gun to his head, there has to be an inquest and it's fearfully boring for all concerned if an entire shooting party has to be questioned by the police.

Far better if he had died at home. Why, it might even allow the jury to bring in a verdict of accidental death. For all sorts of reasons, sentimental, moral and legal, you don't want suicide if you can possibly avoid it.

The chance of any other verdict but *felo-de-se* would depend on the medical evidence. I braced myself to look down at the fatal wound. I make no claims to pathological knowledge, but I've seen plenty of injured animals put out of their misery and I do know what a bullet wound looks like. The hole in Jerry's forehead was circular and singularly neat, suggesting that he had held the revolver at least six inches from his head. If he had pressed the barrel against his forehead, the hole would have been more in the form of a cross or star, due to the gases emitted from the weapon. This was not the case. How fortunate, I thought; anyone examining the body might be led to believe Jerry had fired accidentally. He was always a duffer with guns.

Reader, I can imagine what you are thinking. To be utterly frank with you, I didn't at this juncture entertain any explanation other than suicide. The possibility of murder didn't remotely occur to me. If you had been with me that dread Tuesday and known what I did about Jerry's desolate state of mind, you would have shared my opinion, I'm certain.

Faint voices traveled to us from the depths of the wood, too indistinct to make sense. Marcus must have reached the line and told them their work was over for the day. An unexpected flurry of black and white at the edge of my vision turned out to be a magpie taking to the air. Automatically I swung my hands to the right to receive my gun, regardless that my loader wasn't beside me, and I noticed that Osgot-Edge had done the same. He smiled slightly, then liberally dampened the back of my hand in saying, "S-sorrow."

"You don't need to apologize."

"No, sir. I said s-sorrow."

"I don't think I follow you."

"One m-magpie means sorrow."

I gave him a glazed look. "Really? Is that a superstition? It sounds appropriate, I must say."

"F-from Scotland." With that, he launched into a full rendering of the verse, and I shall spare you the consonantal falterings:

"One's sorrow, two's mirth,
Three's a wedding, four's a birth,
Five's a christening, six a dearth,
Seven's heaven, eight is hell,
And nine's the devil his ane sel'."

I thanked him and said I would rather count plum stones. I didn't mean to sound ungracious after his laborious recitation, so I asked, "Are you a native of Scotland, Mr. Osgot-Edge?"

He looked shocked. "D-definitely not. I c-come from a very old English family. Osgot is mentioned in the D-Domesday Book."

There was another disturbance in the thicket and more birds took to the sky.

Holdfast asked, "What do two wood pigeons signify?"

"Pigeon pie if you can bag them," I said.

We understood the reason for their sudden flight when a few moments later Marcus Pelham came briskly from the covert. He informed us that he had spoken to the gamekeepers. The beaters were trekking back. He'd also seen Bullivant turn back the wagonettes and climb aboard one.

"Excellent." I took out a cigar. "Better give them time to get clear." No one showed much inclination to speak, so I did my best to lift the assembled spirits a little. "This melancholy situation reminds me of a letter I once received at Balmoral in response to an invitation. I have a sneaking impression that Jerry might have appreciated it. 'Sir, may it please Your Royal Highness, the laird is honored to inform you that he does not mean to shoot himself tomorrow; but his gamekeepers will be ordered to accompany you and the usual dogs.' Isn't it priceless?"

"Extremely droll, sir," said Holdfast.

Pelham asked, "Is there a plan, sir?"

I told him what I had in mind and he saw the sense of it at once. "In the circumstances, it's the obvious thing to do."

I didn't care for the "obvious," but I was grateful for his support. Unfortunately there's always some wiseacre who thinks he has a better idea: in this case, Holdfast.

"I've been giving it some thought, sir. Do we really need to move the corpse so far?"

"What do you mean?"

"Why not leave him here, just out of sight in the covert? The gamekeepers will find him soon enough."

"You think that's a better plan, do you?"

"Well, sir, it has the merit of being simple. If he doesn't have a gun beside him it will look as if he died accidentally, the victim of a stray bullet."

I rolled my eyes. "And what sort of nincompoop is supposed to have been shooting at pheasants with revolver bullets?"

He reddened. "Ah. I hadn't thought of that."

Pelham said, "Your plan is best, sir."

I turned to Osgot-Edge. He only needed to tip his head in support. I wasn't asking for anything more. His recital of the verse about the magpie must have gone to his head, because he said, "In v-view of last year we d-don't want another shooting accident."

"Too true," said Pelham.

"What happened last year?" asked Holdfast.

Pelham registered surprise. "Weren't you in the party?"

"I had to miss last year. Wasn't well."

"So did I," said Pelham, and grinned. "Wasn't invited. A beater was shot, a lad of fifteen, one of our own estate workers. Pure bad luck that somebody's swing was out."

"Fatally shot?" I asked.

"Yes. Fortunately he had no parents. Not much was made of the incident." He glanced down at Jerry's body. "This is another kettle of fish." After a glare from me, he added, "So to speak. I mean, the death of the Duke of Bournemouth. Really, I'm surprised Jerry shot himself here when he could have done it at home."

Holdfast said, "I don't suppose he was thinking straight."

Osgot-Edge managed to say, "He m-must have wanted us to find him."

It was a shrewd observation. "Quite possibly," I said. "Typical of Jerry. Considerate to the last. He wouldn't have wanted to scare some wretched chambermaid out of her wits, so he made sure his corpse would be discovered by us. Left it to the last stand so as not to spoil our shooting more than necessary."

Holdfast said with a sigh, "Poor old Jerry. He must have been besotted with Miss Chimes to resort to this."

"C-captivated," said Osgot-Edge more poetically.

Then Pelham, smart aleck, shamed us all with his common sense by asking, "Did he leave a note? Have you searched his pockets yet?"

Not wishing to admit that I hadn't thought of it, I said loftily, "We've been too busy discussing what to do with him. Very well, let's see if there's anything." I stooped to examine the body, which was dressed, like the rest of us, in a Norfolk suit. In one of the top pockets my fingers located a tiny slip of paper. I took it out. Immediately something uncomfortable stirred in the pit of my stomach.

Holdfast asked, "What have you got there, sir? Is something written on it?"

"Just a scrap of newspaper," I remarked, trying to sound unimpressed.

"Anything significant, sir?"

"I doubt it. There's only one word here and that's 'Tuesday.'"

"Strange. Why would he have that in his pocket?"

"I haven't the faintest idea."

"If you ask me," said Holdfast, "it's unimportant. Probably some system devised by his valet for putting out the clothes in the desired sequence."

It was an ingenious suggestion, and I was so grateful for it that I felt like shaking George Holdfast's hand. I knew he was mistaken, of course, but I couldn't myself think of anything remotely plausible. The great thing was that it seemed to satisfy my companions. They were unaware of the piece of paper that had been found when Queenie Chimes collapsed at the dinner table. Only Amelia, her butler and I knew about that. Even Jerry hadn't been told, which made this fresh discovery puzzling, not to say disturbing.

Taking a grip on myself, I resumed my examination of the pockets.

Nothing else of interest was on Jerry's person. I think I found a handkerchief, some coins and his watch.

A church clock chimed. The afternoon was fast drawing to a close, and there was a job to be done before dark. After some trial and error the four of us contrived a way of lifting Jerry's body by employing our shooting sticks crosswise as a sort of improvised stretcher, for none of us particularly wished to take a grip on the stiffened limbs. It proved an efficient method. There was the occasional stumble, but we reached the road in quite a short time, passed our burden across a stone wall and so entered the Bournemouth estate unseen by anyone. Dense ferns delayed our progress somewhat and it was a relief to reach a bridle path that led us more swiftly to the landscaped lawns in front of the house.

Twilight was in session by this time and to anyone who chanced to look out a window we would have presented a weird, not to say gruesome, picture as we moved silently across the turf. Presently we came to a steep, stone-lined bank forming what landscape gardeners call a ha-ha, a shelf in the lawn contrived to be invisible from the house. Without needing to discuss it, we lowered the body to the ground and stretched our aching shoulders.

Holdfast said, "Shall we leave him here, sir?"

"Good Lord, no," I said. "Can't do that. We must get him indoors."

"Break in?"

"Really, George," I said in a pained voice. "One of us must go to the front entrance and ask to see the house steward. You, I think, Marcus."

Young Pelham's eyes whitened in the gloom, whether out of stark surprise or pleasure at being asked I couldn't say.

I told him, "Be sure that you speak to the house steward alone. You will break the new of his master's death and you will say that some of his friends have brought him home and are waiting outside.

If the man has his wits about him, he'll invite us to bring the body at once to the gun room."

"The *gun* room, sir?"

"Yes, the gun room," I repeated as if speaking to a child. "Any steward worthy of the name would rather his master died accidentally whilst cleaning his gun than by his own hand. He won't need telling."

"Very well, sir."

From our position behind the ha-ha we watched Pelham cross the turf and heard his feet reach the gravel drive. In a moment a light appeared at the front entrance and we dipped out of sight.

There was a long, suspenseful wait.

Finally footsteps crunched on the gravel again and after an interval Pelham leaned over the ha-ha and informed us that the house steward was ready to receive the body. Between us we used the shooting sticks to hoist Jerry's mortal remains to the higher level. My three companions stood over him.

"What are you waiting for?" I whispered from below them.

Holdfast cleared his throat. "Aren't you coming with us, sir?"

I said, "It wouldn't be appropriate." Nobody spoke, so I added, "I think I've done my share. And it goes without saying, gentlemen, that my own part in this melancholy episode must not be divulged to a living soul. I shall remain here behind the ha-ha until you emerge again from the house."

Another silence greeted this. They made no move to lift the corpse.

I said, "Is there a difficulty?"

Holdfast looked at the others to see if either of them preferred to speak first. "Well, sir, with three of us . . . we'll have to think of another way to carry him."

"Oh, for pity's sake," I snapped. "Pick him up with your hands."

Nothing was said for a moment. Then Holdfast squatted and placed his hands gingerly under the shins. "He's rigid. Like a piece of timber."

Osgot-Edge said, "Rigor m-m-"

"Much easier to get a grip," I said. You can't be fastidious in emergencies. "What's the matter, Pelham?" He hadn't made a move.

"The gun."

"Which gun?"

"The fatal weapon. It's not much help to us in your pocket, sir."

He was right, but I didn't care for the way he chose to mention it. I passed the weapon to Holdfast and said, "Now get on with it."

They bent to the task and took the strain.

Left alone, I perched on my shooting stick and watched the sky turn from purple to black. A breeze was blowing up from the north. I shivered and wondered bleakly whether tea was yet finished at Desborough Hall. My hip flask was empty. My boots pinched. I wasn't relishing an hour's tramp in the dark.

The next thing I heard some twenty minutes later was the sound of carriage wheels. I raised my head above the ha-ha in time to see a small carriage driven at a canter from the rear of the house. Three men and the driver were aboard. I was incensed. I was pretty damned sure they were Holdfast, Pelham and Osgot-Edge and they must have been given transport back to Desborough.

Surely they didn't propose to abandon me?

I snatched up my shooting stick and set off with bent back along the length of the ha-ha in the direction they were taking. The posture was humiliating. It brought to mind the vulgar riddle that I once accidentally overheard from a drunken undergraduate at Cambridge: what is the difference between the Prince of Wales and an orangutan? A nice shock I gave the fellow when I stepped out from behind a potted fern and demanded to be told the answer, which I have to admit was rather clever, though nobody laughed at the time: the Prince is the Heir Apparent and the ape has a hairy parent. Anyway, the mental picture taunted me now as I loped along with my knuckles grazing the turf. And that was not the worst of it. The carriage showed no sign of halting. In despair I threw caution to the winds, stopped, stood at my full height, shouted and waved my shooting stick, to absolutely no effect. They galloped out of sight along the drive.

No doubt you will be as relieved as I was to find that they finally stopped for me at the end of the drive, just outside the main gates. Plodding towards them like a cab horse destined for the knacker's yard, I heard Pelham's voice say, "That's him!" and then, unbelievably, "Come on, matey, stir your stumps. We haven't got all night."

Insolent pup, I thought. I was about to explode when it was made apparent to me that his words were meant for the ears of the driver. He was playacting to protect my identity. George Holdfast, no actor at all, said woodenly, "Give him a hand up, then. It wasn't Charlie's fault we lost our way."

I climbed up and took a seat beside the poet. While I was recovering my breath, Pelham told me in subdued tones how Jerry Gribble's house steward had received the news. The man was worthy of his calling, thank heavens. He had recognized the wisdom of placing the body in the gun room where one of the gamekeepers would find it. They had deposited Jerry on the floor with the revolver beside him and—a nice touch—a bristle brush in his hand for cleaning the barrel.

We barely had time to agree how much the ladies needed to be told before the carriage drew up at the front of Desborough Hall and Amelia came running down the steps.

"What happened? Has there been an accident?"

I said as I climbed down, "Didn't Claude Bullivant tell you, my dear?"

She spread her hands in a way that conveyed her frustration. "He was very unforthcoming. He simply informed us that you wouldn't be here for tea and then he asked to have a bath. He hasn't appeared for hours."

"That's my fault," I admitted. "I asked him to say the minimum. My dear, we have all had a dreadful shock."

"Someone *is* hurt."

"Jerry Gribble is dead."

She clapped her hand to her mouth.

I put a supporting arm around her and told her gently, "He shot himself, poor fellow. We abandoned our shoot when we learned the dreadful news. We've been to his house and paid our respects. I'm sorry, my dear."

That was the version of events that we had decided would cause the least distress. It was broadly true, if selective with the facts. We had planned it from the highest motives.

The ladies immediately smelled a rat. As if with one mind, they devoted the rest of the evening to wheedling the entire story from us. They were clever. They cornered us separately and got the truth by question and observation. Whilst I was dressing for dinner Alix spotted some blistering on my hands from the stretcher work I'd done with the shooting stick. I didn't admit it right out, of course, but at dinner she took particular note of the other men's hands and they all had blisters except Bullivant and the Reverend Humphrey Paget, who had come in as usual, and was shocked at the news. I think because of the Chaplain's presence, no one accused us of deceit, but significant looks were exchanged. By the time the ladies left the table we men were ready to tell all.

The Reverend Paget left directly after dinner. Perhaps he sensed the crackle of electricity in the air. I can tell you, the brandy did several rounds before we felt sufficiently fortified to rejoin the ladies.

7

Have you ever noticed that yawning is contagious? About an hour after dinner I put my hand to my mouth and said, "Pardon me." Soon everyone was at it, and when I suggested we send for the candles at ten o'clock there was no dissent.

You may think that the shocks and strains of the day had taken their toll. Not in my case. I am blessed with a very resilient constitution. True, my arms and legs still ached a little from the unaccustomed exercise, but I wasn't ready to turn in. I simply wanted everyone out of the way to permit me a private conversation with Amelia Drummond. So after I had wished good night to Alix I changed into my night things, put on a dressing gown and carpet slippers and quietly returned downstairs.

As I expected, she was still in the main drawing room, going through the next day's arrangements with Colwell, her house steward. The moment I appeared, she broke off and stepped towards me, plainly alarmed by the possibility that the hot water had not been left in my room, or some receptacle had not been emptied.

"Your Royal Highness . . . ?"

Behind her, Colwell bowed and started backing discreetly to the door.

I called to him, "Don't go." To Amelia I said, "With your permission, my dear."

She fingered her necklace and tried to appear composed. "Of course, sir."

I beckoned to Colwell. Amazing how distinguished some domestic servants manage to look behind whiskers. Dressed in a frock coat he could easily have passed for Lord Salisbury, the Prime Minister.

If anything, his expression was more noble than Salisbury's. I said, "Yesterday evening when you were clearing the table you found a scrap of newspaper at the place where Miss Chimes had been seated. Is that correct?"

"Quite correct, Your Royal Highness."

"You showed it to Lady Drummond?"

"Yes, sir."

"And to anyone else?"

"No, sir."

"Have you mentioned it to anyone since?"

"No, sir."

"Not even the servants?"

"I never discuss anything with the servants except their duties, sir."

I accepted his word with a nod. "Then I think it would be wise if you continued to keep it to yourself or, better still, forgot about it entirely."

"I shall, sir."

I dismissed him and turned to Amelia. "And now, my dear, if you will forgive me, I would like to put the same question to you."

She looked at me earnestly with her deep brown eyes. "Sir, I have discussed the matter with no one except yourself."

"Not with Jerry Gribble?"

She frowned. "No."

"That is peculiar." I told her what I had found in Jerry's pocket.

Her reception of this information was just as I expected. She blinked, screwed up her face in puzzlement and said, "What on earth can it mean? Was he trying to tell us something?"

"If he was, we knew it already," I commented. "We may not be the best brains in the land, but we didn't need telling that today is Tuesday."

"Perhaps the piece of paper had some other purpose. Did he mean to show that his death was linked with Queenie's?"

"How could he, if none of us had told him about the first scrap of paper?"

"I hadn't thought of that." She reddened.

I said, "You're quite sure you didn't mention it to anyone else? Not even your brother?"

"I swear it, sir."

She looked so hurt at the very suggestion that I grasped her hand and squeezed it. "My dear, I believe you."

Her eyes glistened. "And I am sure Colwell is telling the truth. It *is* a mystery." A tear started sliding down her cheek.

I felt for a handkerchief and found that I didn't have one in the pocket of my dressing gown, so I stopped the tear with my fingertip. "Chin up. Stiff upper lip."

She managed a wan smile. "Sir, I'm sorry."

Sounding more and more like a page from the *Girl's Own Paper* I said, "What's done is done, and we've got to make the best we can of it. It's up to us all to behave as if we don't even know about Jerry's death. We'll have a full day's sport tomorrow just as we planned."

"Oh, yes, sir." Her face lit up again.

I winked. "I wouldn't object to 'Bertie' when we're alone."

I was given a smoldering look. "That's an intimacy I hardly dare to aspire to, sir."

Reader, how did it happen? One moment we were discussing the death of a dear friend and the next I was flirting. Hadn't I resolved to sidestep Amelia's charms? I am burdened with an amorous nature that undermines all my good intentions. I know better than to fight it.

"Don't be so coy," I chided her. "You used the name more than once in my bedroom last night."

"True."

"In private, I'm a man like anyone else, as you will appreciate . . . if you are so inclined." I hoped this declaration didn't sound too rehearsed. It had served me well on similar campaigns.

"Oh." She liked it. She was becoming breathless and her efforts to reinflate herself were visibly improving her charms.

Remembering Alix, I said, "But I don't think my suite is best placed for an intimate conversation."

"Nor mine," she said quickly.

I hesitated. "That is a difficulty."

"Not insurmountable . . . Bertie." The way she spoke that word "insurmountable" syllable by syllable made it sound more suggestive than anything in the dictionary or out of it. The "Bertie" came as quite an anticlimax.

I said with a twinkle, "I believe Desborough has ninety-seven other bedrooms."

"But wickedly cold."

"You mean that the fires have not been lit? My dear, neither of us will notice. If we can agree on a room and both succeed in finding it in, say, an hour from now, a warm outcome is assured, I promise you."

She blushed deeply. "Sir, you flatter me, but I am forced to tell you that tonight is inappropriate."

"Inappropriate?"

"Impossible."

"Ah."

So be it, I thought philosophically. You don't argue with a lady over dates. Perhaps I was feeling more *hors de combat* than I had been prepared to admit a few minutes ago.

With, I hope, good grace, I wished her a pleasant night's sleep and returned to my room. In the corridor I fancied I heard a door open briefly and close again behind me, but I paid no heed to it. Anyone who has stayed in a strange house or hotel knows how at any hour of the night if you need to venture along the corridor somebody else will inevitably choose the same moment to walk past. Doors are repeatedly being opened a fraction and timidly closed again.

I turned off the gas, knelt briefly in prayer, dropped my dressing gown, got into bed and gave a genuine yawn. Sleep must have followed quickly.

Do you know, for the second night running, my sleep was interrupted in the small hours? I was in the middle of a stirring dream of a shoot at Sandringham. I was in splendid form, hitting everything the beaters put up. One glorious cock pheasant, a veritable screamer, flew much higher than the rest. I was supremely certain that I would bring it down. I swung the barrel and squeezed the trigger and instead of the discharge I heard a curious squeak and felt a sudden draft on my face. Then there was a muffled thud. I woke at once. The squeak had come from my door handle. The thud wasn't a pheasant dropping from the sky, but my solid oak door being closed.

I refused to be alarmed. For one thing, the dream had left me in a state of elation. For another, I was confident that I was being visited by Amelia. It had been girlish panic that had prompted her to postpone our assignation. After going to bed she had no doubt lain awake in a lather of frustration. Finally, unable to subdue nature any longer, she had come to me. I smiled in anticipation and lay quite still.

Nothing else happened.

Presently I sat up and peered into the gloom. Sadly for my self-esteem, I had to conclude that nobody was in the room except myself. Yet well-made doors with good fittings don't open themselves for no reason.

She has lost her nerve again, I thought.

I leapt out of bed and without even bothering with my dressing gown, crossed the floor and tried the door. The handle gave a squeak identical to the one I'd heard before. I peered out. No one was in sight, but I fancied I heard a floorboard creak nearby, around a corner. This, I decided, warranted investigation.

Pausing briefly to listen outside dear Alix's door in case the noise had disturbed her (it hadn't), I padded off in pursuit. I knew that Amelia's room was not far along that adjacent corridor and I wanted if possible to catch her before she reached it.

I swung around the corner straight into the arms not of Amelia, but her wretched brother Marcus. Like me, he was in his nightshirt and nothing else.

Imagine my confusion.

"What the devil . . . ?"

He had his finger to his lips. "Shh."

I said, "Someone just opened my bedroom door."

He said in a whisper, "Kindly keep your voice down, sir. It was I."

I said, "Young man, you had better explain yourself at once."

As if only just aware of the gravity of the situation, he swallowed, drew himself up and said, "Sir, I'm profoundly sorry. I didn't mean to disturb you. I wasn't expecting to find you in bed."

"Where the deuce did you expect me to be at this hour?"

He didn't reply directly. He fiddled with the cuffs of his nightshirt and mumbled something about his sister.

"What are you saying?" I demanded.

"I heard you go downstairs after the rest of us had retired. I knew Amelia was down there and I assumed . . ."

"You assumed what?"

Before he answered, a door across the corridor opened and Claude Bullivant looked out. "Who's there?"

I said, "Nobody. Go back to sleep."

He closed the door again.

Marcus took the opportunity to change tack. "You're a man of the world, sir. I regret to say that my sister has become—how shall I put this?—rather too liberal with her favors since her husband passed away. I'm afraid the shock unhinged her in this respect. As her only living relative, I don't want her to bring discredit on herself and the family."

I said, "What are you talking about, man? I'm the future King. Where's the discredit in that?"

Pelham hesitated. "You misunderstand me, sir. I don't mean to offend you. I'm perfectly content—indeed, honored—for my sister to, em . . ."

"Concede me the ultimate favor?"

"Absolutely. What distresses me is when she concedes it to any Tom, Dick or Harry who cares to pass the time of day."

Reader, I could scarcely restrain myself from striking him. "That's a deplorable thing for a man to say about his sister, Pelham, and I happen to know that it isn't true. As a matter of fact, the lady was unwilling to welcome anyone to her bed tonight."

He clicked his tongue defiantly and looked away.

His attitude didn't impress me in the least, so I gave him the dressing-down he deserved. I told him to look me in the eye when I was addressing him. Then I told him curtly, "This prying of yours is more offensive than anything Amelia is alleged to be doing. It is underhanded, unreasonable and unhealthy. If you have a modicum of decency you'll find yourself a mistress of your own as soon as possible and let your sister conduct her private life in the way she pleases. Now get to bed and let us all get some sleep."

He fairly slunk away.

I felt better for having spoken my mind. Little did Amelia realize as she lay asleep that she had a champion defending her. Or was she asleep? I had not gone more than a step towards my room when I heard a short, low-pitched laugh behind me. It was female in origin and it sounded so close that I spun around expecting to see the lady standing there.

The corridor was empty.

The laugh came again, clear as anything, wanton, almost a gurgle of pleasure. That's Amelia, I thought. That is definitely her voice and she is playing a game with me.

One of the first rules of noctambulation is to know who occupies the rooms around one. With the help of my valet, I had acquired a plan of the ladies' rooms on the first night, now usefully committed to memory. Our hostess had her private suite up a couple of steps on the left, so I crept towards her door and listened. Teasingly, she was silent again. I gripped the handle and turned it gently. This handle was well oiled. I eased open the door and stepped inside to find myself in Amelia's dressing room. The fire still glowed sufficiently in the grate for me to recognize the gown she had worn that evening, now hanging outside the wardrobe. A heap of white undergarments lay across an armchair and the lower half of a lady appeared to be standing guard beside them, but was in reality her bustle and petticoat.

Having got thus far, I didn't propose to leave without trying the inner door that led to the bedroom. It was ajar. Temptress, I thought. You ran in here just as I came in.

I wasn't altogether surprised to find the bed unoccupied. My guess was that she would be hiding behind the door without a stitch of clothing on. Certain of the fair sex love to exhibit themselves in as stark and dramatic a fashion as possible. The first time I saw the French beauty, Cora Pearl, was at the Café Anglais in Paris when she was served to me on a silver platter wearing nothing but a rope of pearls and a sprig of parsley.

I said in a gravelly voice, "Come on—surprise me, then."

Amelia was not behind the door. She was not under the bed or in the wardrobe or behind the curtains. She was not on the balcony.

I said, "You can come out, my dear. I'm stumped."

Silence.

By degrees it dawned on me that I had made a mistake. She wasn't in her rooms. Then where the deuce was she? From where had that seductive laugh come?

I returned to the corridor and stood as near as I could estimate to the spot where I'd heard her voice. There were no obvious places to hide. Not a potted palm or a Ming vase to shelter behind.

Mystified, I waited for another sound from her. When it eventually came, it wasn't nearly so audible. It was more of a sigh than a laugh. Helpfully, it was repeated a number of times, faint, but distinct, and the voice was definitely Amelia's.

The sighing settled into a rhythm. I traced it to the other side of a door just across the corridor from where I was standing. The sound slowly increased in tempo and volume.

Marcus, I thought, you could be right about your sister.

I gave a sigh of my own, gritted my teeth and returned to my room.

There, I counted on my fingers. Not Holdfast; his room was at the far end of the corridor. Not Bullivant; he'd looked out of his, which was on the other side. Not the Chaplain, thank goodness; he wasn't staying in the house. And not Marcus Pelham; he'd gone in the other direction. I was just arriving at the inevitable conclusion when my thought processes were rudely interrupted.

Was it my imagination, or did I hear a distant shout of, "M-m-m-marvelous!"?

WEDNESDAY

8

Pardon me if I'm mistaken, reader, but did you anticipate a body at the beginning of this chapter? If so, then *you* were mistaken. We all appeared for breakfast on Wednesday morning, if not bouncing with health and strength, at least capable of buttering toast. Osgot-Edge, I'll grant you, made buttering his slice look as laborious as painting a ceiling. Amelia, on the other hand, was more bobbish than ever. She announced, "I'm planning parlor games this evening, so I don't want anyone sneaking off to the billiard room after dinner."

Lady Holdfast, another who managed to be gratingly boisterous, clapped her hands and cried, "Parlor games—how jolly! Shall we have charades? I'm very good at thinking up words."

"Postman's Knock is more fun," said Bullivant.

"How typical of a man to suggest that."

"Hide and Seek," said Alix, who loves nothing better than a romp.

"Definitely Hide and Seek," said Amelia, giving me one of her looks.

I pretended not to have noticed. The previous night's Hide and Seek hadn't pleased me much.

I wasn't allowed to stay silent. "What's your favorite game, sir?" Amelia demanded.

"Ptarmigan," I said, "cooked in a rich gravy and covered with pie crust."

That put a temporary end to the conversation on parlor games.

We started the day's shoot at the place where we had found Jerry's body the previous afternoon. Nothing resembling a wraith rose up from the fatal spot; just regular puffs of gunsmoke as the birds were flushed out. It was a good bag and my mood improved. I made a point of walking across to the game cart and admiring the Suffolk Punch who hauled it. He was sporting his brasses in my honor. "Is he as strong as he looks?" I asked the driver. "I sincerely hope so. You'll have a full load by lunchtime." And he did, six hundred and seventy-two birds. I know, because I won the sweep to estimate the bag. The day was turning out better than I could have hoped for.

The Chaplain gave us a fright at luncheon by arriving with a companion who turned out to be the district coroner, a cheerful, florid-looking fellow called Elston. They had just come from viewing the gun room where Jerry Gribble's corpse had been discovered by his own head gamekeeper. To our enormous relief, it emerged that Elston was an old friend of Jerry's and was satisfied—or willing to be convinced, at any rate—that the death had been accidental. Then Osgot-Edge incautiously asked him, "C-can you tell us about Miss Ch-Ch-"

"Mischance. He means misadventure," I dextrously cut in. "Is that the verdict in such cases, Mr. Elston?"

"Misadventure? Quite possibly, yes, sir."

"There you are then, Wilfred. Have some more game pie."

That muzzled Osgot-Edge for the rest of the meal. How imbecilic, to be on the point of mentioning Miss Chimes's death almost in the same breath as Jerry's when we had gone to such pains to separate the two fatalities.

I must say, it made me nervous, as well as annoyed. People are so unpredictable. I might have expected someone like Moira Holdfast to make such a gaffe, but I took Osgot-Edge for a man of intelligence. I could only ascribe his lapse to lack of sleep, and he didn't get my sympathy for that.

All was forgiven by teatime, for that afternoon we increased our bag to over a thousand. Marcus Pelham had arranged for a photographer to record the event, and when we five guns lined up beside the results of our marksmanship you would never have guessed that a cross word had passed between us.

With hearts swelling and heads ringing, we repaired to the house and received the ladies' congratulations over tea. Certain of them, not least my own dear wife, appeared more excited about the parlor games in prospect than our performance in the field, but we forgave them, for they gave us a splendid welcome and the drawing room hummed with good humor. I wouldn't want it to be thought that we had forgotten the tragedies of the previous days; we were all in black ties out of respect—the ladies in subdued colors—and most of the blinds were down, but when all's said and done, you can't toll the knell twenty-four hours a day.

I picked a chair beside Miss Dundas, who greeted me with an amused curl of the lip as if I were some elderly masher about to inflict myself on her company. I didn't expect her to spring up and curtsy, but I'm not used to being treated so casually, and I could have found it irksome. Instead it was curiously stimulating.

She didn't appear to be eating anything, so I recommended the cucumber sandwiches, lowering my voice to add that I really preferred tea seated at a table, rather than having to wait for a parlor maid to pass the plate around the entire room before one saw it again.

She said the way the tea was served was a matter of indifference to her.

"Aren't you eating at all, then?" I asked. "You're not tempted by the egg and cress or the salmon?"

"No, sir."

"You're not unwell, I hope?"

"On the contrary. I feel extremely well. It's just that I prefer not to eat at this time."

"Don't be like Alix," I warned her, speaking close to her ear. "She hasn't touched any cooked food since Monday."

"I am sorry to hear that. Is she ill?"

"Merely careful in view of what happened. She's surviving on bread rolls and sugar lumps. I don't know how long she'll keep it up. Those small macaroons are delicious. Won't you be tempted?"

"Really, sir, I don't require one."

"Yes, but I do. Be an angel and take one for me when the girl comes by."

A crack appeared in her stony facade; she smiled faintly to reveal a tantalizing glimpse of those snow-white teeth. She collected the macaroon and held it elegantly between finger and thumb whilst I consumed the two I had taken. She will be so much more of a conquest than Amelia, I thought as I chewed.

She asked, "Shall I pass it to you now? Then I can take another when they come round again."

"Capital. I had no idea you were so resourceful. The great disadvantage of a shooting party is that it deprives us of the ladies' company for much of the day. How did you spend the morning?"

"Pleasantly enough, sir. Lady Drummond took us on a tour of the house."

"Did she, indeed? Now I suppose you know all the best places to hide—the priest's hole, the secret panels."

She frowned, evidently at a loss to understand me.

I said, "The parlor games tonight. Hide and Seek. I shall never find you."

"Oh. Are we certain to play Hide and Seek?"

"Alix will insist on it. Won't you tell me where you propose to hide?"

With the slightest tilt of the eyebrows she commented, "Surely that would spoil the game, sir?"

"Not for me, Isabella."

At the mention of her name a tinge of color sprang to her cheeks. It was the right moment to move on. One needs to judge these encounters with finesse. After all, there was an entire evening to come. I said, "I really must go over and congratulate our hostess on the macaroons. Isabella, you will remember what I said, won't you? I shall be looking to you for hints."

After tea and before sunset I took a solitary walk along the drive. Not for exercise or recreation; it was a little obligation that I always put upon myself when visiting a house. In the course of a day I see most of my personal servants, but it's quite possible to go through the week without once encountering the man from the Household Police entrusted with my safety. Inspector Sweeney was on duty at the Lodge, watching the comings and goings, a dreary task.

He came to the door in his braces, with the smell of fried bacon wafting from behind him. His eyes bulged. "Holy kicker!"

I relished the moment. Sweeney is a limpet. There's no other word to describe the way he attaches himself to me whenever I step into a public street. Consequently he is better informed about the intricacies of my private life than anyone else in the kingdom. It was rare—and rather gratifying—to see beneath *his* shell.

"Your Royal Highness—I thought you were safe in the house."

"At ease, Mr. Sweeney. I am perfectly safe," I told him indulgently. "We can afford to relax in the country. I say, have you been cooking?"

"My supper, sir."

"It smells rather appetizing. I think I'll step inside."

I sat warming my hands at the range and watched him finish crisping the bacon, followed by kidneys, tomatoes and potatoes.

The Lodge had been put entirely at his disposal during my visit. He was under instructions to remain there except in an emergency. I didn't want him stumbling through the coverts and startling the game.

"Will that be sufficient, sir?"

"Yes. I shall be eating dinner in an hour. Are you quite certain there's enough for both of us? I'll have a rabbit sent up to you if you wish. This is a very toothsome offering, Sweeney. Scrumptious."

The sharing of food has a curious way of encouraging confidences. I found myself talking about poor Miss Chimes and what happened at dinner on Monday evening.

John Sweeney was wise to everything, of course. I believe he knew all about Jerry's death as well, but he was tactful enough not to allude to it.

"Does anyone know what killed the young lady, sir?"

"Not yet. We shall have to wait for the postmortem examination."

"When is that to be, sir?"

"As soon as possible. The coroner will want a report."

"He was here today, sir, with the Chaplain. I challenged them at the gate."

"Good man. Yes, they joined us for lunch, half expecting another corpse, I dare say."

Sweeney grinned and said, "Dying is their living, isn't that a fact, sir?" Which I thought rather witty, and very Irish.

Half past nine the same evening found me sitting cross-legged on a cushion making a spluttering attempt to smoke a hookah—to the undisguised mirth of the rest of the company, seated around me. On my head was a crimson fez with a tassel.

"Turk," shouted Bullivant.

"Sultan?" called Alix.

"Wait a minute," I protested. "We haven't started yet."

The Chaplain struck some chords on the piano that were meant to suggest Asia Minor and Amelia Drummond made an astounding entrance. She was dressed (if that is the word) in the authentic costume of a Turkish belly dancer with *yashmak*, spangled bodice and purple harem trousers. Her feet and ankles were quite bare. She was rattling a tambourine. Our choice of word in the charade had been suggested by Amelia herself and now I understood why. She must have ordered the outfit specially from a theatrical costumier. She surprised even me and, I think, shocked some of the company as she stood a yard or so in front of me beating the tambourine and shaking her hips in a most vigorous and distracting manner.

"Oh, I say!" cried Lady Moira Holdfast.

"Corking!" said her husband.

Bullivant called out, "Take a look at Bertie. The smoke is coming out of his ears!"

The game was fast getting out of control, so I stood up and said, "Thank you, Rector. That was the first syllable. We shall proceed at once to the second."

As I ushered Amelia to the door, Bullivant called out, "Encore, if you please!"

What he got instead was Wilfred Osgot-Edge in a solo rendition of the second syllable. Dressed in the suit he had worn for dinner, the poet gave a performance more notable for its understatement than anything else as he paced the room staring at the floor, then got down on hands and knees apparently to examine the carpet. Finally he stood up and stamped his foot.

"Is that all?" asked Marcus.

"Pheasant," said Miss Dundas.

"I beg your pardon."

"The answer is pheasant. The first syllable was 'fez' and the second 'ant.'"

Alix clapped. "Oh, Isabella, how clever of you!"

"But you didn't wait for the whole word," I protested. "We didn't act the whole word in one."

"We got it without that," Alix pointed out. "Is it correct?"

"Well, yes," I said grudgingly. I could see she was bent on mischief.

She said, "We don't want to see the whole word acted now. I think you should pay a forfeit instead. What does everyone else say?"

Forfeits, of course, are immensely popular when someone else has to pay them. I regret to say that parlor games bring out a decidedly cruel tendency in the national character. The British would rather see punishments inflicted than prizes handed out. There were shouts of support from every side, and the Chaplain gleefully rubbed his hands.

George Holdfast had been appointed forfeit master at the start of the evening. We had agreed to pay our dues as we incurred them, rather than all at the end. "Very well," George said with due severity. "The three of you are to put four chairs in a row, take off your shoes and jump over them."

There was a moment's stunned silence.

"George," protested Lady Moira. "You can't ask His Royal Highness to do that."

"Moira, I'll thank you not to interfere," said her husband through gritted teeth.

"And you can't possibly ask a lady to perform acrobatics."

Goaded into a callous remark that I'm sure he regretted later, Holdfast said, "Why not? She's dressed for it."

I turned to Amelia. "Well, my dear, it seems that no appeal is possible. Do you think you could do it?"

She shook her head. "I think I'd rather be given another forfeit."

"Like kissing me?" suggested Bullivant.

"She'd rather jump in the moat," said Marcus sourly. "Are you going to try, sir?"

"What—kissing your sister?" I said like a shot. "That wouldn't be a forfeit at all."

Marcus scowled and turned pink.

"Put out the chairs," I said, "and let's see if it's possible."

"You have to try," insisted my loving wife.

Just to look at the four chairs side by side brought me out in gooseflesh. "You'd have to be a kangaroo," I said.

Then Osgot-Edge spoke up. "I b-b-believe I can do it."

I could have poleaxed him. This was no time to break ranks. "It seems that we do, after all, have a kangaroo in our midst. Show us how, if you insist," I said airily.

"C-could we hear the f-forfeit again?"

"With pleasure," said Holdfast. "You are to put four chairs in a row, take off your shoes and jump over them."

"I th-thought I heard right." With that, Osgot-Edge removed his shoes, put them side by side and jumped over them. *Over the shoes.*

"Oh, bravo, Wilfred!" cried Holdfast. "He saw through it. A trick forfeit!"

Everyone clapped, including the two of us who hadn't had the wit to guess the catch. Sheepishly Amelia and I performed the ritual of jumping over the shoes and so paid our dues. I felt extremely peeved that Osgot-Edge—of all people—had bested me.

Lady Moira proposed another round of charades, but she was voted down. After the belly dance, anything at all was going to be an anticlimax.

Alix suggested tentatively that we move on to Hide and Seek.

Marcus Pelham brusquely overruled her. "Spinning the Trencher. Then we can have more forfeits while Amelia changes into something more suitable."

If looks could kill, three of us would have murdered young Pelham on the spot. Alix was piqued at being ignored; I was angry on her behalf; and Amelia, I'm certain, had intended wearing her Turkish costume for the rest of the evening. But in the interest of social harmony we all submitted without a murmur. A silver tray was provided and we arranged ourselves in a large circle, taking turns to spin the "trencher" on its edge and call out the name of another player until each of the party had failed to catch it at least once and so incurred a forfeit. By turns we submitted to whatever indignity was demanded until Amelia reappeared wearing her dinner gown.

"Time for a different game, I think," said Holdfast, and loud support came from every side.

"Hide and Seek?" said Alix.

"I don't know about the rest of you, but I'm parched," said Pelham, pointedly ignoring her again. "Let's have something to drink and then see if anyone can think of a decent game to play." He pulled the bell rope.

His rudeness to Alix had become insupportable. I said in a voice that brooked no interference, "By all means send for the drinks. They will refresh us for the Hide and Seek that we shall play immediately after."

A silver punch bowl on a trolley was wheeled in. In my time I can fairly claim to have sampled as many punches as a fistfighter, and I've learned to treat them warily. When you take a straight brandy at least you know what you are drinking. If someone hands you a cup of warm liquid with strips of orange and lemon floating on the surface, there's little to distinguish it from the sort of pick-me-up you give an ailing child in the nursery—that is, until it picks you up and throws you through the ceiling.

This particular concoction was heavily based on French brandy, with, I think, additions of white wine and Jamaica rum. I'm willing to concede that there was a hint of calves-foot jelly in the flavor, and a few leaves of mint lay beguilingly among the orange peel, but it didn't beguile me. My eyes watered before I put the cup to my lips.

To my surprise two of the ladies drained their cups and put them out for more. Less to my surprise, they became increasingly noisy, not to say tipsy. Which two? Why, the Ladies Amelia Drummond and Moira Holdfast. Alix had put hers aside after a mere sip and Miss Dundas had asked for water.

There are almost as many ways of playing Hide and Seek as there are of making punch, so we had to agree to a set of rules. Alix didn't mind which version we played. I think it was Amelia who gave a bosky smile and suggested Sardines.

George Holdfast looked around in puzzlement. "Sardines?"

"Don't you know?" said Bullivant, amazed at such ignorance. "Oh, Sardines is quite the most jolly form of Hide and Seek. It has to be played in the dark."

"Galopshus!" muttered Lady Holdfast.

"One of us has to hide and we all count to ninety-nine and then begin the search. The first to find the hider will quietly join him—or her—in the hiding place. Both must remain as silent as possible. The next to find them squeezes in beside them, and so it goes on until all but one are wedged into the hiding place. Hence the name of the game."

"And the last pays a forfeit," cried Amelia. "Let's turn out the lights and begin."

Sensibly, Bullivant suggested that we first set some limits, or the game would range over the entire house and none of us would ever find each other. It was agreed to restrict the hiding places to the main rooms downstairs. The kitchens and servants' quarters were to be out of bounds.

"Splendid. Who shall go first?" said Holdfast.

"I propose Alix," said Miss Dundas to compensate a little for Pelham's rudeness.

"That's very kind," said Alix, "but I would rather be a seeker the first time."

Lady Holdfast said in a slurred voice, "One of the gentlemen. It ought to be one of the gentlemen. There are more of you."

"How about you, Bertie?" said Bullivant.

Before I opened my mouth, Alix scotched that suggestion. "He's too easy to find. Follow the stale cigar smoke and there he is. We want somebody who'll test us to the full."

"Then it must be Wilfred," Amelia declared. "He's a wonderfully quiet mover."

"Don't we know it," murmured Marcus Pelham close to my ear, before turning to Osgot-Edge and asking, "Are you game?"

The poet checked that his bow tie was still straight. "If you w-wish."

"Very well." Marcus turned to one of the maidservants who had come in to collect the punch bowl and asked her to have the lights turned off. "Better get on your way, Wilfred. We won't start counting until we're all in darkness."

"F-find me if you can, then." And Osgot-Edge hurried away like the White Rabbit.

"That's the morning room that way," young Pelham helpfully informed us. "It leads to the conservatory and the billiard room."

Holdfast said, "Ah, but he might double back in the dark and go through one of the other doors."

"He could, too," said Amelia, sounding quite proud of her poet. "He's like a panther."

About three minutes passed after the trolley had been trundled out. Then one of the maids returned and informed us that all the lights had been extinguished except for the drawing room in which we stood. Pelham dismissed her and turned it off himself.

We started counting in unison. When we got to ninety-nine, Pelham shouted, "Coming!"—and we applied ourselves to the hunt.

I'm sure you'll have gathered, reader, that half the entertainment in the game of Sardines is blundering into other seekers and the other half is squeezing up to the hiders (preferably ladies) after one has found the hiding place. Truth to tell, we weren't in total darkness as we searched, but it was dark enough to excuse a certain amount of horseplay. Before I had moved a step I found myself entangled with Lady Holdfast. Believe me, this was through no desire on my part. The woman rushed at me like a chimpanzee to its trainer and refused to let go. She was aptly named.

I was trapped in the curve of the grand piano, shocked and winded by the force of the attack. To add to my discomfiture, the shrieks and giggles all around were evidence enough that others were having highjinks whilst I was locked in this unwelcome embrace. I wouldn't have credited such strength in a lady of Moira Holdfast's maturity. But she wasn't content to hug me. She had her hands inside my dinner jacket. "I'm going to tickle you," she told me, and added, "but you'd better not tickle me."

Next, I felt my shirtfront tugged out of my trousers and cold fingers on my bare flesh. I flinched at the touch. I quivered. I'm extremely ticklish. I started making hooting sounds.

She said, "I've got you at my mercy now."

Then a voice beside us said, "Is that you, Moira?"

The voice was Sir George Holdfast's.

Lady Moira hesitated.

I didn't. I pushed her hands away and dodged clear. Stuffing my shirt back where it belonged, I bolted across the room and collided with someone at the door to the breakfast room. Someone pretty substantial.

"Who's that?" I asked.

"Your Royal Highness? Oh, my word, I beg your pardon. After you," said he, and I recognized the Chaplain's voice.

"Where have you looked, Rector?" I asked him.

"Behind the curtains in the morning room and in the window seat. He isn't there, sir."

"That's obvious," I said, "or you wouldn't be here. I shall search the billiard room." I groped my way towards a chair and crossed the morning room by passing from one piece of furniture to another. Was it my imagination, or did I hear voices ahead?

There was a swishing sound that might have been a curtain being drawn across, or possibly somebody appealing for silence as they heard me approach.

I reached the conservatory—a cold place filled with musty-smelling potted plants that had a gray, dead look in the moonlight through the glass roof. I doubted whether anyone would choose such an inhospitable room to hide in, so I moved on, through the door to the billiard room. This was a windowless room, pitch-black.

With my hands probing the space in front of me, I found the table and started feeling my way along its length. Some billiard rooms are equipped with cupboards large enough for several people to hide in and I proposed to investigate the far end.

There was no need to. I was moving crabwise alongside the billiard table when I felt a touch on my leg.

I said, "God Almighty!"

There were some stifled laughs.

I had found the hiding place. They were under the table. An obvious place to hide, you might be thinking, but allow me to point out that it was extremely clever. If they hadn't given themselves away by laughing, I would have gone straight past. I couldn't see anything when I bent to look.

A voice said, "Who is it?"

"Your husband, my dear," I answered to Alix. "Who else is here?"

"Sh! Someone's coming."

I ducked under the table and in so doing found myself intimately close to a lady. I knew she was a lady because my hand came inadvertently to rest on—forgive me—her thigh and I could feel warm flesh through a fabric that was certainly not the cloth of evening trousers. She placed a cool hand over mine and removed it. Her touch was too light for Alix and not warm enough to be Amelia, and Moira Holdfast in her present inebriated state wouldn't have removed my hand at all.

So she could only be Isabella Dundas.

In the spirit of the game, I edged closer. I got a delicious whiff of some Parisian scent and a sudden jab in the ribs from her bustle, which I was unlucky enough to press against. I gasped.

"Found you!" cried the Chaplain, who had followed me into the billiard room, and was standing beside the table. Just to make sure, he swung his leg and caught my other set of ribs with the point of his shoe.

I protested painfully.

The Chaplain said, "So sorry, whoever you are. I say, is there room under there for a little one?" He scrambled in, bowled me over and practically suffocated me.

Now there was pandemonium. Others had heard my shout and dashed into the room, desperate not to be last. Bodies hurled themselves into the hiding place, unaware that like some victim of a medieval torture I was bent backwards over the steel bars of Isabella's bustle.

I yelled for mercy.

"Somebody's hurt!" one of the company said superfluously.

"Take care!" said another voice. "It sounds like Bertie."

They made a united effort to find some space for me and I succeeded in rolling off the metal hump.

"Better?" somebody enquired. People do say asinine things at such times.

I didn't reply.

I think it was Marcus Pelham who presently observed, "Well, if there's anyone still trying to find us after that, I'll eat my hat."

"Who's here, then?" asked the Chaplain. "Let's see. Be so good as to answer your names. Lady Drummond?"

One by one, we answered to the roll call like children in school.

"That's everyone," said the Chaplain.

"No," said Isabella. "You called nine names. There are ten of us."

"Nine of us and Mr. Osgot-Edge, who was the hider. There was no need to call his name, because he must have been the first here. Isn't that so, Wilfred?"

There was no response.

"Wilfred?"

"Stop playing games, Wilfred," said George Holdfast.

"Damnit, we *are* playing games," said Pelham testily.

"But we play fair. Speak up, Wilfred. Are you under here?"

"He *must* be, or what are the rest of us doing?"

Nobody supplied an answer. There was a thoughtful interval of about half a minute.

Then one of the ladies made a sound like a steam engine and it soon became obvious to all that she was trying to stifle a giggle. She gave up the attempt and laughed out loud.

"Is that you, Amelia?" said Pelham.

Amelia erupted into laughter. "He isn't here!" she managed to say between shrieks of mirth. "Claude and I were under here first. We wanted a place for a cuddle. Then Alix came along and we had to pretend we were playing the game." She broke into another peal of laughter. "Wilfred is still hiding somewhere, wondering if anyone will ever find him!"

We had all been well and truly gulled, and now we all joined in the laughter, except, I suppose, for young Pelham, who must have disapproved strongly of his sister's spooning with Bullivant. Even I shook with laughter and hurt my bruised ribs in the process.

"Come now, let's all stand up and see if we can do better this time," the Chaplain exhorted us as if we were at choir practice.

Bullivant said, "I like it here."

"Saucebox!" said Amelia dotingly. My assessment of her as a flirt was amply justified.

"The Rector is right," said Holdfast. "Come on, everyone. One of us will have to pay a forfeit, remember."

There was a distinct reluctance to move. Crushed together as we were, united in the silly error we had made, the party had in some mysterious way attained a feeling of kinship. How odd, that civilized people should become comfortable with each other sitting in the dark under a table—more at ease than they were at dinner, or in the drawing room. If one of us had started to sing, I'm sure we would all have joined in.

However, the game was still on. We turned out to resume the hunt.

"I'm going to look in the library," said Moira Holdfast.

I rather think that she had said it for my ears, so I resolved to go in the opposite direction. I retraced my way through the conservatory to the breakfast room. Someone was ahead of me—George Holdfast, as it turned out, because I heard his voice presently.

He had stepped across to the food lift and opened the door. I heard him haul on the rope and bring up the dumbwaiter. He sounded pleased with what he discovered there. "By George, here you are!"

If this meant he had found Osgot-Edge I was surprised, not to say shirty. This wasn't playing fair. There wasn't space enough inside the dumbwaiter for more than two or three to hide. And it would be far from safe.

Yet as I crossed the room to join them I sensed that something was wrong.

Holdfast spoke in an urgent whisper, "Wake up, Wilfred." Then, "Oh, Jupiter!"

I was at his side. "What is it?"

He gasped, "Horrible!" Then he grasped my arm. "For pity's sake, keep the ladies away."

9

I struck a match and held it close to the lift, a damp match, it turned out—or perhaps I moistened it with my hot hand—because the flame refused to ignite the wood. It flared for a second and died, but in that brief effulgence it showed me what George Holdfast had discovered. The dumbwaiter contained the hunched, motionless body of Wilfred Osgot-Edge. The handle of a knife jutted from his chest. A thin streak of blood had trickled down his shirt.

Reader, you may think me obtuse, but I hesitated to believe the evidence of my eyes. I suspected a prank. To understand this, you ought to be aware that it pleases me immensely to play practical jokes on my friends, the more elaborate the better. Anyone as expert as I in leg-pulling needs no telling that a private house party is a heaven-sent opportunity. One needs to be more than ever on one's guard against other jokers. So a stabbed man in a dumbwaiter may not be all that he seems. In a bored voice, I said, "Send him down, George."

"What, sir?"

"The lift. See if you can lower it."

He obeyed. The mechanism rumbled and squeaked.

I said, "Not all the way down. We don't want it to reach the kitchen. Stop it halfway." I struck another match. "Nicely done. Now we shan't have to turn the ladies away."

His eyes gleamed like coach lamps. "Didn't you see the knife, sir? Someone stabbed him."

"I wouldn't leap to conclusions if I were you, George."

"That was real blood, sir. Look at my fingers. Still wet."

It took the evidence of his bloodstained fingers to convince me that what I had just seen was no tomfoolery. Real blood has a smell that any hunting man can recognize. Suddenly the true horror of what we had just seen struck at me like a serpent. My hand twitched and the match went out.

Somewhere behind us, a board creaked.

Holdfast caught his breath.

I muttered to him, "Say nothing."

"Who's that?" asked Amelia's voice. "Who's cheating? Who's been lighting matches?" She fairly charged across the floor, caught at my sleeve and giggled. "Got you! It's Bertie, isn't it? Let's feel if you've got whiskers."

"There's no need." I struck the next match.

She said, "Two of you! This is all against the rules, you know, two gentlemen collaborating. We ladies are entitled to some help."

I said grimly, "My dear Lady Drummond, I think we should arrange for you to have a cup of strong, black coffee."

"Fiddlesticks!" She laughed. "Bertie, I'm not drunk, just a little merry, and where's the harm in that? Besides, we're in the middle of a game. We haven't found Wilfred yet." She gave me a stare. "Have we?"

The black coffee wasn't required. She sobered up appreciably when I told her what had happened. She said, "What in the name of God are we going to do?"

My brain was temporarily addled. I made a performance of lighting another match in hopes of Holdfast suggesting something, but he was no help at all.

From another room came the coarse, now-incongruous laughter of people still trying to play Sardines. Amelia answered her own question. "First, we must stop this ridiculous game and get the lights on. Oh, Bertie, they'll be *so* alarmed."

Holdfast said, "We ought to fetch the police."

"My thought exactly," said I, crossing to the sideboard to a candlestick I had spotted. I managed to light it before the match went out. "By Jove, yes, we'd better send for Sweeney. He'll help to calm things down."

"Who is Sweeney?"

"My man from the Royal Household Police."

"I hope he can catch the murderer," said Holdfast.

At this, Amelia gave a horrified cry, turned away from us and vomited. Happily the jug from which the porridge was served at breakfast was at hand. That it was murder seemed to have eluded our poor, benighted hostess until this moment. One had to be sympathetic. You don't expect such things to happen under your own roof—least of all when you're entertaining the Heir Apparent.

Amelia soon learned that my presence in the house was more of an asset than an embarrassment. In the next hour I took command, summoning one of the butlers to restore the gaslight; dispatching a footman to fetch Sweeney from the lodge; calling the guests into the large drawing room and announcing what had happened. There was no point in sparing the ladies' feelings.

There were gasps of astonishment all round, and Lady Holdfast swooned, or appeared to (she may have succumbed to alcoholic stupor). Calmly and reassuringly I informed them that the matter was already under investigation.

"Might one be so bold as to enquire who is in charge, sir?" asked the Chaplain.

Without pause for thought I answered, "I am." Then, seeing several jaws drop in surprise, I quietly added, ". . . assisted by Inspector Sweeney, whom you will all meet presently. We shall question everyone in the house and bring this investigation to a speedy conclusion." Taking care not to look in Alix's direction, I then stated my own credentials. "I am not without experience in detective investigations."

"Sir, I hope you'll question the servants first," said Bullivant. "You're not going to find a murderer among present company."

Lady Holdfast, restored to consciousness, piped up, "I think the policeman should be instructed to protect us, or we shall all be murdered in our beds."

"I shall see that a patrol is put on the corridors," I promised. "And as to your suggestion, Claude, yes, we shall shortly summon the servants and question them rigorously."

"Have you any conception how many there are?" said Pelham with his usual want of charm.

"That is immaterial," said I.

"Thirty-seven are permanently in service here," he insisted on telling me. "Twenty more have been hired for the week. To that figure must be added a further thirty or so who are visitors—the retinues you brought with you. I make that eighty-seven at the very least."

"Then have them assemble in the Hall in fifteen minutes," I retorted crisply.

He glared, reddened and marched out.

I glanced at the clock on the mantelpiece. Half past ten. "Unless you have anything germane to impart to me, ladies and gentlemen, I shall now confer with Inspector Sweeney."

That worthy officer, when I received him in the anteroom, was anxiety personified. With his toes turned inwards and a tortured look on his features he gave the impression that he needed urgently to shake hands with an old friend, as the saying goes.

"Not a living soul came in or out of the main gate tonight, Your Royal Highness. It was shut and bolted."

I assured him that nobody held him personally to blame. "I sent for you, Sweeney, because I shall require your help in investigating this brutal crime."

"Me, sir?" he said, performing a terrified jig.

"You're an inspector of police."

"I'm no detective, sir. Bodyguarding is my speciality. I think we should call in the criminal investigation boys."

"Allow me to be the judge of that," I told him brusquely. "What has happened is desperately unfortunate, for Lady Drummond, for her honored guests and not least for me. We can't have it broadcast to all and sundry that I was within an ace of being murdered tonight—because that is what the press will make of it if the word gets out."

"Jesus, Joseph and Mary!" muttered Sweeney, transparently thinking not of me, but his career as a Royal bodyguard.

To reinforce the point I sketched a small, but vivid, word picture. "Imagine Her Majesty the Queen opening the *Times* tomorrow morning. No, Inspector, this is not a case for the common police. You and I are going to solve it together and bring the murderer to account."

"Begging your pardon, if we do, sir, it's bound to come out. There would have to be a trial."

"Not necessarily."

"I don't follow you, sir."

"Better if you don't," I said cryptically.

It was necessary for me to stand halfway up the main staircase to address all the assembled servants, and I had to concede that young Pelham had made a valid point. Normally one has no conception how many domestics are involved in a house party because they are never seen *en masse*. The scale of the investigation came home to me forcefully when I looked down on those serried ranks, the liveried staff to the fore, and behind them so many white caps that I thought of Cowes and felt a touch of *mal de mer*.

I didn't need to inform them of what had happened, of course. The electric telegraph is nothing to the buzz of servants' tongues. I ordered them on pain of instant dismissal without character to say not one word more—except to me or Sweeney—of what had happened. They were not to speak of it to a living soul, now or ever after. I said that we should require from each of them a precise and complete account of their movements between nine and ten P.M. that evening. Those untutored in writing were instructed to obtain assistance. The statements would be collected by the house steward and handed to Sweeney by midnight.

After dismissing them I beckoned to Colwell and told him to send four men to the breakfast room to remove the body after I had examined it.

He cleared his throat in the way senior servants do when some impediment to duty is exercising them.

"Well?" I asked.

"May I be so bold as to enquire the destination of the deceased, Your Royal Highness?"

"His destination?" I knew very well what he meant, but I couldn't resist saying, "That's a question for a higher authority than I, Mr. Colwell. Try St. Peter. Or were you merely asking where the men should take the body?"

"That was my meaning, sir."

"I suggest somewhere removed from the house, some outbuilding that will serve as a temporary mortuary. What's that place beyond the kitchen garden?"

"The game larder, sir."

"Ah."

"There is a harness room attached to the coach house that is not in use, sir."

"Well, then. You've answered your own question."

"Yes, sir."

He still seemed reluctant to move, so I said, "Is there something else?"

Colwell cleared his throat again. "If I may venture to make a suggestion, sir . . ."

"What?"

"You asked me to send four men to the breakfast room."

"Yes."

"That would involve conveying the gentleman's remains through the state rooms to the main entrance and down the steps. If, instead, sir, we lowered the dumbwaiter to the scullery, the men could carry their melancholy burden through the tradesmen's entrance without further inconvenience to the guests."

It was a fine point of decorum, weighing respect for the dead against the sensibilities of the living. As a means of conveyance for a corpse, and a gentleman's corpse at that, the dumbwaiter was hideously inappropriate. However, since Osgot-Edge was already in there, he might as well be removed at the most convenient level.

I gave my consent. "We'll do it as tastefully as the circumstances allow. I shall proceed to the breakfast room with Inspector Sweeney and examine the body there, at the top of the shaft."

"Very good, sir."

"You will assemble your men in the scullery and when the signal is given, er . . . what is the signal?"

"There is a speaking tube, sir."

"I shall give the instruction down the tube and you will lower the dumbwaiter."

With that settled, I snapped my fingers at Sweeney, who was edging towards the cloak room, and we returned at once to the breakfast room. There, I instructed him to close all the doors and raise the dumbwaiter.

My confidence drained as Sweeney hauled on the rope. Suppose, after all, this *had* been a practical joke, and Osgot-Edge was poised to leap out, alive and smiling. Or suppose the merry jester had contrived to escape, leaving the dumbwaiter empty. I would look pretty silly after my solemn speeches to all and sundry. I'm sure it was this uncertainty that stopped me from feeling a proper sense of grief or regret at his passing. I couldn't shake off the suspicion that I was being duped.

So you will understand why I breathed a sigh of relief—no, let's be truthful, I practically cheered—when the corpse came into view with the knife still protruding from the chest. It was propped up in a sitting position in the cramped space, but it looked decidedly more dead than it had by match light.

"God help us," said Sweeney in a whisper.

I ordered him to withdraw the knife from the body.

"Is that wise, sir?" he asked. "Shouldn't we be leaving it for the police to see?"

"Sweeney, you are the police."

"That is a fact, sir."

"Do you have a handkerchief?"

He was silent for a moment. "What would I be wanting with a handkerchief, sir?"

"You wipe the blade with it. We don't want to ruin our clothes.

Take the one from his top pocket, then. Keep it ready in your left hand and withdraw the knife with your right."

He braced himself and grasped the hilt. The blade came out easily.

He wiped it clean and handed it to me.

So far as I could judge, it was a bone-handled kitchen knife, used, presumably, for cutting meat or vegetables. I ought to say much used, for the blade had been worn to a virtual spike. It was extremely sharp. No great strength would have been required to have plunged such a weapon into a man's chest, so I could not exclude the possibility that a woman had committed the crime.

"We must ask the cook whether this is one of her knives," I told Sweeney.

"I'll attend to that at once, sir."

"No you won't. Not yet. Go through the pockets."

Starting with the jacket, he made a painstaking search of Osgot-Edge's clothes, handing each item to me. Truth to tell, the harvest didn't amount to much: another handkerchief, a pencil and some loose change.

"Are you sure there's nothing else in the top pocket? No slip of paper?"

He pulled out the lining to show me.

I decided to tell him about the pieces of paper found with Queenie Chimes and Jerry Gribble. "I was half expecting to find another scrap with 'Wednesday' written on it," I admitted. "It's a good thing we didn't."

"It is and it isn't," he said with Irish logic. "If it was there it would raise the unpleasant possibility that Miss Chimes and the Duke were murdered; but as it isn't, we don't have much to go on."

"Come now, we've hardly begun our inquiries," I said with my usual optimism. "Can you use a whistle?"

His blue eyes regarded me with mystification.

I reached for the speaking tube and handed it to him. I've never been obliged to whistle for anything.

Comprehension flooded over his features. He pulled the whistle from the tube and blew on it.

I took it from him. "Colwell, are you there?"

The answer came up, "Your Royal Highness?"

"We have finished up here."

"Very good, sir."

The ropes tightened, the pulleys squeaked and Osgot-Edge went down like the setting sun.

* * *

"Is the scoundrel apprehended?" was the question that was flung at me when I returned to the drawing room. It came from the Chaplain.

The tense faces of the guests regarded me in a way that I didn't find at all agreeable. It was as if they blamed me for what had happened. Obviously they had worked themselves up into a frightful lather. Even Alix looked faintly skeptical of my authority.

I informed them that inquiries were vigorously underway. Written statements had been demanded from all the servants and by the morning we expected to have a list of possible suspects. Meanwhile it would be sensible if each guest appointed a trusted servant from his own retinue to stand guard outside his bedroom door for the night.

"I've arranged that anyway," said Holdfast. "I think we should issue them with weapons from the gun room."

"Oh, do you?" said Amelia. "And what do you suppose will happen if one of us is compelled to visit the bathroom in the night?"

"Forget the guns," said Bullivant. "Better issue us with jerries instead."

It was a measure of the crisis that nobody smiled.

The guns were rejected by common consent. Presently the footmen arrived with the candles to escort us to our rooms. Holdfast took out his watch. "Good Lord, it's almost Thursday already."

While the party was starting to disperse, Alix chose her moment to draw me aside. "Bertie, I insist that you send for the police. This isn't the time to play your detective games."

I reminded her that Sweeney was a policeman.

She said, "Sweeney wouldn't recognize a clue if it turned a double somersault and bit him on the nose. He's a bodyguard, not an investigator."

I said, "I hope you haven't spoken in these terms to anybody else."

"Of course not! They'd panic if they knew. You're trifling with their lives, Bertie—with all our lives. There could be another murder in the night."

"My dear, I'll make you a solemn promise. If anyone else is killed tonight I shall send for the detective police at once."

"That will be too late for the unfortunate victim."

It was no use arguing with her. I said, "I think I shall sleep in your bed tonight."

Just as I hoped, she was derailed by the remark. We've had separate rooms for years. "Where do you propose that *I* should sleep?"

"Next to me."

"Bertie, how *could* you—when a murderer is at large?"

"I think you misunderstand me, my dear," I said piously. "My thoughts are exclusively devoted to the personal safety of the lady I love and cherish more than any other."

Her lip trembled as it does when I remember our wedding anniversary. No more was said about sending for the police.

There was a diplomatic cough from somewhere behind me. I turned and saw Colwell the steward and took a few steps towards him, well out of Alix's earshot.

"Did you convey the body safely to the coach house?"

"Yes, sir. I have locked the harness room."

"And have the servants produced their statements?"

"Almost all have been handed in, sir."

"Excellent. Give them to Sweeney as soon as possible. Tell me, do some of the servants live out?"

"There are some from the village, yes, sir."

"Are they discreet?"

"I believe I can vouch for them, sir. We had an unfortunate incident last year and it was kept from the village. We pride ourselves on a very loyal household."

"That may be so," I said, "but tonight's affair is rather more sensational than some boy shot by accident. Mr. Osgot-Edge was murdered, no question of it."

"I still have confidence in my staff, sir."

"Good, but it may be prudent to issue a further warning to anyone leaving the house."

"No one is going off duty tonight, sir."

I gave an approving nod. Colwell was a credit to his office.

He lingered, glancing about him to see if he could be overheard.

A warning pulse started beating in my temple. I said, "Is there some other matter that you wish to bring to my attention?"

"There is, sir. We made a rather disturbing discovery when we removed the body from the dumbwaiter. A piece of paper, tucked under his leg. I took the precaution of pocketing it before anyone else had an opportunity to read it. In view of the scrap of paper I found on Monday evening when Miss Chimes collapsed, I thought this may be relevant to the investigation."

"What did it say?"

"I have it here, sir." He handed me a piece of newspaper.

And of course you are correct, reader. It had been cut from the *Times* and the word printed on it was "Wednesday." But that was not all. Something else had been added by hand, in black ink, so that the message in its entirety read: *Wednesday's Corpse.*

I was forced to conclude that I was dealing not with one murder, but three. *Wednesday's Corpse* implied that the deaths labeled *Monday* and *Tuesday* had been planned and executed by the same evil assassin.

THURSDAY

10

I believe it was about 1:30 A.M. when Alix said, "Bertie, if you don't mind, I would like to get some sleep tonight."

I told her not to be such a killjoy.

"But I can scarcely breathe! I really must object."

"My dear, you never used to. In fact I was given to understand that you found it quite agreeable."

"Yes, but not in bed. How much longer are you going to be?"

"I suppose I've finished," I said, reaching for an ashtray to extinguish the objectionable cigar butt. "I thought it would help me concentrate, but I can't say I've reached any rational conclusion."

She grasped the bedclothes tightly and made a performance of turning over. "Murder isn't rational. Kindly turn out the lamp, would you?"

I obliged. But I remained sitting up in the dark, unable to rest until I had made more sense of the evening's appalling discovery. Queenie Chimes had not, after all, collapsed from natural causes; she had been poisoned. Jerry Gribble hadn't committed suicide; he had been shot. Osgot-Edge had been stabbed, and the murderer had claimed all three like a sportsman bagging game.

I shuddered.

Murder isn't rational, Alix had pointed out, yet calculation must have played a part in these killings, for the pieces of newspaper had clearly been cut from the *Times* beforehand and left like calling cards. The killer was boasting: *Look at my tally—a murder a day. Be sure and credit the deaths on Monday and Tuesday to me as well as Wednesday, won't you?*

I couldn't imagine why anyone should want to murder three innocent people—a trio so different as a pretty actress, a middle-aged Duke and a poet. Admittedly Queenie and Jerry were lovers, so they may have been killed as a brace, if you'll pardon my persisting with the sporting idiom. But I could think of no other connections.

Well, you'll have gathered the direction my thoughts were taking. It seemed to me that the victims had been picked off like prey, impersonally, for no other reason than that they happened to be guests in Desborough Hall at this time. Such callous slaughter is not unknown. I can't expect my twentieth-century reader to have heard of the East End murders committed in 1888 by a seeker of publicity known to the press as Jack the Ripper. At the time they made a considerable sensation. He wrote letters challenging the police to catch him, but up to now he is still at liberty. I tell you candidly, sitting in that darkened room, I could foresee a campaign just as brutal and alarming as the Ripper's—in fact more alarming, because it was aimed not at streetwalkers, but people of refinement.

If this murderer is a publicity seeker, I told myself, then my conduct in the case is amply justified. Silence catches the mouse. He wanted the world to know about these daily killings and the telltale scraps of newspaper left beside the bodies. I frustrated his plan. Not even my fellow guests are fully aware of what he has done. So I have trapped him into adding something to his calling card.

Wednesday's *Corpse*.

The addition had been written in a crude, spidery copperplate hand, probably disguised. John Sweeney had by now collected his statements from the servants, but I doubted if we would learn much by comparing their handwriting with that of the murderer. Half of them were sure to be illiterate, and must have asked others to assist them.

Alix interrupted my thoughts by saying, "Bertie, are you proposing to sit up all night?"

I said, "I'm thinking."

"Can't you think lying down? There's a draft down my back. . . . What are you thinking about?"

"A piece of paper."

"Notepaper?"

"It's of no importance."

She clicked her tongue in annoyance. "It must be important, to keep you awake like this. Does it have some bearing on what happened to poor Wilfred?"

"I can't say."

"Bertie, you're hiding something from me."

I groaned inwardly. My dear wife is remarkably tolerant of my activities. She seldom protests or interferes, but she will not abide flannel.

She would have prized the truth from me, syllable by syllable, so I surrendered the whole bloodcurdling story of the week's events without more ado, and I must say she took it with commendable *sang-froid.*

"*Wednesday's Corpse?*" she repeated. "How melodramatic—as if every day brings a fresh fatality."

"It does," I said.

"I do dislike that word 'corpse.' It sounds so final."

I said, "It's curtains for some poor blighter, however you put it."

"Yes, but 'body' is less horrid, don't you think? *Wednesday's Body.* This murderer has no feeling for the English language."

"That's rich," I said, "coming from a Dane."

"Who are you to criticize, a Saxe-Coburg who rolls his 'r's?"

Alix and I have had this exchange many times before. It descends rapidly into mild vulgarity, but we find it amusing. I think we both welcomed it as a temporary relief from the grim events of the day. Finally the banter ran out and we went silent.

After an interval I asked her, "Were you trying to make a serious point?"

"About the word he used? I don't know. It sounds out of place. And yet . . ."

"And yet what?"

"I'm not sure."

She yawned.

I eased myself under the bedclothes, stretched and turned on my side. I was almost asleep when Alix piped up from her side of the bed.

"It scans."

"Mm?"

"'Corpse.' It's only one syllable, so it scans. Like the word 'child' in the rhyme. *That*'s why he used it."

"Which rhyme?"

"Oh, Bertie, don't be so dense! You know it. Everyone knows it:

"*Monday's child is fair of face.*
Tuesday's child is full of grace.
Wednesday's child is full of woe.
Thursday's child has far to go.

Friday's child is loving and giving.
Saturday's child works hard for a living.
But the child that is born on the Sabbath Day
Is bonny and blithe and good and gay."

In the darkness I scratched my beard thoughtfully. Of course I knew the verse. I'd had it recited to me often enough in the nursery. I was a Tuesday child, full of grace. I'd rarely listened to what was said about the children born on other days of the week.

Sounding very like my old governess, Alix said, "Now substitute the word 'corpse' for 'child.'"

I saw the point. However, I wasn't much impressed by it yet, though I did my best not to trample on Alix's feelings. "Yes, it fits up to a point. Monday's corpse was Queenie Chimes, fair of face, certainly. Tuesday's was Jerry, and if His Grace the Duke of Bournemouth doesn't fit the rhyme, I don't know who does. Full of grace by birthright, bless him. But there the coincidences end, I'm sorry to say. I wouldn't describe Osgot-Edge as full of woe. He was a cheerful fellow, a bit of a lady's man on the quiet. No, my dear, it doesn't match up, I'm afraid."

She said, "Perhaps his poetry was full of woe."

"Woeful, I'll grant you," I quipped. "No, to be fair what he wrote was meant to be amusing. Do you recall the poem that was read out to us on Sunday evening? That line about the lion saying 'Let us prey' probably went over your head, my dear, being Danish. It was a pun. Did your English tutor teach you about puns?"

Alix said, "Something you feed to an elephant?"—and I suspect that she smiled in the dark.

We lapsed into a drowsy silence. I may even have dozed a little.

Suddenly Alix startled me by saying aloud, "I've got it! Wilfred Osgot-Edge."

I said, "You're talking in your sleep."

She said, "His initials. It's his initials—W.O.E."

"Woe?" I propped myself up. "*Full of woe!* Alix, you're right! You must be!"

"Don't sound so surprised, then."

There was another pause, filled, this time, with a spate of mental activity.

Finally I said, "What day is it?"

"Bertie, you know. It's already tomorrow. Thursday."

"Refresh my memory. What was the line about Thursday?"

"'*Thursday's child*'—or *corpse*—'has far to go.'"

"Far to go . . . Oh, my hat!—Miss Dundas, the explorer!"

I give Alix her due. She objected strenuously to my calling on Miss Dundas in the middle of the night. I would have expected no less. Clearly I was putting my personal safety—not to mention the future of the realm—at risk. I could have been struck down by the killer as soon as I stepped outside the bedroom door.

However, I was adamant. Perhaps I'm too gallant for my own safety, but I rather relished myself in the role of protector to Miss Dundas. And as I explained to Alix, no one else except the murderer knew the danger the lady was in. I had a responsibility to warn her. A moral responsibility.

For that, I was treated to a few uncomplimentary remarks about my morals that need not be repeated here. Alix also complained that I wasn't showing sufficient concern for *her* safety, and refused to spend the rest of the night alone, so I had to ring for her woman-of-the-bedchamber, Charlotte Knollys. Poor Charlotte, plucked from a warm bed upstairs, burst in seconds later in a flannel nightgown expecting heaven knows what emergency. Upon seeing me she gave a cry of dismay and put her hand to her curlers. In the confusion I stepped past her through the open door.

Immediately four or five faces stared at me. I'd quite forgotten the servants on guard outside the bedroom doors. Decently clad as I was in dressing gown and slippers, I nevertheless felt slightly foolish carrying the poker I'd picked up for protection; however, I think they were more ill at ease than I. Tucking the poker under my arm like a swagger stick, I marched past them without a word along the corridor to Isabella Dundas's room.

It was disturbing to discover that hers was the only door without a guard. I tapped lightly and got no response, so I tried a second time, with a firmer knock.

Nothing.

I glanced over my shoulder and immediately the five pale faces watching me rotated like lighthouse lamps and looked the other way. I gripped the door handle, fully expecting to find the door locked.

It opened. I stepped inside, into a more profound darkness. "Miss Dundas?"

No reply. This was not encouraging.

I took a step inwards, hands probing the space in front of me, while behind me the door shut with a thump loud enough to waken the dead.

I said, "Isabella?" and still elicited no response.

Becoming increasingly perturbed, I felt in my pocket for matches and then cursed my negligence; I'd left them in Alix's bedroom.

I suppose it was pride that stopped me from returning immediately to fetch them. I didn't relish the looks I would get in the corridor. Instead I chose to proceed as well as I could without a light. After all, it was just another bedroom to negotiate in the dark, I told myself, to keep up the proverbial pecker. This wouldn't be the first, or, one trusted, the last.

Such blind faith!

One step forward was all I took. Without warning I felt my ankles gripped by a cord of some description. It tightened so suddenly that I keeled off balance and crashed to the floor. Immediately I was smothered by some all-enveloping fabric and trussed up, notwithstanding my strongly voiced objections.

And would you believe nobody came to my aid? That's the penalty of being of the blood Royal: people are only too happy to dance attendance on you for as long as you conduct yourself according to protocol, but the moment anything untoward occurs they are too timid to come forward. I had to wait, practically suffocating, until my captor chose to loosen the bonds. Fortunately, it wasn't long. I was aware of a sawing motion at my neck that I sensibly and correctly took to be the cord being severed. Then the blanket—for that was what covered my head and torso—was drawn back from my face like a cowl and I found myself staring first at a knife blade gleaming in candlelight, and beyond it at Miss Dundas.

She said without a trace of remorse, "So it *is* you."

"Would you have liked a fanfare?" I said with sarcasm. "If you were here all the time, why the deuce didn't you speak up?"

She said, "Sir, I had to be certain. After all, it could have been someone impersonating you. I'm sorry if you had a shock, but an undefended lady is entitled to take reasonable steps to protect herself when a murderer is afoot."

"Reasonable!"

She said, "You're more fortunate than you realize. You could have found yourself dangling by your heels from that beam above you. If you'd been a baboon I wouldn't have hesitated. Don't look like that, sir. I was about to explain that this is a simple hunter's trap. I used to rig one up when I camped in the jungle. Ideally I'd have used rope and a good, strong net, but sashcord and a blanket had to suffice tonight. Allow me to finish untying you and then you can tell me why you're here."

With as much dignity as I could salvage, I remarked, "I merely looked in to save your life. I have reason to believe that you are next on the murderer's list."

She gave that amused curl of the lip that I had noted before. In the circumstances I excused it as a nervous reaction. "Surely there isn't a list?"

"I'm afraid that is the inescapable conclusion," I told her. I explained about the cuttings from the *Times* and the rhyme linking each of the victims to days of the week.

"So you interpret 'far to go' as fitting me?" she said with that smile still lingering about her mouth.

"No one else in the party has traveled so far, or is ever likely to," I answered.

After a moment's reflection she said, "Perhaps the words are meant to apply in another sense. Have you considered that?"

"You had better explain."

"Well, without wishing to alarm you, sir, it might be thought by some that the throne of England is the very height of society. In that sense you, the Heir Apparent . . ."

I said, "No, no. That's too farfetched for words."

She finished loosening the cord around my ankles. "Well, sir, now that you have warned me—and I thank you for that—I shall rig up my trap again."

"Extremely wise."

"Then I think we can safely go to bed."

After this astonishing remark I stared saucer-eyed at Miss Dundas. In my time I've met more than my share of ladies who fit the appellation of "fast," but never one who came to the point without a hint of passion, not a sigh, nor a blush. It was as matter-of-fact as putting on a shoe, and, to be candid, just about as stimulating. After all, I was here on a mission of life and death. True, there was a certain piquancy to visiting a lady in her bedroom, but I wasn't expecting a tumble. Even a courtesan would have pulled up the drawbridge under present circumstances. To hold her at bay, I said, "That's very agreeable, my dear, but rather sudden. Wouldn't you care for some liquid refreshment? I see you have a decanter and some glasses here."

She cleared her throat. "It seems that I expressed myself badly. I propose, sir, that you return to your bed and I to mine."

"Ah." A misunderstanding. The wind returned to my sails. "No, I shall remain here."

"I beg your pardon."

"I said I shall stay here. Your life is in grave danger, Isabella."

She gave a sigh and ran her hand through her hair, which hung loose over her nightgown. "Sir—"

"Bertie."

"Bertie, then. I appreciate your concern, but it won't be necessary."

I said, "I'll be the judge of that, my dear."

"I can protect myself."

"Of that I am certain," I said. "However, I have taken it as my solemn duty to protect everyone in this house by apprehending the murderer. Having rather cleverly deduced that this room is earmarked for the next crime, I intend to remain here until I've made an arrest."

"Couldn't you wait outside the door?"

"And advertise my presence? No, no. I must surprise the villain."

Overwhelmed by the force of my reasoning, Miss Dundas applied herself to re-erecting her man trap, with some assistance from me. When the job was done, she said, "I think I will investigate that decanter. Will you join me? By a fortunate oversight two glasses seem to have been provided."

A fortunate oversight! You might be familiar with jungles, I thought, but you don't know much about the secret ways of country house parties, Isabella.

She climbed into bed with her Madeira and I sat high-mindedly in the armchair.

"Who will it be?" she asked presently. "Whom do you suspect?"

"If I knew for certain," I answered guardedly, "I would already have made the arrest."

"I can't think who would wish to murder me," she said after taking a sip of Madeira.

"I dare say each of the victims would have ventured the same comment."

"Oh." She drew up her knees and clasped them over the bedclothes. "Are these murders without cause, then?"

I didn't answer. I didn't know.

"Really," she went on, "one ought to consider what the victims had in common, apart from being here this week. An actress, a duke and a poet. What about Queenie, the first to be killed. What do we know about her? She was with Irving's company at the Lyceum, wasn't she?"

"I gather so, in a small capacity, a non-speaking role. I found her charming and inoffensive."

"I didn't speak to her," said Miss Dundas. "She was shepherded closely by Jerry Gribble."

"'Shepherded,'" I said. "That's a delicate way of putting it. Jerry would have liked that. Yes, there's no doubt she was included in the party as company for Jerry. They met at a cricket match six months ago, he told me. She was selling tombola tickets. Poor fellow, he had a fatal weakness for the ladies."

She tilted an eyebrow.

"Well he was twice divorced," I said. "He made it clear to Queenie that he wouldn't be getting spliced a third time."

She asked, "What happened to the ex-wives? Perhaps there was resentment if they fell on hard times later."

"And saw him shepherding pretty young actresses, do you mean? Good thinking. But I have to tell you that Angela, the first Duchess, died in childbirth after she married a French count; and Polly, the second, lives very comfortably in New Orleans, happily married to a ship owner."

"I wonder whether anyone else bore some grudge against Jerry?" she persisted.

"That's hard to imagine. He was a dear fellow, a gentleman in every sense, the salt of the earth."

"Twice divorced?"

"But utterly without blame. The judge found the wives at fault in each case."

She rolled her eyes upwards; precisely why, I couldn't say. "Well, Bertie, if you're right, Miss Chimes and Jerry Gribble were two delightful people who gave no offense to anyone. What of Wilfred Osgot-Edge? He was a more complex person than the others, was he not?"

I pondered this for a moment. "Because he was a poet, d'you mean? That may be so, but I found him straightforward enough. When he succeeded in putting more than two words together, he generally had something practical to say."

"Yes, I rather admired the efforts he made to be sociable. I think what I mean is that poetry and shooting are difficult to reconcile—the one creative and the other destructive."

"Forms of self-expression," I explained. "Perfectly understandable for a fellow who is tongue-tied to write down his thoughts in verse. And what a tonic for his confidence to shoot better than the blighters who show him up in conversation. He was devilish fast on the trigger."

Miss Dundas signaled a spicy remark by clearing her throat. "I formed the impression that he wasn't exactly slow in other matters."

"Matters of the heart?" said I, mindful of what I had heard in the corridor the night before.

She smiled faintly. I'm sure she knew Osgot-Edge had winkled his way into Amelia's bed. Nothing in a country house at night escapes the notice of the fair sex.

Never one to beat about the bush, I said, "Our charming hostess might be able to enlighten us further on that subject. Come to think of it, the frolics yesterday night might have given someone else a motive for murder."

"Jealousy?"

"Exactly."

We had no need to say it. We both thought of Amelia's brother, Marcus.

"Be that as it may," I said. "There's still no connection I can see with the other deaths."

She evidently agreed, for she said, "Looking at it another way, have you made a list of possible suspects?"

Impressed, I commented, "My word, Isabella, you *are* well informed. Do you read the police reports?"

"No," she said. "Detective stories. Cheap and trivial, but they pass the time on long sea voyages. It seems to me that this is a case in which opportunity may be more indicative than motive."

"My thought exactly," said I. "Would you care to elaborate?"

"If you kindly pour me another Madeira." She held up a finger. "I mean nothing else, Bertie. I can drink this stuff and stay sober till kingdom come."

I said as I collected the decanter, "I'm the Prince of Wales, my dear. It's my destiny to wait for kingdom come."

When she'd taken a sip, she said, "Opportunity, then. Queenie Chimes, it appears, was poisoned. Something, presumably, was added to one of the dishes she had at dinner. Who was in a position to poison her food?"

"Someone in the kitchen. The waiters. The dinner guests."

"Can you recall who was sitting on either side of her? I think one was Jerry Gribble."

"Who was the other? I know—Claude Bullivant! By George, he

was, and doing his best to frighten us all by saying there was a ghost in the house. Frighten us, or distract us, I ask myself."

She moved on without showing much respect for my observation. I had already noticed that she was rather partial to Bullivant. "Then there was the shooting of Jerry Gribble. Was opportunity a factor there?"

"Less so," I said. "He'd been dead some time when we found him." I tossed in my bit of medical jargon as if I was constantly using the term. "*Rigor mortis* had set in. My estimate is that he died shortly after breakfast, before we started the shoot. Almost anyone could have fired the fatal shot—servants, beaters, people from the village, or any of the party."

"Probably not one of the kitchen staff, however," said Miss Dundas astutely. "After breakfast they must have been fully occupied preparing the picnic lunch."

"Which brings us back to the guests," I mused. "And the third murder. Whoever stabbed Osgot-Edge succeeded in doing it under cover of darkness as we were playing Sardines. There shouldn't have been any servants about. It points emphatically to someone involved in the game." I clicked my fingers. "Who was it who suggested Osgot-Edge should hide first?"

"Not I," said Miss Dundas. "I suggested your wife, Her Royal Highness, if you remember, and she declined."

"Yes, and then Bullivant suggested me, and Alix made some comment about a trail of cigar smoke. Do you know, I think it was Amelia who put Wilfred's name forward?"

"It was."

The full import of this took a moment or so to digest. I fingered the top button of my nightshirt. "And it was Amelia who drew up the guest list and invited us here in the first place."

11

My suspicions of Amelia may strike the reader as deplorable. She had gone to no end of trouble and expense to provide a good week's sport, welcomed us warmly to her house and put the best rooms at our disposal, and now I was willing to regard her as a modern Lady Macbeth. I can only say in mitigation that if the wretched King of Scotland (his name escapes me) who came to stay with the Macbeths had been as circumspect as I, then he would have survived and Shakespeare could have put his talent to better use. Too many of the Bard's plays are about the untimely ends of kings and princes for my liking. Personally, I find more to admire in Gilbert and Sullivan, but that's to digress.

Back to Amelia. If our hostess *had* been planning the demise of several ladies and gentlemen of her acquaintance, she was well placed to do it. She had issued the invitations, subject to my approval, of course, planned the menus, allocated the rooms and she, better than anyone, knew the house, its corridors and staircases, entrances and exits. The poisoning of Miss Chimes, the shooting of Jerry Gribble and the stabbing of Osgot-Edge were all within her capability, given that she was better placed than anyone else to choose the appropriate moment and make good her escape from the scene of the crime.

Was I being uncharitable? You will have an opportunity to judge.

Meanwhile, I prepared to stay awake seated in the armchair, waiting for the murderer to spring the trap. In my right hand was the length of sashcord I would pull at the critical moment. Across my knees lay the poker I had brought from Alix's room.

Miss Dundas said, "Would you mind if I blow out the candle?"

I gave my consent and promised to remain alert, adding the wish that she would sleep soundly. To be frank, I hadn't the slightest expectation that she would. It amazed me soon afterwards to hear her breathing lengthen and take on the regular tempo of slumber. What self-possession, I thought—to be capable of sleep when a murderer might enter the room at any moment! Quite extraordinary. I could only put it down to habituation, the many times she must have bedded down in her tent in the Amazon jungle while untold dangers lurked outside. Or because she felt safe with me as her protector.

Quite soon the armchair began to be uncomfortable. Pins and needles spread up my left leg even though I shifted my position several times. Moreover I was wrestling mentally with the knowledge that only half the bed was occupied and the probability that Miss Dundas was only pretending to be asleep in an effort to suppress her natural excitement at my physical proximity. I found myself wondering whether I could work the man trap from a recumbent posture.

Of course it was out of the question and I didn't seriously entertain it. I took my responsibility seriously, which was just as well, because presently I heard a sound, muffled, but not to be dismissed. Outside, close to the bedroom, something had moved. I tightened my grip on the poker and watched the door.

Miss Dundas stirred. "What was that?"

"I don't know," I whispered.

"Let them step right in before you pull the cord," she cautioned.

I held my breath.

Another sound came, a thud, too heavy to be a creaking floorboard. I felt the hair rise on the back of my neck. You see, the sound didn't come from outside the door. It came from the French window. Someone was on the balcony. Slowly and with stealth, the handle was being turned.

There was I, seated with my back to it, waiting to trap someone at the door. Reader, I did the only sensible thing—dropped the sashcord and ducked behind the bed.

I heard the curtains flap. I was conscious of a draft from the window and with it a distinct whiff of scent. Everything I had deduced was coming true except the means of entry. The only uncertainty left was the weapon Amelia proposed to use. I decided against raising my head to find out.

You may imagine the shock it was to hear a masculine voice say in a curiously unthreatening tone, "Isabella, are you awake?"

To say that I was taken by surprise is an understatement. I was dumbfounded.

He repeated her name and I was too stupefied to recognize his voice until he said, "Bit of a liberty, eh? Didn't like to think of you alone in here, not after some of the looks you gave me. You're a damned fine looker, if you want to know."

I boiled inwardly. The voice was Bullivant's.

"Be a peach," he went on in this disgraceful vein, "Say you're gasping for me. Don't hold it in. I brought you these. Picked by moonlight."

He'd filched the last roses from the garden, the blighter, which explained the perfume I'd noticed.

Miss Dundas said, "Kindly keep your distance, Mr. Bullivant. I am holding a knife."

"I'll be jiggered!" said Bullivant on a high note of indignation. "You're not afraid, are you? Good God, I wouldn't take a lady by force. That's not the ticket, not the ticket at all. I wouldn't say a kiss and a cuddle is the summit of my ambition, but if that's as far as you care to go on this occasion, Isabella, I'm your man."

You may imagine my outrage at this unseemly declaration. It took a moment to satisfy myself that Bullivant wasn't bent on murder, but when I fathomed that his boorish behavior was meant to win the lady's favors I was almost as appalled as if he *had* meant to kill her. In the nature of things one doesn't normally hear how other fellows broach the question, but if this was typical of the English gentleman then all of us might as well go back to painting ourselves with woad and clubbing any passing lady we admire. Whatever became of old-fashioned chivalry, sweet nothings and honeyed words? One bunch of roses stolen from someone else's garden didn't impress me much—nor Miss Dundas it seemed, who said acidly, "You're *not* my man, Mr. Bullivant, and you won't be anybody else's if you so much as touch me."

To which he said, "Fiddlesticks. What have you got to lose, my beauty? Surely not your Sunday School certificate?"

This was more than I could stomach. I stood up, no, sprang up, and said, "That's unforgivable, Bullivant."

He uttered my name as if a fire had broken out.

Fairly flinging my words across the bed, I continued, "If I hadn't been speechless with disgust I'd have stopped you earlier. How dare you molest this lady?"

"Sir, I didn't know you were here," he protested lamely.

"That's immaterial," I told him.

"I didn't molest her," he said, more confident now.

I said, "You did worse. You insulted the lady. You molested her verbally, cast an aspersion on her reputation. I heard it."

"You weren't meant to."

"You'd better apologize at once."

"Sir, I do, most humbly."

"*To the lady*, Bullivant, to the lady."

Miss Dundas surprised us both by striking a match to light the candle at her bedside. She said, "No apology is necessary, or desired. There has obviously been a misunderstanding for which I must bear some responsibility, at least. Mr. Bullivant and I have had several conversations in the last few days and it is not impossible that he gained the impression that I was amused by his blandishments. Not that I had in mind a visitation by night, I hasten to add."

Her statement silenced us both, so she went on, "Three unexplained deaths in the house are not conducive to romantic trysts, I would have thought. And with all those servants standing guard in the corridors—"

"That's why I climbed over the balcony," said Bullivant. He turned to me, the blighted hopes still lingering on his features. "But if I'd known you were here, sir, I wouldn't have ventured from my room. Frightful gaffe."

I pointed out firmly, "I was engaged in investigating the crimes."

"Ah." Bullivant sounded as if a doctor were examining his tonsils. As an expression of belief it failed to carry conviction.

"What is more," I informed him, "my detective duties require me to remain here for the rest of the night."

Bullivant seemed to understand this, even if he didn't altogether appreciate it. He said, "You'd like me to return to my room, sir?"

I nodded. "By the same route you entered, and you can take the roses with you. They're covered in greenfly."

12

You may wonder how I felt towards Isabella Dundas after that unseemly incident with Bullivant. After all, she had admitted to the possibility that her light behavior had encouraged the man. I had been led to assume that she was indifferent to my own good looks and winning ways. Well, not to mince words, I was peeved. I'd gone to her room from the highest motives, ready to deal with a murderer. I hadn't bargained on a lover. All this, of course, was trivial compared to the matter under investigation, but one has one's pride. I resumed my armchair vigil in a chastened mood. It improved towards morning, about 5:30 A.M., when the lady offered to change places with me. She'd slept sufficiently, she told me, and now I deserved a turn in the bed. I didn't decline the offer.

Nobody else disturbed us until the maid came with tea and bread and butter. Miss Dundas had stepped deftly around the trap to take the tray in at the door. She offered me the cup (there was only one), but since I prefer cold milk to tea in the morning, I took what was in the jug and used the glass tumbler beside the bed.

All things considered, I felt agreeably refreshed. In one sense the chance to snatch some sleep had been a blessing, but it was all time that I could ill afford from my investigations. The murderer remained at large and the threat to Miss Dundas was not removed. If my judgment counted for anything, she would be in mortal danger for the rest of Thursday. I told her firmly that I wouldn't be leaving her side until Inspector Sweeney reported for duty.

Madam said with a click of the tongue, "That's going to be inconvenient." But as she had already dressed by this time, it was clear that the inconvenience would be mainly on my side. She said, "Would it simplify matters if I packed my things and left?"

"Went home, do you mean? No, no," I told her. "That's no guarantee of safety. Come along to my rooms while I get into some clothes."

She rightly pointed out that we ought to dismantle the trap in case the chambermaid became enmeshed in it. "What an anticlimax," she remarked as we untied the cords. "You were the only catch all night."

Everyone had gone to breakfast by the time we emerged from her room, so we were spared any embarrassment. I'm not unused to being caught out, as they say, but I would resent winks and nudges after a night of what the lady aptly, if unkindly, characterized as anticlimax.

Whilst I dressed with the door ajar, she leafed through a magazine in the adjacent sitting room, turning the pages with a quickness that conveyed her ill humor. She called out to me, "Really it's no different from the so-called savages of the Amazon."

"What?" I said, caught hauling up my trousers. I looked to see if some mirror was embarrassingly positioned.

"These pictures of fox hunting in—what is it called?—*Fur and Feather*."

I said, "You're not comparing what goes on in the jungle with the hunt?"

"Why ever not?" she answered. "The meet is a tribal ritual, after all—the Master of Foxhounds and the stirrup cup and the horn and the 'Tally-Ho' and the 'View Halloo'."

"That's sport."

"Dressed up to the nines to chase a verminous animal across country, catch it, kill it, cut off its tail and blood the novices? The only difference I can see is that the Amazon hunters catch their prey to eat. You stuff it and call it sport."

"You're talking like a blasted socialist," I told her testily.

She started to laugh and then stopped abruptly with a sharp intake of breath.

"What is it?" I said. It was a horrid moment. Dreadful possibilities flitted through my brain.

Then I heard a too-familiar voice ask stiffly, "Is the Prince of Wales through there?"

Alix didn't wait for a reply. She stepped into my dressing room and said, sounding depressingly like my mama, "Bertie, I have been waiting for you to accompany me to breakfast. It's five past nine already. Everyone must be waiting downstairs."

"My word," I said, recovering my wits. "Is it so late? I overslept, my dear."

"You were supposed to have been preventing another murder."

"Oh, I did," I answered. "Miss Dundas has come through the night safely, as you see. I guarded her room while she slept. Took a nap towards morning, when I was satisfied that the immediate danger was past. How are you this morning, Alix? Did you manage to get some sleep yourself?"

Ignoring that, she asked, "How do you propose to pass the day—taking care of Miss Dundas?"

I told her with dignity that I would be delegating that responsibility to Sweeney at the earliest opportunity. "I must start my inquiries in earnest. I shall interview everyone."

"You'll have to hurry, then," she said. "The Holdfasts are about to leave, if they haven't gone already. Their carriage is at the front door and their trunk has been loaded. I saw it from my window."

"I can't allow that," I said. "Damn them, they can't! Stay with Miss Dundas, would you?" and with that, I fairly stormed downstairs.

Sir George Holdfast was in the entrance hall, already in his overcoat saying goodbye to Amelia. When I demanded what the deuce was going on he gave a feeble shrug and blamed his wife. "Moira is extremely agitated, Bertie. She hardly slept at all last night. She is resolved to leave."

I said adamantly, "You must tell her that I cannot allow it. As I made clear last night, I have instituted an inquiry into these regrettable deaths. You will each be required to make a statement about your movements and what you remember of the circumstances leading up to the murders."

He said in a shocked voice, "You don't regard Moira and me as suspicious persons?"

"George," I answered slowly, spacing out my words, "it would look suspicious if you defied my instructions and left the house."

I had him collared and he knew it. "I'll speak to Moira," was all he said.

Having weathered that crisis successfully, I went in to breakfast, where everyone waited ravenously for morning prayers. I gave them a profuse apology. One short prayer from the Chaplain and we all dipped in the trough, so to speak. After the first pangs were satisfied, I thought I had better take precautions in case anyone else had ideas about leaving. I ordered them to assemble in the morning room at half past ten, a measure of my resolve considering that it restricted breakfast to a meager hour.

Subdued and ill at ease, they filed in.

"It isn't more bad news?" Amelia asked me in confidence. She was still my principal suspect, but I have to admit that her concern sounded genuine enough.

I shook my head and gestured to her to sit down. "Are we all assembled?" I asked. "We seem to be short of several people."

Marcus Pelham grinned unpleasantly. "Haven't you heard?"

Amelia gave him a glare and said, "There should be eight of us, sir. The Chaplain asked me to give you his apologies. He has to take his Scripture class at the village school."

"Eight it is," said Holdfast after a glance around the room. At bottom he was a sound fellow and a good support.

"Splendid." I launched into my announcement, putting it to them in a positive manner that brooked no interference. The investigation, I informed them, was already well advanced. Statements had been collected from the servants, and Inspector Sweeney (who was at my side, looking pale) had spent much of the night comparing them. We were now about to begin the second stage of our inquiry, namely the questioning of the present company. It was imperative that they remained in the house for the rest of the day.

The moment I stopped talking, Pelham inquired, "What have you learned so far, Your Royal Highness? Have you found any clues?"

"Clues? What are they?" cried Lady Holdfast, lifting her feet off the floor and staring about her as if they were cockroaches.

"Ignore him," said Amelia. "He reads the police reports in the newspaper and he wants to impress you all."

"Actually, a clew," Pelham insisted on telling us and spelling the word, "is a ball of thread. Anyone who knows the classics must remember the clew that Ariadne gave Theseus to unwind behind him as he went through the labyrinth at Crete. So in its modern rendering, Lady Holdfast, a clue—c-l-u-e—is anything that guides or directs one in an intricate case. Proper detectives always look for clues."

"Oh. Have you discovered any?" asked Lady Holdfast, trying to sound calm again. "Do tell us, Your Royal Highness!"

I was cautious. For one thing I didn't want to alarm people by telling them about the pieces of paper found with each of the bodies and the significance I attached to them; for another, I meant to deprive the murderer of the attention she (or he) was seeking. In that way, we might lure her (or him) into the open. So I said, "We are far advanced with our investigation and we only require your help to bring it to a swift conclusion."

"You can speak frankly to us," said Pelham.

"That is exactly what I have done."

"And we support you to a man," said George Holdfast. "Who do you want to question first, Bertie?"

"Our hostess," said I.

Amelia turned pink.

"And, in due course, each of you," I added.

"Don't leave out the Chaplain, will you?" said Pelham. "He could be a vital witness. He was here last night, remember, and he was at the table on Monday when Miss Chimes collapsed. He's as warm a suspect as anyone else."

"Fie on you!" said Lady Holdfast. "A man of the Church?"

"The Chaplain will be invited to assist us," said I.

Then Alix quietly added, "And Claude Bullivant?"

"Claude?" I said. "Isn't he here? I thought we were all present."

"Oh, my word!" cried Lady Holdfast. "What's happened to Mr. Bullivant?"

"We counted eight," said Amelia, "But we must have included Inspector Sweeney."

Her brother said, "Then where the devil is Bullivant? Did anyone tell him about the meeting?"

George Holdfast asked, "Has anyone seen him since last night?"

Miss Dundas cleared her throat to speak. I cut in gallantly, "Yes, I saw him in the small hours. I expect he overslept, like me. Better send a servant up to his room."

So we adjourned. The man sent to rouse Bullivant returned shortly to report that he wasn't in his bedroom. I was unperturbed. Bullivant wasn't earmarked as the next victim of our killer; in no conceivable way had he "far to go." But it did cross my mind that he might have come to grief climbing over balconies by night. So I ordered a search of the immediate grounds. Another mishap, from whatever cause, would not be good for morale.

Amelia lingered in the morning room, waiting to be questioned. Catching her eye, I said, "It's a fine morning. Why don't you put on a coat and we'll take a walk outside?" I turned to Sweeney and instructed him to stay with Miss Dundas.

"Shall I question her, sir?"

"Better not. Just guard her like a crock of gold, Sweeney."

"Depend upon it, sir." And he couldn't resist adding, "Protection duty is my proper function."

So I stepped outside the house with its pretty owner and escorted her slowly along the gravel path that led past the croquet lawn to a rock garden. "This is a fine pickle, Amelia," I said without preamble. "What's behind it?"

She looked up at me uncertainly, her hazel-green eyes glistening moistly. I must say she appeared a picture of fragility in her black coat with beaver trim and matching hat. "I wish I could understand."

I said sternly, "You had better try. The plain fact is that you invited a number of guests to your house and three of them are dead. They were not killed at random. They were chosen victims. If I understand it right, you prepared the guest list."

She took a quick, frightened breath, yet still had the temerity to say, "It was sent to Marlborough House for your approval, sir."

"I know that," I said curtly. "The names were your choice, were they not?"

She hesitated. "Well, yes."

"No one else influenced your choice? Your brother, possibly?"

"Marcus? No, I didn't consult him. The list was my own absolutely."

"Hm." This was becoming more damning by the moment. Time for a smoke, I thought—one reason why I'd suggested an interview outside. I put a match to a Tsar that I had ready in my pocket. "You had better tell me why you chose this particular set of people."

We walked on for some distance before she replied, "They had to be guests who would meet your approval, sir."

A pretty low punch. I refused to let it wind me. "That wasn't the only criterion, surely?"

She said, "As it was a shooting party, I nominated the guns first. Your name was top of the list. Then I selected several gentlemen I considered worthy to stand with you, old friends who shot here when Freddie was alive. Sir George, Wilfred, Claude and Jerry. All distinguished people. Marcus had to be included to act as host. Oh, and the Chaplain attends all the social events at Desborough. Really it was quite obvious who should come. I did include another neighbor on the original list."

"The V.C.?"

"Colonel Roberts, yes. He's new in the county. I met him at the Hunt Ball. Knowing that he was a sportsman and a gallant soldier, I thought he might be suitable, but you struck him out."

"So I did. Thirteen on the list. That was tempting the fates. I did your Colonel a good turn, as things turned out. He might have been dead by now."

She shivered. "Don't! It's too horrible to contemplate."

We had come to a bench overlooking the croquet lawn, so I suggested we sit down. "Now you can tell me how you selected the ladies. That is, apart from Alix and Lady Holdfast."

"Who does that leave? Queenie Chimes and Isabella Dundas. Well, sir, I first met Queenie at the Church garden party. It was well known locally that she came to stay at Jerry Gribble's house for occasional weekends, and the poor man really wasn't himself without her. As for Isabella, I wanted to include a lady of character, someone with sand in her boots, so to speak. She gave a very impressive lecture at the Beaconsfield Geographical Society last January and I was introduced to her afterwards. We corresponded and she accepted my invitation. Without disrespect to the other ladies, I felt that her presence would add intellectual weight to the female side of the party."

"But you didn't know her before last January?"

"I'd read about her in the magazines, that was all."

"You bear her no ill will?"

"Quite the contrary! Why do you ask?"

"No matter. And you say that your acquaintance with Queenie Chimes was slight?"

"I met her on three or four social occasions in this neighborhood."

"You didn't disapprove of her morals?"

"Sir, if I had, I would not have invited her to Desborough. I'm not a prude." She looked away, across the croquet lawn. "I believe I know what you're thinking. But if I'd wanted to do away with Queenie for some unfathomable reason, I'd be a fool to do it in my own house in full view of all those guests. And I wouldn't have dreamed of shooting poor Jerry. He was a darling, one of our oldest and best-loved friends."

"Since you've mentioned Jerry," I said, "was there any breath of scandal locally about his liaison with Queenie?"

"I couldn't say. I don't listen to gossip."

"I was thinking of people who knew the wives he divorced and may have felt angry that he should now take up with an actress."

"Plenty have behaved worse than that," she replied. "It wasn't as if he was still married." Then she shot her hand to her mouth. "Oh, dear! I mean nothing personal, sir, really, I don't."

I shook my head. "You won't embarrass me, Amelia. But I shall expect you to answer a personal question with the same candor.

Was there ever any suggestion that Jerry might marry you after Freddie died?"

Her cheeks turned scarlet. "Jerry? He was twice my age."

"He was twice Queenie's age."

"I was speaking for myself."

"Ah, but from Jerry's point of view, you were his neighbor, a pretty widow he'd known for years. It would be strange indeed if he hadn't given some thought to your future. May I have an answer to my question? Did he ask you to marry him?"

There was a pause, followed by a sigh. "It's painful to speak of. He didn't propose. He said after two marriages he had a horror of front pews. He wanted me to live with him, to live in sin. Of course I refused. I made light of it, and we remained friends. He was charming about it. I don't know to this day how serious he was. Please, I wouldn't want this mentioned to anyone else. I was never Jerry's lover."

Her statement impressed me. Jerry's maxim about the front pew sounded so typical of the things he trotted out. But if I believed Amelia, my theory ran aground. If she hadn't been jealous of Queenie Chimes and angry with Jerry, what motive had she for killing them?

Stumped for the moment, I moved obliquely to the matter of the other victim. "If you were to take a lover, he would have to be a younger man?"

She stood up. "I'd like to walk on, if you don't mind. It's cold sitting still."

"Such as your poet," I said, flicking the ash from my cigar.

She didn't deny it, which was a point in her favor. Instead she asked, "Sir, perhaps you will tell me what is behind that observation?"

"Certainly. I happen to know that Osgot-Edge visited your room the night before he died." I saw the muscles flex at the side of her face. "Suppose, for the sake of argument, you *had* killed the other two, and Osgot-Edge found out and was profoundly shocked that the lady he loved could be capable of murder—"

"You are wrong!"

"—then you had a motive for killing him as well."

"I did not!" Her eyes managed to glisten with tears and burn like beacons at the same time. "Yes, he was my lover. That is the *only* thing you said that is true. Wilfred was a kind, courageous, gentle-hearted man. Whoever killed him is a demon." With that, she broke into a fit of weeping and ran away from me.

This was dreadful. I had overstepped the mark. I couldn't allow the interview to end like this. I tossed away the cigar and ran after her. "Amelia!"

Unhappily, my running is usually done astride a hack. The lady was too fast for me. She ran up the steps of the house and through the door before I reached the staircase. She was still sobbing pitiably.

I pounded up the steps after her, sounding like a bulldog with bronchitis, through the hall and into the morning room. Six pairs of eyes stared at me.

"Next?" said Marcus Pelham.

13

"Has Bullivant appeared yet?" I asked.

Inspector Sweeney gave me a persecuted look, then told me not only that the search for Bullivant had been unproductive, but that people were becoming agitated.

"Probably he went for a long walk," I said. "I dare say he'll appear for luncheon."

"Might I have a private word with you, sir?" Sweeney asked. Before we had withdrawn to the far end of the room he said, "I wouldn't describe myself as a detective, sir—"

"I know that," I said through gritted teeth, "but you don't have to broadcast it to all and sundry. Keep your voice down."

"This Lady Holdfast, sir. She's acting like a guilty person, saying over and over that she wants to leave the house as soon as possible. She's giving her husband the devil of a time, sir."

"Pure nerves," I told him.

"I'd be nervous myself if I'd murdered three people, sir. She has a wild look in her eye. I wouldn't care to meet her with a dagger in a dark room."

"That may be so, Sweeney, but I need something more to go on than a wild look."

"I thought I'd mention it."

"And you have."

"You could question her next, sir."

"And give her the excuse to leave? No, she'll have to wait. Return to your bodyguarding. That's what you do best. Leave the conduct of the case to me."

I fingered my watch chain and thought what on earth shall I do next? Interview another suspect. Young Pelham will do. But when I crossed the room, he had gone.

"If you're looking for Marcus, he went up to see what he could do for Amelia," Alix informed me without looking up from her needlework. "She was plainly distressed when she came in."

The notion of Marcus Pelham comforting his sister was so unlikely that it warranted investigating. Instead of sending for him, I went upstairs myself. Just as I approached Amelia's room, the door opened and Pelham emerged. He closed it, hastily, I thought. "How is your sister?" I inquired.

"Resting. She wants to be quiet for a while. She seems wrought-up. I promised her she wouldn't be disturbed before luncheon."

"How thankful she must be."

He frowned at me. "Thankful?"

"To have a dear brother to comfort and protect her," said I with a straight face. "You had better escort me downstairs, hadn't you, seeing that I was the instrument of her distress? I want to put some questions to you anyway. Let's see how you stand up to the inquisition."

He grinned sourly.

I took him through a different part of the garden, past borders where forlorn chrysanthemums lingered into the autumn on stems with shriveled leaves. "Where does this lead?" I asked.

"I couldn't say."

Ungracious pup. "Have the good manners to address me properly, would you? Surely you know the garden well?"

He shook his head.

I warned him, "You're testing my patience, laddie."

"It's true," he said defiantly, and then added tamely as I conveyed my displeasure with a look, "Sir. I'm as much of a stranger here as yourself. This is the first year I've been invited to shoot at Desborough. I wasn't welcome when Freddie was alive and I'm only here now because my sister needs a man to act as host."

"What was Freddie's objection to you?"

"He found out that Amelia was paying off my debts from time to time. Bloody Freddie would cheerfully have seen me in the poorhouse."

"How did the debts arise? Do you gamble?"

"Not to excess." Sensing, correctly, that I would erupt if I heard one more boorish word from him, he added "sir" as an afterthought and volunteered some information. "This may seem difficult to credit, but my sister and I had a strict upbringing. Our father was an archdeacon. In the last century there was money to burn in our family, huge estates, rents, all a gentleman could want. Then one morning out of the blue, Grandfather Pelham—Sir Hugh, as he was—heard the call of God. He renounced his life as one of the gentry and studied to become a parson. He found the scriptures difficult to master, so he was never admitted to holy orders, but he made sure that my father and my three uncles all wore the cloth. The Pelham estates were given to the Church because the Bible tells us not to lay up treasures upon earth."

"That's a text I've pondered more than once," said I. "I'm not much of a theologist, I admit, but I would have thought that handing over one's inheritance to the Church of England would put the Church itself in danger of laying up treasures. No, I take it as an injunction to spend generously while one has the means, don't you?"

Young Pelham wasn't much of a theologist either. He sidestepped the question. "Well, enough was provided for my school fees and Oxford and then I was supposed to take holy orders myself, but I rebelled. I wasn't suited for preaching, damn it."

"That is evident."

"I'm with my eighteenth century ancestors in spirit."

"In spirit, but not in funds."

He nodded.

I said, "How thoughtful of your sister to have married a rich man like Freddie Drummond!" Provocative, I grant you, but the sarcasm rolled off this young man. We walked on in silence for a stretch and entered a walled vegetable garden. I may have appeared quiet, but as we strolled among the ranks of savoys I was busy revising my opinion of Marcus Pelham. Until then I had put him down as a man unhealthily infatuated with his own sister and jealous of any fellow who showed the slightest interest in her. Apparently I had been mistaken. The interest wasn't incestuous. It was pecuniary. He was afraid of someone marrying her and putting a stop to the payments.

I said, "Don't you have any private income at all?"

"A few stocks and shares, sir. Not enough to survive on."

"You're being uncommonly frank."

"I've seen the way certain people are looking at me. I don't mind being unpopular, but I dislike being under suspicion. I want you to know why I'm here, and it isn't to murder the guests."

"You know on which side your bread is buttered."

"Exactly."

"And at the same time you can observe what progress, if any, her lovers are making."

He gave me a surprised look. "Now *you're* being uncommonly frank, sir."

"Isn't that a fair comment?"

"Well, yes."

I said, "Let's speak plainly, shall we? We both know that your sister has a liking for masculine company."

He muttered resentfully, "You could put it more plainly than that."

"That's plain enough. We're gentlemen, when all's said and done. My point is this. Any lover of Amelia's who is not a married man must be considered a potential threat to your income. Isn't that so?"

He picked a Brussels sprout off its stalk and tossed it at the wall. "Not necessarily."

Unmoved, I went on, "Freddie conveniently died. But there were others lining up to replace him. Jerry Gribble was a widower and Osgot-Edge a bachelor. You may well have decided to protect your future by killing them both."

He made a show of being amused. "Jerry and the poet—to stop them marrying my sister? That's rich!"

I waited for the bluster to subside.

It took a moment or two for the gravity of the charge to penetrate. Then he said more earnestly, "Before you put a noose around my neck, sir, there's an obvious flaw in this. What about the other victim? Why should I have killed Queenie Chimes? She was Jerry's mistress. If what you say is true, I would have wanted Queenie to stay alive and keep Jerry out of Amelia's skirts."

I mulled it over for a few paces. "That has a certain logic, I grant you. However, a really cunning murderer knows that logic will defeat him, so he commits an illogical crime. One more death is neither here nor there to a man who is resolved to murder twice. He kills Miss Chimes to obscure the pattern of his crimes." This ingenious theory sprang practically unbidden from my lips. I found it so persuasive that I said, "You'd better give an account of yourself. Where were you sitting at the table that first evening when Queenie collapsed?"

Perhaps it was the chill of the air, but I fancy that the color rose to his cheeks now that he sensed how serious I was. His tongue flicked nervously across his lips. "The Chaplain was on my right and the Princess of Wales on my left. If you want to know who sat on either side of Queenie it was Jerry and Claude Bullivant," he added.

"That is of small consequence," I pointed out. "Anyone could have tampered with the food before it was served."

"Only if they visited the kitchen. I did not."

"Then the poison could have been placed in the drink she had in the anteroom."

"You had better speak to Colwell about that. He served the aperitifs."

"I have every intention of doing so," I said, slightly ruffled, wishing I'd thought of this before.

A certain smugness spread across his features. "When all's said and done, Colwell is just a glorified butler. Have you considered the possibility that the house steward did it? Perhaps he has a grudge against the upper classes."

I ignored the observation and pressed on. "Let us consider Jerry's murder. It was perfectly possible for you to have fired the fatal shot on Tuesday in the hour between breakfast and the start of the shoot."

"It was perfectly possible for any of us to have fired it, not excluding the ladies. And as for the stabbing last night," he said, anticipating my question, "the same holds true. We were all there in the dark. It wasn't my suggestion to play Sardines, by the way, Your Royal Highness. I dislike the game. The only game I suggested all evening was Spinning the Trencher, and if that incriminates me, what hope is there for any of us?"

This, I thought, was too bumptious by far, so I commented, "You may not want a noose around your neck, Pelham, but you sound increasingly like the counsel for your defense. Have you been rehearsing?"

His lower lip protruded sulkily. After an interval I asked, "Do you happen to remember who did suggest Sardines?"

"My sister." To this unbrotherly admission he saw fit to add, "Anyone might have made the suggestion, given that we'd promised to play some form of Hide and Seek."

"Quite." I didn't need reminding that the Hide and Seek had been Alix's suggestion.

He said, "I don't think Amelia is capable of killing anyone. She wouldn't hurt a fly."

We had reached the limit of the vegetable garden, so we returned by a second path, a decision we might have reconsidered had we known that it led past the pigsties. I said wryly, "You were speaking of flies?"

Pelham pulled a face and said, "It's offensive. She'll have to get rid of them."

I remarked, "I happen to have quite a healthy respect for pigs. We rear them on the Sandringham estate. Highly intelligent creatures. You can train them, you know. And they make few demands. They'll eat anything you give them. Anything. You could put a dead sheep in there and not a bone would remain."

"I'm obliged to you for the information, sir, but I definitely don't kill sheep," said Pelham.

I gave him a sharp look and his eyes glittered in amusement. It *was* amusing in a morbid way, and I was forced to smile as well. If he supposed my suspicions were any the less, he was mistaken. As soon as we reached the fresher air of the flower borders, I brought up the vital question of the guest list. "When did you first see it?"

"Towards the end of May, I should think."

"Five months ago. Were you consulted about the choice of guests?"

"No, sir. My sister showed me the final list after you had approved it."

"But you were given the names as early as last May?"

"Amelia had persuaded me to act as host. The least she could do was tell me who had been invited."

"Had you met any of them before?"

He thought for a moment. "All of them except yourself and Her Royal Highness."

"Every one—including the three who are dead?"

He nodded.

"Queenie Chimes?" I said in surprise. "Where did you meet her?"

"The first time? On the landing outside my rooms in Chelsea. She dropped her umbrella down the stairs and I opened my door and picked it up. She sent me a ticket for the Lyceum and we had supper after the play."

"When was this?"

"Last winter. January, I think. The play was *Julius Caesar* and she was in the crowd scenes."

"'Friends, Romans, countrymen . . .'?"

Ignoring my apt quotation, he went on, "As it happens, she was impossible to spot in the costumes they wore, but of course in Romano's afterwards I praised her performance to the skies. She was easily pleased. I saw her in something else on another occasion—*Much Ado About Nothing*. She played a gentlewoman then. I wasn't so flush that week, so we had a one-and-sixpenny supper in Kettner's and walked home. In case you care to know, sir, there was never anything improper between us."

"A pretty girl like that? Surely you didn't take no for an answer?" Leaving that aside, I turned to the interesting implication of what he had just told me. "It emerges, then, that you knew Queenie before Jerry did. They met at a cricket match a mere six months ago—something about tombola tickets."

"Queenie told me, yes."

"So you knew she was Jerry's mistress?"

"I gathered as much, and my sister confirmed it when she showed me the guest list."

"Weren't you infuriated? I'm sure I would have been."

He shook his head. "As I tried to explain just now, my association with Queenie amounted to nothing more than a few visits to the Lyceum, followed by supper. One doesn't turn down the chance of seeing Irving. Queenie was gracious enough to invite me, so I treated her to supper. That's all. I wasn't jealous of Jerry Gribble and I wasn't angry with Queenie."

"You don't need to raise your voice," I told him. "The point is taken."

He said, "From the way you spoke, sir, I thought you were still accusing me of murder."

"Everyone is under suspicion except me, laddie," I told him. "And I want to know more about the guest list. Quite obviously, the whole case hinges on it. You got the names from your sister in May, you said? Did you discuss them with Queenie Chimes?"

"Naturally, when I knew she was included. She was curious to know who else was coming and I told her. It didn't mean much to her. I don't think she'd met any of us except Amelia, Jerry and me."

This young man and his sweeping statements! I was forced to put him right. "On the contrary, I suggest that a list like that would mean a great deal to any young lady capable of reading the newspapers. She must have heard of Miss Dundas, the explorer, and probably Osgot-Edge. George Holdfast's name appears on just about every list you see of subscribers to charitable causes. And I haven't even mentioned the Princess of Wales and myself."

That silenced him, which hadn't been my intention. We were fast approaching the house again and I still had a crucial question to put to him about the guest list. To gain a few minutes, I asked, "What's that small building at the end of the rose arbor?"

He took it for a trick question. "I wouldn't know, sir. As I told you I'm almost a stranger here."

"Of course. Shall we find out?" As we stepped out, I said, "Does the name of Colonel Roberts mean anything to you?"

"The V.C.?"

"Evidently it does. Do you know the man?"

He was bright pink again. "No, sir. I heard from my sister that you struck him out of the original guest list, that was all."

"You wanted to know why, no doubt?"

"I was curious, yes."

"Thinking perhaps that Roberts was a social pariah for some unsavory episode in his past? You were wrong, then. It was simply a matter of reducing a list of thirteen names to twelve. I happen to be superstitious."

"I see."

Looking at the wood and stone structure ahead, I said, "I believe it's a well."

"So it is."

"Did you mention Colonel Roberts to Queenie Chimes?"

"No, sir."

"He's a local man, isn't he? Is it likely that he would have heard that his name was put forward and rejected?"

"I don't know, sir. You had better ask my sister."

Pelham may have added something else. If he did, I have no record of it. My attention had switched to something quite different, and much more arresting. On the low brick wall surrounding the well was a scrap of newspaper weighted down with a stone. I moved the stone aside and picked up the piece of paper.

Do I need to tell you the word that was ringed there?

14

"Thursday?" Puzzlement was written large on Marcus Pelham's features and horror much larger on mine. He shook his head. "What can this possibly mean?"

I rattled out an order. "Get some men here with ropes and grappling hooks. Hurry!" Even as I spoke I was striding with all speed towards the house. In the morning room, five anxious faces, alerted by the urgency of my approach, stared at me: Alix, the Holdfasts, Sweeney and—I was heartily relieved to see—Isabella Dundas.

Explanations had to come later. I told them simply that I believed someone had fallen down the well.

Predictably, Moira Holdfast whimpered and sank facedown into her husband's lap. The others stood up and fairly showered me with questions: how did I know, and where was the well and was it an accident and was the person alive and shouldn't we call for help?

I appealed for silence and asked, "Has anyone seen Amelia since she went upstairs?"

The clamor ceased.

She spoke from behind me, and gave me quite a start. "I'm here." She had followed me in. She said, "It isn't Marcus, is it?"

I shook my head. Pandemonium returned.

Shortly after, however, utter silence reigned as we stood around that stupid well like characters in a nursery rhyme, except that it was a human being down there and a grappling hook was being lowered. Marcus had rallied the head gamekeeper and three of his men. From the way coil after coil of rope dropped out of sight it was evident that the well was exceedingly deep. The chance of anyone surviving a fall was negligible.

At length, the gamekeeper gave the order to stop unfurling. The end of the rope was passed across the windlass and two of the men commenced to haul it up. "It's no good," said one. "There's no weight on the end." So they lowered it again. They had no better success. This procedure must have been repeated a dozen times. Then they brought the hook to the surface and discovered nothing more on it than mud.

An hour passed. Alix complained of the cold and returned to the house with Amelia. Most of the others followed soon after, but I remained, and so did Pelham. In desperation more hooks were lowered. The clash of steel carried up to us faintly, depressingly faintly. Three hooks proved to be no more productive than one. In fact the ropes became entangled and hindered the operation.

In the next hour a hamper of lunch was sent out to us and the men ate and worked the ropes by turns. Nobody had the temerity to suggest that I might have been in error, but the comments each time an empty hook was brought to the surface became increasingly despairing. It wasn't a matter of offensive language or outright defiance. The skepticism a man can put into the simple word "no" is quite sufficient to express his feelings. I was left in no doubt that if I had relaxed my vigil and left them to their work I could expect no result whatsoever.

I don't exaggerate when I say that almost four hours elapsed before I was proved to be correct. An evening mist was closing in on us when one of the men announced, "It feels like something."

We all moved closer and peered into the void.

"Careful, now," I cautioned. "Don't snatch at the rope. Bring it up gradually, hand over hand."

To be just, they did their best. For a few seconds they appeared to be raising a considerable weight. Then the rope slackened abruptly.

"Bloody hell!" said Pelham, and I think he spoke for everyone.

At my insistence they hauled the grapnel to the surface, and a good thing, too, for one of the flukes had a torn scrap of fabric attached to it, a strip of silk, maroon in color, patterned with small white stars. It was some three inches long, tapering to a point. Clearly it had been ripped from a garment, for there was a buttonhole at the wider end that I observed had been torn at the edge, presumably when the weight of the body was taken up. I eased the piece of material over the point of the fluke and examined it. Then I passed it to Pelham, who remarked that from the size of the buttonhole it appeared to have come from a waistcoat.

"Yes, but do you recognize it?" said I.

He did not. He muttered something about clothes having no interest for him.

I said, "I shall show it to Alix. She is acutely observant of people's dress. She will certainly know if she's seen it before."

And Alix did, when I returned to the house and showed it to her. Without hesitation she told me, "It's from Claude Bullivant's waistcoat. I know the pattern. He wore it on Tuesday evening. Bertie, how dreadful!"

I answered cryptically, "Yes . . . and no." I had better mention here that I hadn't passed those hours beside the well in a state of passivity. From the moment I had seen who was left alive in the morning room I had concluded that the body down there could be no one else but Bullivant's. After that I had set my mental powers the more demanding task of accounting for his death. The explanation had not come quickly, but when it did, it had all the simplicity of the truth. And, as I indicated to my dear wife, my conclusion was not wholly pessimistic.

I decided to communicate my findings to the company; they had not had much to cheer about. When they were assembled in the drawing room, comfortable in their chairs, teacups in hand, I took up a position beside the fire. "My friends, I propose to tell you a story. Bear with me, please. It has a particular relevance to things I wish to tell you later. Some years ago I heard of a sportsman, a shooting man, who was unwise enough to speculate heavily on some venture in the Stock Market that failed. He was ruined, irredeemably. So he put on his Norfolk suit and collected his shotgun and whistled to his favorite retriever and spent the day on his estate contentedly bagging game until the sun set. Then he returned to the house and took his bag book off the shelf and entered his tally. I believe it amounted to some fifty wildfowl and a dozen rabbits. Finally he added his own name to the list. Then he blotted the ink, replaced the book on the shelf and shot himself."

I smiled, so George Holdfast took the cue and chuckled, encouraging some of the others to titter self-consciously. No doubt the story would have gone down better after a good dinner when the ladies had left the table.

"What is more, there was an inquest and they brought in an open verdict." I capped it with all the aplomb of a music hall comedian. "Nobody had thought to look in the bag book."

After an uneasy silence Alix asked, "And what is the point of the story, Bertie? Does it have a moral?"

"I was about to come to that," I said. "First, I must offer a small apology to most of you. In the course of my investigation of the shocking events of this week I thought fit to keep certain information to myself. The murderer left some clues."

Moira Holdfast dipped down and gathered her skirt against her ankles. Swarms of clues still infested her fevered imagination.

I continued, "I deemed it prudent to say nothing about these clues at the time. On the evening when Miss Chimes collapsed at the table, a scrap of newspaper with the word 'Monday' on it was found at her place setting. The next day, when Jerry Gribble was found dead, a similar piece of paper was in his pocket."

George Holdfast perked up. "I remember. It said 'Tuesday.'"

I nodded. "And after Mr. Osgot-Edge was stabbed, we found yet another piece of newspaper bearing the day of the week, except that this time a word had been appended, so that it read 'Wednesday's Corpse.'"

Horrified gasps compelled me to pause.

"It was obvious to me by this time," I continued in the same calm, authoritative tone, "that this was a murderer who was not satisfied with mere killing. He wished to advertise his crimes. He was issuing a challenge. The pieces of paper left beside the bodies were, in effect, a conundrum, and it was the work of a few minutes to resolve the puzzle." Out of the corner of my eye I noticed Alix set down her teacup and fold her arms. I hoped she wasn't about to interrupt. "The key to the puzzle is the rhyme familiar to us all. 'Monday's child is fair of face' and so forth, the word 'corpse' being substituted for 'child.' So simple." Alix shifted again and I moved on swiftly to explain the relevance of each line of the verse to the respective victim.

They stared at me like owls in a thunderstorm.

"So when I was walking in the grounds this morning with Marcus and spotted yet another scrap of newspaper, this time on the walled surround of the well, I knew exactly what had happened."

"I don't quite follow," Pelham interrupted me. "I thought the rhyme to which you referred went 'Thursday's child has far to go'?"

"So it does."

"But we believe that Claude Bullivant is at the bottom of the well. I cannot conceive of any sense in which that line of verse can be applied to him."

Not without satisfaction, I said, "Then it would seem that our murderer is too clever for you, Marcus. Let us remember how ingenious—or devious—he has been up to now. 'Fair of face' we can take as a literal description of the first victim, poor Miss Chimes. The second line, 'full of grace,' was a play on words, a reference to Jerry's Dukedom. And 'full of woe' was, we deduced, a reference to Wilfred's initials. Each interpretation of the verse has been different, so why shouldn't Thursday's bring yet another variation?"

"Well, it's all Greek to me. 'Far to go'?" said Pelham, and the murmurs around the room suggested that it was all Greek to the rest of them.

"If any one of us fitted the description, it would have to be Isabella," added Holdfast.

"A reasonable assumption," I acknowledged. "I made it myself at one stage, and of course I took sensible precautions to safeguard Miss Dundas. However, the murderer had someone else in mind—Claude Bullivant. And the phrase 'far to go' is a reference not to his way of life, but to the way he met his death."

After some hesitation, Alix said, "By falling down the well?"

"Now you see it. The man had far to go, indeed. That well is extremely deep. I doubt whether we shall ever recover his body, which is, perhaps, what he intended." I remained alone in a sea of blank faces, so I said helpfully, "Cast your minds back to the story I told you a few minutes ago about the man who entered his own death in the bag book. That, I suggest, is what Bullivant did."

"Killed himself?" said Holdfast, his voice rising in astonishment.

"After putting out the piece of newspaper," said I.

"With all respect, Bertie, I find that uncommonly difficult to believe," said Holdfast. "He wasn't a melancholic sort at all. Far from it. I can't see Claude doing away with himself."

"What you can't see, George, is the totality of the mystery. I don't blame you. It would tax many a trained investigator. Before Claude Bullivant did away with himself, as you put it, he had done away with three others. I put it to you that he is the murderer."

"Claude?"

The faces around the room were satisfyingly aghast.

I said, "Just like the man in the story he went on a solitary hunt and then added himself to the tally."

"You're telling us he killed Miss Chimes and Jerry and Osgot-Edge? Why?"

"Why does anyone resort to murder? Either he was mad, or bad. I cannot be more precise than that. His motive is somewhat clouded, I grant you, but one is confident of a clear view before much longer. At this moment I wanted mainly to reassure you that your lives—indeed, all our lives—are no longer at risk."

"Thank God for that!" cried Moira Holdfast.

"Let's also thank His Royal Highness," said her husband with his customary tact.

There were murmurs of support, rather muted, I have to say.

Miss Dundas, who had sat through my explanation in conspicuous silence studying the tea leaves in her cup, now joined the conversation—using a tone I didn't care for at all. "Apart from the fact that he is dead," she remarked, "is there anything whatsoever about Mr. Bullivant that would suggest he killed people?"

This, I thought, was pretty unsporting considering what she and I knew about Bullivant's erratic behavior in the night. I wasn't so ungallant as to let the company know that he'd climbed over the lady's balcony expecting a tumble, but to my mind it was a strong indication of guilt. Of all the party, only the murderer could have known that it was safe to philander.

Rather to my surprise, Marcus Pelham sprang to my defense. "I'll tell you one thing. Bullivant was sitting next to Queenie Chimes on the night she died. He was better placed than any of us to tamper with her food."

"So he was!" said Amelia.

"Don't sound so surprised," her brother rounded on her. "You drew up the seating plan."

Miss Dundas remained unconvinced. "But why would he have wished to kill Miss Chimes?"

George Holdfast gently chided her, "My dear, you're asking for the motive. Bertie just told us that he doesn't know yet. The main thing is that it's all over. We can sleep safely in our beds tonight."

A comforting statement, you might think, but it almost caused a domestic tiff. Moira Holdfast said, "If you think I'm willing to spend another night in this house after what has happened, George, you're woefully mistaken. Our things are packed and we're leaving within the hour."

Amelia was up from her chair before the words were out. "What are you implying, Lady Holdfast? I've heard more than enough of your slurs on my hospitality. Nobody was murdered in bed. Nobody. You make it sound as if my house is verminous."

"Your manners are," retorted Moira Holdfast. "Not to mention your morals."

"Moira!" George rebuked her.

Amelia caught her breath at the enormity of the insult. She would certainly have struck Lady Holdfast had I not intervened. Just as she raised her wrist I grabbed it. I appealed to them both, "Ladies, please! Decorum, decorum!" To salvage a little dignity for them I added, "We have all been subjected to intolerable strains, but the danger is over now. Let us be thankful that we are alive." I was about to add, ". . . to tell the story," but stopped myself in time. I didn't want anyone telling the story. I'm only telling it now in the knowledge that it will be under lock and key until long after all of us are dead.

Lady Holdfast redeemed herself slightly by saying that she regretted her last remark, but she still intended to leave as soon as possible. Amelia was led to a chair where she remained sullen and ashen-faced.

Then Alix enquired of me brightly in her singsong accent, "Is the house party over, then? You found your murderer, Bertie. That is all we have to decide, is it not?" She can be embarrassingly direct with her remarks.

I strolled back to the fireplace, thinking actively. "Well, the case has been brought to a conclusion, it is true. It's out of the question, of course, to resume the shooting tomorrow . . ." I hesitated.

Miss Dundas—another lady whose questions struck into you like bolts from a crossbow—said, "May I ask what you propose to do about Mr. Osgot-Edge?"

"Osgot-Edge?"

"Unless I am misinformed, his body is still in an out-house somewhere. What is to become of it if we all go home?"

"Fair comment," I said, buying time to think.

"Sir, we ought to inform the police," said a voice at my ear that had not spoken for some time.

"Sweeney, how many times do I have to remind you that you *are* the police?" I smiled at Miss Dundas. "You're absolutely right, my dear. Of course the poor man must have a decent burial. I shall speak to the Chaplain. We'll have a private funeral before the weekend."

"Shouldn't there be an inquest?" asked Alix.

I gave her a look that she recognizes—not one that I am often forced to resort to—and she was silent. Turning to Amelia, I said, "You knew Wilfred better than any of us. Did he have any family?"

"There's a brother in the Indian Civil Service."

"Based abroad, then?"

"In Bombay, I was informed."

"That's all right. You can write him a letter. He wouldn't get back in time for a funeral in any case. Be so good as to send word to the Chaplain that I would like to speak to him urgently, would you?" To Alix, I said, "That, I think, is the answer to your question, my dear. Some of us may wish to stay on for the funeral. I see no reason why Lady Moira should remain, if it would upset her, or any of the ladies, come to that."

So it was agreed that the Holdfast carriage should be summoned. George very decently insisted on staying. His insufferable wife, he said (he didn't really say it; I did), was capable of traveling to their London residence in the company of her maids. As for himself, there might be some way in which he could be useful to me and Amelia. I thanked him for his support.

Then Alix announced that she, too, proposed to leave. I suppose I ought to have expected it; there wasn't much prospect of parlor games in the next day or two. I tried to persuade her to delay her departure until the morning, but she was insistent that she would rather spend the night in her own bed at Marlborough House however late she got there, so I ordered the carriage. In the privacy of her suite I told her I hoped she understood why it was necessary for me to remain.

Making a fine distinction she said, "I understand why you feel it is necessary to stay. I didn't expect you to return with me."

I squeezed her hand to show my appreciation. "What will you say when they ask why you came home?"

She lifted her shoulders. "If anyone really wants to know, I shall say the party didn't turn out as I expected."

"That's true."

"I think we should all respect the truth, Bertie."

"I couldn't agree more, my dear."

"Will you keep yourself to yourself when I am gone?"

I frowned and tried to look puzzled.

She said, "Leave them alone, Bertie. One is too clever and the other is anybody's. Get some sleep, you old ram. You are looking tired."

"Tired, but not unsatisfied," said I, letting the remark make its impact before I added, "You haven't congratulated me yet."

She stiffened—and when Alexandra stiffens she could stand in a sentry box. "Congratulate you—what for?"

"My detective work, of course. Another case brought to a brilliant conclusion."

She sighed. "Oh, Bertie, I despair of you. You don't really believe Claude Bullivant was a murderer? He was killed like the others. Isabella Dundas was right. There's no motive. All the evidence you have is circumstantial."

This from my own wife set me back on my heels. "Of course there's a motive," I told her scornfully. "I shall find it. See if I don't." I was so astounded by what she had said that I felt like quitting the room immediately. I believe I would have done so if I hadn't thought of a devastating riposte. "If there's any truth in what you say," I told her, "the murderer is still at large. How can you even think of going back to London knowing that your husband is in risk of his life?"

She tilted her head defiantly and said, "You're welcome to come with me."

"My dear Alix, it's utterly out of the question. I shall be here until Osgot-Edge has had a Christian burial and all the other matters are tidied up."

"Tidied up—or hushed up?" she said insensitively. "It's the same old story wherever we go, isn't it, Bertie? Avoid a scandal at all costs."

"This time I'm blameless. I can't be faulted."

"That's a matter of opinion. I warned you not to play at being a detective. You brought this botheration on yourself, beloved, and now you want to sweep it under the carpet. Stay here if you must. I don't think you'll be murdered. All the murders up to now have fitted that rhyme and if there are to be any more, I don't suppose the murderer will deviate from it. What's tomorrow?"

"Friday."

"Friday's corpse is loving and giving. The loving might apply to you, but not the giving. You're not ungenerous, but I wouldn't say you're noted for it. That must be someone else. Then there's Saturday. Saturday's corpse works hard for a living. Even less likely. And the corpse that is killed on the Sabbath Day is bonny and blithe and good and gay. Bonny and blithe I grant you. Gay, yes. Much more gay than good." She made a wafer-thin space between her thumb and forefinger. "The good is a small measure."

"Well," I said cuttingly, "if I want home truths, I always know where to get them."

"Yes," said Alix. "But I don't want you to think I'm indifferent to the perils of this place, Bertie. Just to be sure, I've had a quiet word with Sweeney. After I've left he's going to move into my suite and keep a special watch on you."

15

I was pocketing my handkerchief after waving goodbye to Alix when a pony and trap trundled up the drive with the Reverend Humphrey Paget aboard, so I remained at the foot of the staircase to thank him for answering my summons so swiftly. Having eased his weight ponderously from the carriage to the gravel, the Chaplain performed an odd maneuver. He dipped his head, as if uncertain whether protocol required him to bow to me, and then proceeded to rub each shoe in turn against the back of his opposite trouser leg. No doubt about it—the fellow was buffing up his toecaps to discourage me from another demonstration of the science of deduction.

We mounted the stairs together and entered the hall, where Amelia received him in what was by her standards a lackluster manner, a fleeting smile and a limp hand.

As soon as we were alone in the drawing room the Chaplain commented, "Poor Lady Drummond! The burden of these tragedies is more than she should be asked to bear. It's too cruel!"

"Did you hear about Bullivant?" I ventured.

"The dreadful news was in the note she sent. Such a cheerful fellow I always thought, may the Lord rest his soul. Is he still . . . ?" He pointed downwards.

I nodded. "The men will try again tomorrow, no doubt. In many ways it might be a mercy if he is never brought up. Probably you didn't hear that we suspect him of having killed the other three."

His eyebrows reared up like flying buttresses. "My word, no! That is unbelievable."

"On the contrary, Padre. It is obvious."

Now his fat features absorbed the shock and became more guarded and the eyes narrowed. "Did you deduce it, sir?"

I was beginning to find the Chaplain tiresome. I said as if to a child, "It's the only possible explanation. But to return to the topic of Amelia and her distress, I should like for her sake to keep the events of this unhappy week from being bandied abroad."

"How very considerate."

"I shall do everything within my power, Padre, and I look to you for support."

"You shall have it, sir." And in case I doubted his credentials he declared sanctimoniously, "As a pastor it behooves me to give comfort and succor to all who require it in this transitory life."

"Capital. So I dare say you wouldn't mind burying one whose life turned out to be more transitory than any of us expected?"

"Oh?"

"I should be obliged if you would lay the poet to rest as soon as possible."

"Mr. Osgot-Edge?"

I nodded, tempted to say that I didn't know of any other dead poets wanting a quick funeral. "Would you care for a cigar?"

He took one and his hand shook. "Has Mr. Elston the coroner been informed, sir?"

"About Wilfred? No, we haven't troubled the coroner. He's busy enough, I am sure, with Queenie Chimes and Jerry Gribble."

He clasped his free hand to his mouth and drew the fingers downwards as if trying to locate his chin in the fleshy surrounds. "Forgive me, wouldn't it be somewhat presumptuous to consign a stabbed man to his grave without an inquest, sir? Not that I wish to be obstructive."

"I'm glad to hear it, Padre." I struck a match. As he drew close to light up the cigar I added, "On occasions one is justified in bending the rules. You and I know that Osgot-Edge was murdered in this house and we know who did it. But the whole of the kingdom doesn't have to be told. Fearfully distressing for Lady Drummond, not to mention the rest of us."

"Does he have a family?"

"Osgot-Edge? A brother in India. I'm willing to serve as chief mourner myself. A private ceremony in the village church tomorrow. What say you?"

There was a pause. Then: "Might I help myself to some brandy, sir?"

"I'll join you. Didn't I hear from somebody that you organized a private funeral last year for a young gamekeeper who was shot?"

"Accidentally shot, sir. On that occasion there was no question of deliberate murder. The boy happened to stray ahead of the beaters. One of the guns heard something in the thicket and took a shot at what he supposed was a wounded bird."

"Who fired the shot?"

"I didn't witness the incident, sir." He had his back to me, pouring from the decanter. Interesting, isn't it, how much you can tell about a man's state of mind by looking at his back?

"But you know who fired it?"

"The members of the shooting party resolved to treat the incident as a closed book after the boy was buried." He handed me a glass. "The poor lad was an orphan so we laid him to rest in the village churchyard the next day."

"I must insist that you answer my question, Padre. Who was it who shot the boy?"

He sighed. "Sir, in all humility I beg of you to respect the confidentiality of this information. It was Mr. Bullivant."

"Bullivant?" I got up and walked to the window. "I should have guessed. Things are beginning to fall into place. Who else was of the party—Jerry Gribble?"

"Jerry, yes."

"Freddie Drummond, of course?"

"Er—yes."

"Osgot-Edge?"

"Yes." You'd have thought every yes was a slate from the roof of his church.

"Any other guns?"

"No, sir," he said with relief.

But I hadn't finished. "And the ladies, apart from Amelia? Miss Chimes, perhaps?"

"No, sir. There were no other ladies present."

"How dreary. I do think a complement of ladies makes for a more agreeable atmosphere, don't you?"

He didn't answer. Perhaps it wasn't a fair question, though I've known parsons who would have answered strongly in the affirmative.

Returning to matters more pressing, I said, "Well, Padre, how soon can we have the funeral?"

Dinner was destined to be a subdued occasion that evening, so I had no qualms about telling them between courses that we would bury Osgot-Edge on Saturday at noon in the village churchyard. The ladies—that is to say Amelia and Miss Dundas—immediately fell to debating what they would wear. Marcus Pelham quizzed me on the formalities—the need to obtain a death certificate from a doctor and the difficulties attendant on employing an undertaker. Fortunately I was able to pass on the reassurance that the Reverend Humphrey Paget (who had murmured something about a choir practice and taken to his heels after the interview with me) was hand in glove with Dr. Perkins and Mr. Hibbert, the gentlemen who fulfilled those offices in the district. Osgot-Edge's death would go down as heart failure and he would be buried in a nightshirt buttoned to the chin. The Chaplain, the doctor and the undertaker were not unused to cooperating to cause the least embarrassment to the families of the departed. In country districts such as this, death had an inconvenient habit of occurring during bouts of inebriation or infidelity that would have caused no end of humiliation to the bereaved had our resourceful trio not combined to circumvent it.

George Holdfast then remarked, "And Bullivant? Will he be buried at the same time?"

I said, "Between ourselves, George, I think it unlikely that we will succeed in raising him. As I mentioned to the Chaplain, the sensible procedure may be to say the burial service at the top of the well."

"And block it up after?"

"Exactly."

Amelia broke off her description of a crepe bonnet to say, "Nobody has used it for years."

Holdfast said, "What's your source of water, then? Are you on the mains, my dear?"

"I've never enquired."

"Might be prudent to find out."

To finish the evening on a less depressing note I suggested a few rubbers of bridge. How often have I been grateful for my pack of playing cards when more boisterous entertainment is unsuitable to the occasion. One has to say it: the Royal Family is so numerous that Court mourning is practically the norm. And when one is obliged to show respect each time some European Grand Duke gives up the ghost, it's no wonder that I can deal the cards as smoothly as a Mississippi sharp.

Seeing that we were five in number, Pelham said with more tact than I thought he possessed that he would go and look for Sweeney for a game of billiards, leaving Holdfast and yours truly to get up a four with the two ladies. I partnered Isabella Dundas, who seemed to understand my calls like the sounds of the jungle and we lost only one rubber all evening. There was no acrimony from the other side, either. In fact, Amelia's good humor was quite restored, for Holdfast repeatedly praised her play and claimed that all the mistakes were his own. I'm sure it was a tonic for us all to pass two hours without once referring to the dreadful events of recent days.

We had a final drink and some warm sausage rolls soon after midnight and sent for the candles. Cheery good nights were exchanged, though I have to say that we sounded awfully like provincial actors speaking lines.

Upstairs, it was comforting to see a light under the door to the rooms Alix had so recently occupied. I dismissed the footman and went in to have a few words with Sweeney, whom I discovered to be mother-naked, a curious, hairy specimen of manhood among the pink bed hangings and cornflower-blue walls. He grabbed his nightshirt and apologized.

"Not at all," I told him. "I never knock on bedroom doors, so it isn't the first time, although I will say I've made prettier discoveries. I hope you gave young Pelham a pasting."

"The billiards, sir? Not at all. I should have played him for matchsticks. He's a regular demon with the cue. Did you learn anything over the card table?"

"Quite the reverse. Miss Dundas and I gave a lesson in bridge to Sir George Holdfast and Lady Drummond, if that's what you mean."

"I'm glad to hear it, sir. Actually I was enquiring about the case."

"The investigation? That's over, Sweeney. Didn't you hear? Bullivant killed the others and then did away with himself. What is more, I have now deduced the motive. Would you be interested to hear it?"

"I'm all ears, sir."

"I wouldn't have said so when I opened the door just now." I got a sheepish grin for the quip. It was slow in coming, but no matter. I used the time to settle into an armchair and light a cigar. "Be seated, man. You don't have to stand on ceremony now. You can get into bed for all I care. Now, the key to this case is a very unfortunate incident that happened a year ago. It was mentioned to me first by Osgot-Edge after Jerry was shot. Pelham gave me the gist of the story and later the house steward referred to it obliquely, but I had to prize the crucial facts from the Chaplain this evening. A boy was accidentally shot and killed at last year's shooting party. By Claude Bullivant. Did you know that?"

"I did not, sir."

"The lad was without parents, so the Chaplain was persuaded to conduct a funeral with all speed and in the utmost privacy and the members of the shooting party pledged themselves to regard the incident as a close secret. And of course the servants were instructed on pain of dismissal not to mention it to anyone. Bullivant must have spent some sleepless nights, but as time passed and nothing more was said, it seemed that the accident really had been successfully swept under the carpet. So successfully, in fact, that Lady Drummond had no qualms about holding another shooting party at Desborough this autumn and inviting me as her principal guest and Bullivant as one of the guns. So we all arrived expecting a fine week of sport and on the first evening one of the party was poisoned—Miss Queenie Chimes, the Duke of Bournemouth's doxy. And who was seated on her left at dinner? Claude Bullivant."

Sweeney's face was a study.

"Why was the lady murdered?" I mused. "Have you any suggestion, Inspector?"

"None, sir."

I shamed him with a shake of the head. "You must tell me what you think of mine, then. There was rather more to Miss Queenie Chimes than met the eye. She was a scheming young woman, an adventuress, as Her Majesty the Queen would put it, and I'll tell you how I know. I have it from Marcus Pelham that before Miss Chimes met Jerry she contrived a meeting with Marcus and invited him to the Lyceum. Did I tell you she was an actress in Irving's company? Well, he was presented with tickets on several other occasions and she met him for supper after the performance each time. However, I have Pelham's word that it wasn't a romantic fling and I believe him. Queenie was pumping him for information, Sweeney. He put it down to natural curiosity. I'm convinced he was mistaken. Somehow or other that young woman had learned about the shooting accident. Someone had talked. So this minor actress, trying to exist on the paltry money Irving pays his underlings—and Irving is notoriously close—this hard-up, scheming little supernumerary saw a way of putting the information to profitable use."

"Blackmail, sir?"

"Pray allow me to continue. She befriended Marcus, thinking that he would be her *entrée* to this year's shooting party, but inconveniently for her plans, Marcus isn't a lady's man, so she had to look elsewhere. She settled on Jerry, who had chalked up two marriages and two divorces and still hadn't learned to resist the flutter of eyelashes. In no time she was at his side wherever he appeared. And when the invitations to the shooting party were sent out, Queenie was on the list."

I paused. "What I am about to say now is conjecture, Sweeney, but I think you will agree that it provides a credible explanation of the ghastly events that happened later. I believe this artful young woman must also have made some sort of approach to Claude Bullivant and thoroughly alarmed him. Months ago, before she met Jerry, I think she tried her damnedest to win her way into Bullivant's affections, and when that didn't work because he guessed what she was up to, she threatened to expose him as the man who shot an innocent youth and failed to report it to the proper authorities."

Mystification had been creeping over Sweeney's features. "What I don't understand, if I may interrupt, sir, is why Miss Chimes went to all these lengths just to get an invitation to a shooting party."

Policemen can be deplorably dense on occasions. "It wasn't just a shooting party. She heard that I—the Prince of Wales—was being invited."

"Oh."

His mouth still stood open like a crocodile's, but I kept my temper and explained, "She saw it as a way of insinuating herself into my company. She'd calculated that a Royal patron could work wonders for her prospects as an actress. Without mentioning anyone in particular, she wouldn't have been the first to benefit from my interest in the stage, I'm bound to admit. Does that explain it to your satisfaction?"

"Thank you, sir."

"Let us examine the consequence. When Bullivant learned to his horror that Miss Chimes was being invited to Desborough, he was in ferment. He was convinced that she would blurt out the story of what happened last year, to the extreme embarrassment of himself and all the others who had helped to conceal the incident from public knowledge. He could foresee the effect upon me, Sweeney. I was certain to be outraged at finding myself embroiled in a scandal through no fault of my own. I would be compelled to leave at once. And Bullivant would become a social pariah."

"What did you say, sir?"

I sighed. "A pariah, Inspector. An outcast. Society is not merely founded on family, school and so forth. It requires consent. I could rattle off a dozen names of people of impeccable pedigree who have forfeited that consent by misconduct of various kinds that has become public knowledge. They are pariahs. When invitation lists are drawn up, their names are not included. If they ask to join our clubs we blackball them. If they appear in public, at the races or the theater, we cut them. That is the prospect Bullivant faced—through one interfering actress. Understandably, he was beside himself with anger and humiliation. So he decided to silence the woman. He obtained some poison and brought it with him to Desborough. He slipped it into her food or her drink at the first opportunity, at dinner on Monday evening, when he happened to be sitting next to her. She collapsed, as you know, and died on the way to the doctor's, in Jerry Gribble's arms. And the next morning, Jerry himself was shot through the head. Can you account for it now?"

"Mr. Bullivant killed them both?" said Sweeney, in manifest disbelief.

"Yes, and I'll tell you why. I think Jerry didn't tell me the truth when he got back that night. He said that Miss Chimes died without recovering consciousness. I believe she did speak. Before she died, she managed to tell him that Bullivant must have poisoned her, and why. What a terrible accusation! No wonder Jerry was in such a distracted state. And no wonder he concealed the truth from me. He decided to confront Bullivant with it at the first opportunity, which was in the morning, after breakfast. They must have walked or driven away from the house to discuss it. And when Bullivant realized that Jerry knew he had committed murder, he took a gun from his pocket and shot him. Two deaths."

"Two deaths," Sweeney echoed. "And two to go."

"Let us consider the next, then. Osgot-Edge must have been killed for the same reason. He was one of the party last year. He was part of the conspiracy. Osgot-Edge was a shrewd fellow, Sweeney. After two mysterious deaths, he must have been deeply suspicious. Unfortunately, he made the same mistake as Jerry, attempting to take the matter up with Bullivant. It sealed his fate. Bullivant plunged a knife into him the same evening. And with Osgot-Edge's death, each of the guns from last year had perished, except Bullivant himself."

Sweeney gave a long, low whistle. "That is a fact, sir. There's no denying it."

I said, "You can go through the survivors: Pelham wasn't invited last year because Freddie couldn't stand the sight of him; George Holdfast went down with shingles; and I was at Sandringham."

"Speaking of the late Lord Drummond, sir, do you think his death could have been murder?"

"No, no. He was gored by a bull last winter. Pure accident. Any other questions?"

"Well, sir, there's Mr. Bullivant's death."

"Yes?"

"How do you account for that, sir?"

He was being fearfully obtuse and I let him know it with my tone of voice. "Obviously suicide. He knew that I was on the trail and getting closer by the minute. There was no escape, so he jumped."

There was an interval of silence.

Sweeney said finally, "It's a peach of a theory, sir. Beautiful."

"It's more than a theory, Sweeney. It's the explanation."

"The explanation, yes." He lowered his eyes as if something embarrassed him and fingered the hem of his nightshirt.

I said, "Out with it, Inspector. Have you thought of a snag?"

"Not at all, sir. Not a snag. More of a loose end. It's the little pieces of paper. I'm trying to think why he left them beside the bodies."

"Well, I suppose as some sort of distraction, to deflect us from the truth."

"But they fitted the rhyme, sir—which you cleverly identified. Monday's corpse is fair of face. If the theory—pardon me, the explanation—is right, Mr. Bullivant poisoned Miss Chimes to keep his secret safe. He wasn't expecting to kill the others. That happened later, when they tumbled to what had happened."

"That is correct."

There was another pause. "Well, sir, I may be out of order here, but it seems to me that the person who left those bits of newspaper must have known on Monday that he was going to kill his second victim on Tuesday and his third on Wednesday." He hesitated. "And another on Thursday."

I stared at him, stunned. He was absolutely right.

He added, "And so on."

FRIDAY

16

"*And so on.*" The force of those words, spoken so softly in Sweeney's Irish lilt, as if on a note of apology, was devastating. My beautiful explanation was in ruins. The murders hadn't been contrived to silence people who found things out; they must have been premeditated, intricately and cold-bloodedly planned. Alix's words came back to taunt me: *"Oh, Bertie, you don't really believe Claude Bullivant was a murderer? He was killed like the others."*

I suppose if I were asked which of my personal qualities has contributed most to such successes as I have chalked up as a detective I would have to say in all modesty my quicksilver reactions. When I am blown off course—and it happens to the best of investigators—I refuse to be run aground. I instantly reach for the tiller, so to speak, and chart a more promising course.

"Sweeney," I said, "you and I must act at once, or I fear the murderer may strike again."

"You're right, sir."

"Of course I'm right. It's past midnight and this is Friday. Another day, and another victim—unless we prevent it. Friday, Friday—what does that suggest?"

"Would you be thinking of the little verse, sir?"

"I would, Sweeney, I would. 'Friday's child'—Friday's corpse—'is loving and giving.' Which of the party could be so described? That is the burning question."

"No doubt about it, sir."

"You have the answer?"

"No, sir. It's the burning question, that's for sure."

I sighed. Plainly it was too much to expect that my bog-trotting assistant would have a constructive idea in his head. He'd picked a hole in my hypothesis, but ask him for a thought of his own and he was stumped. He fingered his left ear lobe as if it might assist his mental process.

"Well now, there aren't many of us left to choose from," I pointed out with the patience of an old nanny. "Lady Drummond and her brother Marcus, Miss Dundas, Sir George Holdfast and myself. I don't include you."

"Thank you, sir."

"Although the murderer might," I added, seeing the look of complacency that was spreading across his features. "Your turn may come tomorrow. Saturday's corpse works hard for a living. That would exclude everyone else but you." I paused to let it take root. "However, let's not anticipate. The obvious candidate for tonight is Sir George. I can't think of anyone in the country more loving and giving. I wouldn't mind a guinea for every charity he supports. You must have seen his name on the horse troughs."

At that moment Sweeney wouldn't have known a horse trough from an elephant. He was thinking about Saturday's corpse.

"We have a duty to warn him," I went on, raising my voice. "Sir George Holdfast, Sweeney. His life is threatened."

He had stopped fidgeting with his ear. He was tugging at his lower lip now.

I said, "Do you hear?"

He said, "Do you suppose it could be referring to one of the servants, sir?"

"What?"

"Works hard for a living."

"Sweeney, I despair of you. I don't believe you heard a word I was saying. Do you possess a dressing gown?"

"No, sir."

"Never mind. Pick up the candle and follow me."

Few places are so drafty as the corridor of a country house by night. The candle was blown out straight away and we had to pause to reignite it. Holdfast's bedroom was around a turn and at the end. I stepped out boldly. Anyone hearing my tread could have been in no doubt that my purpose was urgent. Sweeney padded barefoot behind me, doing his best to keep up and guard the flickering flame.

I halted at Holdfast's door and instructed Sweeney to knock. There was no reply from within, so we entered.

"Nobody here," Sweeney intoned in a voice of doom.

"I can see that," I said tersely, flinging open the wardrobe. The suit George had worn that evening was hanging there among the others. "No obvious sign of foul play," I commented in the reassuring manner of Scotland Yard, though my heart was pounding a knell. I looked into the cupboards, under the bed and out on the balcony. "He could be anywhere in the house or grounds."

"Do you think we're too late, sir?" Sweeney asked.

I said phlegmatically, "I think we are justified in ascertaining which of the guests are where they should be, in their bedrooms."

Sweeney's eyes gleamed in the waxlight. "Sure and if anyone is missing, we'll know why. We'll be arresting the murderer tonight and putting a stop to his crimes, sir." His voice positively throbbed with expectation.

Without another word I strode out to the corridor and stopped at the first door on the right, which I knew to be Pelham's, and thrust it open. Bed springs creaked and Marcus's voice demanded, "What the deuce . . .?"

Sweeney held the candle high.

"Merely making sure," I announced. "You may go back to sleep." We withdrew and closed the door.

We ignored the room opposite, the one formerly occupied by Osgot-Edge. Sweeney, a veritable bloodhound now, trotted ahead of me and grasped the handle of the next.

"One moment," I cautioned him just in time as I saw which door it was. "I think it would not be wise to make a sudden entrance here." In my mind's eye I saw Sweeney hanging by his heels from the beam while Miss Dundas prepared to eviscerate him with her hunting knife. "Better knock and wait."

Presently the lady's voice sang out clearly from within, "If that is who I think it is, I'm honored by your gallantry, sir, but I'd rather fend for myself. I wouldn't care to repeat what happened last night."

"As you wish, my dear." With a look at Sweeney that defied him to put any construction on it, I gestured to him to move on. Isabella Dundas was in her room and that was all we needed to know. There remained one room to check—Amelia's—and the attentive reader will recall that I had originally plumped for her as my principal suspect before succumbing to the theory that Bullivant was responsible.

Sweeney stationed himself on the step outside our hostess's door and gave me a doglike look.

"Leave this to me," I told him, reaching for the handle, but it turned before my hand made contact.

The door opened six inches and a face stared out, the broad, ruddy-cheeked face of Sir George Holdfast. He looked at me as bold as a cabman and spoke my name.

And I spoke his. For the moment I had nothing to add. Sudden death was so much the vogue in this house that I'd mentally killed him off. It was like seeing a ghost.

He asked, "Is everything all right, sir?"

I said, "That is a question I should address to you. You weren't in your bedroom." And even as I spoke, the mystification cleared. He was barefoot and wearing a nightshirt. What an old goat! No sooner had he waved goodbye to his wife than he was partnering Amelia at cards, trumpeting every hand she played and buying his ticket for a mattress jig.

"Were you looking for me, sir?"

"Out of concern for your personal safety, George," I told him. "I had reason to believe that your life is threatened, and when I walked into an empty bedroom I feared the worst. Obviously I need not have worried. Lady Drummond is within, I take it?"

He lowered his voice. "Yes, sir, but things are not as they appear."

I said, "Save your breath, George. You and I are men of the world and Sweeney wasn't born yesterday."

His face twitched as if a wasp had stung him. "Sir, the reason I'm here is that Amelia invited me to come."

I said acidly, "Bully for you!"

"No, please allow me to make this clear. She isn't entirely convinced that Bullivant committed the murders, and she reasoned that I—with my reputation for supporting good causes—fitted the epithet loving and giving."

"Which you obviously do. I'm sorry we interrupted."

"Sir, you interrupted nothing!" The old hypocrite's motives were as spotless as the bottom of a birdcage, but he would insist on justifying his tumble with our winsome hostess. "What I am trying to say is that Amelia blames herself for these tragedies. She feels that if she hadn't invited us to Desborough to shoot, none of this would have happened. In spite of your reassurances to the contrary, she is fearful of yet another dreadful event tonight, and for her peace of mind I was persuaded to pass the night in here upon a made-up bed on the ottoman, where I shall come to no harm."

I gave him a penetrating look and said in a voice that only he and I could hear, "That remains to be seen."

His eyes widened and I saw the first spark of doubt there. He whispered, "Surely you don't suspect . . ." He pointed over his shoulder.

"George, I wouldn't be in your shoes for all the tea in China." It was an unsuitable thing to say because he wasn't wearing shoes, but it made its point.

"Oh, Jerusalem!"

Just then Amelia called out, "Georgie, darling, I'm getting cold like this. There's a wicked draft."

He clapped a hand to his face. The fruits of passion had suddenly turned sour. In desperation, he asked me, "What can I do?"

"Not much to please a lady, if I'm any judge." Cruel, I admit, but it was rather galling to hear Amelia call him to her bed. More helpfully, I added, "Make an excuse."

To my utter surprise and confusion, he did. He turned and informed Amelia, "It's His Royal Highness, my dear. I believe he has something of a confidential nature to impart to you. He has recommended me to return to my room, so I'll wish you good night." With that, he stepped into the corridor, dipped his head in some kind of salutation and moved off at speed towards his bedroom.

"Shall I make sure he comes to no harm, sir?" volunteered Sweeney, quick to seize on a chance of bodyguarding as a change from looking into bedrooms.

I nodded. Holdfast had to be protected. Sweeney handed me the candle and set off in pursuit.

Events were moving with bewildering speed, like a lantern show that is running out of time. Next, I heard a movement from inside the room and Amelia looked around the door, her black hair hanging free like a gypsy girl's. "Bertie, you're dressed."

I said, "I haven't been to bed."

"Do come in. Corridors are so public." She grabbed my free hand and drew me firmly inside and closed the door. She was wearing a silk kimono like the young ladies in Mr. Whistler's pictures. It was quiveringly clear that she was unconfined by other items of clothing, but as you will have perceived from my reference to fine art I meant to keep my thoughts on a higher plane.

"What a lark!" she gushed. "What on earth did you say to George to get rid of him? Never mind. I've had some fizz, so you'll have to forgive me if I'm too forward. Or would you like me to send for some more?" Her eyes gleamed.

It's no secret that I excite the fair sex to an exceptional degree. I'm used to them becoming quite giddy in my presence. Whether this interesting effect arises from my Royal blood, or the cut of my clothes, or my blue eyes, or the charm of my personality is not for me to say; whatever its origin, I cheerfully accept it as a fact of life.

I suppose I had better give you the reverse of the coin: I'm readily aroused by a pretty woman, sometimes too readily for my own good. This time, I meant to keep myself in check, for this pretty woman might also be a murderess. "Thank you," I said in answer to her offer of champagne, "but I'd rather have a cup of cocoa, if you would be so kind. And more of those sausage rolls." While she rang for a maidservant, I placed the candlestick on the mantelpiece, picked up a poker and attended vigorously to the fire, which had burned low.

She said, "I'm going to blow out the candle. I love the firelight, don't you?" She came so close as I crouched on the hearthrug that she nudged my shoulder with what I shall politely call her hips. She said, "What a splendid flame! I shall warm my knees." She parted her kimono to reveal as pretty a set of pins as you would ever see. "Bertie, this is such a surprise! I didn't think it possible that you would visit me like this."

"Why not?"

"After our talk in the garden today—or is it yesterday now?—I thought you had decided I was to blame for all the horrid things that have happened."

I said in all sincerity, "Yes, I spoke too harshly. I came after you to apologize. I came up here to explain, but your brother said you wouldn't wish to be disturbed." On an inspiration I added, "This is the first opportunity I have had to make amends."

"How gallant." She put a hand on my shoulder and slid it over my collar, letting a fingertip stroke the curls at the back of my neck, a pleasant sensation were it not that my knees wouldn't support me any longer in the crouching attitude.

I stood up and she took it as a cue to move towards me, almost nose to nose, saying, "Do you feel safe with me now—or would you care to search me?"

Such temptation! You'll be encouraged to learn that I resisted. Well, to be strictly accurate, her maid knocked and she went to the door to give the order. I took the opportunity to seat myself in an armchair and take out my cigar case. "You don't mind if I smoke?" I asked her when the door was closed again.

She gave her permission, of course, and made some remark about the cold, so I told her to find a shawl, or something, to which she said coquettishly that she knew better ways of getting warm and ran across the room to the fire and pulled the kimono fully open, stretching it out like a flag. I had the draped view from the rear, I must hasten to emphasize, but I was still subjected to the shape of her body behind the silk silhouetted by the flames, and very provoking it was, I can tell you.

To subdue nature, I made a performance of lighting the cigar. I was reluctant to speak in case she turned about and gave me the front view. But she wrapped herself up again and said, "Bertie, in case you are wondering why, the reason I invited George to my room was because I'd abandoned hope."

I couldn't resist a chuckle at that.

She said solemnly, "I had better rephrase that. I didn't dare hope or aspire to a visit from you. Oh dear, I confess that I have been thinking of it constantly, ever since Monday night when I came to your room with the news that Miss Chimes was dead and you appeared for a moment to misinterpret my reason for being there. But it seemed so unthinkable, so open to censure until . . . ."

"Until this evening when Alix left," said I, matter-of-factly, to help her out.

"Well, yes—and you appeared anyway to suspect me of murder."

"I suspect everyone," I told her genially.

"But mainly me?"

Ducking that, I said, "I can't think why a lady would invite a number of old friends to her house and kill them one by one."

"She wouldn't and she didn't," said Amelia. She hesitated, and then added in a small, tight voice, "But she's guilty, and ready to confess."

Every muscle in my body tensed. "What?"

"Yes. A confession, Bertie. Do you want to hear it?"

I glanced rapidly about the room, suspecting a trick, looking for the hidden weapon that she meant to kill me with the moment she had told me the truth.

She approached and leaned right over me, with her hands on the arms of the chair, her face within inches of mine, the faint fumes of champagne on her breath. "I plead guilty to desires of the flesh, Bertie."

"Oh."

"There! I've said it." And having said it, she flopped into my lap like a Channel swimmer who has reached the shore. I was quite unable to prevent it without risk to each of us from my cigar. She pressed her face against mine as I shifted my legs to accommodate the rest of her anatomy.

I would like it to be known that even under this extreme provocation I endeavored to keep my detective duty paramount. I said, "Is that all?"

She didn't answer. She was unbuttoning my waistcoat.

I persisted, "Is there nothing else that you meant to confess?"

She answered, "There is nothing else. Please don't cause me to weep again. This has been such a wretched, ill-fated week, but tonight I want to forget all the horrors we have had to endure. You have been a tower of strength, Bertie, so resolute and so manly."

"Decent of you to say so," I remarked, caught slightly off guard.

Her hand moved inside my shirt. "Please take me to bed," she murmured.

I was fast succumbing. There are limits to every man's resistance and my limits are shorter than most. In ordinary circumstances I wouldn't have held out for half so long. It's not in my nature to disappoint a lady. However, I had one more card up my sleeve. "What about the cocoa and sausage rolls?"

She giggled. "I told the maid to leave them outside the door."

That giggle was irresistible.

And now in the interests of decorum we move forward in time by an interval I am unable to document. I lost track of time, and when I might have consulted my watch it was still in my waistcoat pocket somewhere on the floor across the room.

Amelia said, "Do you mind cold cocoa, or shall I send for some more?"

I said, "I'll take it cold. I'm devilish thirsty."

"No wonder!" She went to the door and picked up the tray and carried it to the commode on her side of the bed. "Sugar?"

I propped myself up on one elbow, mainly, I confess, to look at her in the pink, and a sublime spectacle she was. "Sugar—yes."

I was feeling agreeably fatigued, as one does, and relaxed, so it says much for my vigilance that I spotted what she was doing. *She had a bottle in her hand and she was pouring a pale liquid into one of the cups*. You may imagine what I immediately suspected.

My first impulse was to shout, "Poison!" and snatch it from her, but some instinct made me decide on a less dramatic course of action. I sat back submissively against the pillows and allowed her to hand me whichever cup she selected. I then asked her if she would fetch my cigar case from my jacket.

She said with a smile, "I do believe you enjoy seeing me prance about the room in a state of nature."

"Emphatically."

The moment her back was turned, I leaned across and switched her cup of cocoa for mine. Cruel, do you think? If it *was* poison, it had been meant for me. If it wasn't, no harm would come to her.

She climbed into bed. We each had a sausage roll and drank our cocoa. I found mine slightly bitter to the taste and added some sugar.

Presently I found myself slipping down in the bed. My eyes were heavy-lidded.

Amelia said, "Aren't you going to smoke a cigar after all?"

"No, I feel drowsy now, uncommonly drowsy."

"That's good," she said. "We should both get a good sleep. I took a large dose of chloral with mine. It's a habit, I'm afraid. I had trouble sleeping after Freddie died, but this stuff really knocks me out. Sweet dreams, Bertie."

17

Normally I am one of the charmed few who can wake refreshed at the crack of dawn unable to fathom why the rest of humanity prefers to linger in bed. So it was puzzling, not to say infuriating, for me that Friday morning to find that lifting a leg off the mattress was a feat to be equated with tossing a caber. I made a number of attempts and, shameful to relate, dozed in the intervals.

By degrees I dimly registered that the cause of my lethargy must have been the chloral hydrate I had swallowed the night before. The taking of sleeping drafts is, I gather, a widespread practice among the fair sex, but I have never had any truck with it. So when at the umpteenth attempt I succeeded in getting a foot to the floor, my mood was thunderous. Nor was it helped by the discovery that Amelia's side of the bed was empty; she, it appeared, having had no difficulty in getting up.

Mother naked, I stumbled across the room and looked into her dressing room, which felt like the North Pole, and revived childhood memories of winter mornings in Buckingham Palace. The balcony windows were wide open.

I braved the cold and put my head outside in the hope that fresh air might sharpen my wits. The balcony afforded a frost-blanched view of a small walled garden with bits of stone statuary and gravel walks lined with box hedges. A pond at the center had gray ice floating on the surface.

One deep breath was enough. My legs wobbled. The scene changed to a snowstorm, as if someone had given a shake to one of those ornamental glass orbs containing water and a miniature village. The snow, of course, was in my head. I staggered forward and grabbed the iron railing, telling myself that a cigar would have been a better remedy than fresh air.

Presently my vision clarified. I could see the gravel below the balcony. And—reader, forgive me for the shock this will cause you, for it was a paralyzing shock to me—I saw another corpse.

She lay in a posture of terrible finality, with her head turned at an angle that could only mean that her neck was broken. One arm was trapped beneath her body and the other was fully extended, the palm resting upwards. She was still in her nightdress, leaving one of her legs exposed almost to the knee.

My first impulse was to rush downstairs and cover her decently. Pausing only to pull on a few clothes of my own, I dragged a blanket from the bed and hared down the nearest staircase, through the first door I reached, which happened to be a baize one, and out through the servants' hall past a group of goggle-eyed maids. My mental faculties were responding to the emergency, thank heaven, and my legs were functioning too.

Outside, I scarcely had time to spread the blanket over Amelia's body before Colwell the house steward joined me, summoned, I suppose, by the maids. With admirable *sang-froid*, he asked whether he could assist me in some capacity.

"You can tell me where everyone is," said I. "Mr. Marcus Pelham, for one."

"Mr. Pelham is in the breakfast room waiting for morning prayers, sir, together with Sir George Holdfast. They are being observed by Inspector Sweeney from the serving hatch."

"Ah." The last I had seen of Sweeney was when he had volunteered to make sure Holdfast came to no harm. He was still on duty, no doubt blithely believing that he had thwarted the murderer.

"Miss Dundas has ordered breakfast in her room this morning," Colwell continued.

"But someone has seen her?"

"One of the maids."

"Good." I paused to consider which course of action was appropriate to this latest outrage, which had shocked me more profoundly than any of the others, as you will appreciate, for reasons of a character too intimate to dwell upon. That it was murder I had no doubt. Murder had been done within a few feet of the place where I had lain drugged and asleep.

Colwell cleared his throat. "Might I enquire what is under the blanket, sir?"

I stooped and uncovered the face.

"I feared so," he said in a flat voice.

I replaced the blanket. "That's a curious remark. Surely you didn't know that Lady Drummond was killed?"

He raised his eyes to the balcony above us. "I didn't know it, sir, but in all the circumstances, it was a reasonable deduction."

I refrained from asking him how he deduced it. I said, "I think it would not be prudent to speculate any further. Leave the detective work to me, Colwell."

"I shall, sir."

"And be so good as to ask Inspector Sweeney to join me here at once."

Later that morning at my request our tragically dwindling party assembled in the drawing room—a mere half dozen of us, and that included the Chaplain, who had remained after breakfast to discuss the arrangements for Saturday's funeral. They may have been few in number, yet they spread themselves around the whole of the room, not, I have to say, to appear more numerous, but to keep at a safe distance from each other.

"You all know by now that our dear hostess is dead," I said.

"Rest her soul," added Sweeney, earning an "Amen" from the Chaplain.

"I discovered Lady Drummond in her private garden under the balcony of her dressing room. Having examined the scene, I concluded that the fatal act had been committed within the hour. The signs were very instructive. For one thing, her clothes were almost unmarked by the frost."

"And for another?" said Pelham with his usual impertinence.

"May I remind you, Mr. Pelham, that we are in mixed company? Graphic descriptions of violent death are manifestly unsuitable for the drawing room. Take my word for it that your sister was killed between six and seven o'clock this morning."

"Killed?" spoke up Miss Dundas. "Are you quite certain it wasn't an accident, sir?"

"Utterly."

"She could have fallen from the balcony, could she not?"

"That was a possibility until we examined the, em, body," said I.

"So far as I am concerned, you may speak frankly, sir, since I am the only lady present."

I gave a shrug. "As you wish. Inspector, would you explain?"

Sweeney said, "She hit the ground head first and her neck was broken. We found pieces of gravel embedded in the scalp on the left side of the skull. But we also found injuries on the other side of the head that could not have been caused by the fall. It seems that she was first attacked in the dressing room."

I took up the account. "I went to the dressing room and found the weapon—a poker. It was lying on the floor. Her attacker evidently struck her twice and then opened the balcony windows and pitched her over the railing to make certain she was dead."

With a glance in the direction of Miss Dundas, George Holdfast put in, "Or perhaps to give the impression that she caused her own death."

I shook my head. "This murderer doesn't wish us to be in any doubt, George. We found the usual calling card, the scrap of newspaper with 'Friday' printed on it. It was wrapped around the poker."

They heard this in horrified silence.

Holdfast said in what sounded suspiciously like a complaint, "Bertie, I don't understand the logic of this. Last night you came to warn me that I was the likely victim. Friday is the one who is loving and giving. It fitted me. And now we find that Amelia was killed."

Marcus Pelham had observed an understandable silence since learning of his sister's murder. Now he said, "If it's love you're talking about, no one was more loving than Amelia."

"How true!" the Chaplain said sanctimoniously and got a glare from Pelham.

"Loving and giving," said Pelham. "She gave herself to all and sundry."

The Chaplain gasped.

"Shame on you, sir!" The rebuke came from Holdfast, and I think he spoke for us all.

Pelham glared at him. "That's the giddy limit, coming from you. Where were you last night when His Royal Highness knocked on your bedroom door? Let's have the truth."

Not liking the drift of this at all, I said, "I'll ask the questions, gentlemen."

"But it's obvious," the loathsome fellow insisted on continuing. "Find out who was sleeping with Amelia and we've got our man. Who else could have attacked her in her own dressing room?"

"Pelham," I addressed him coldly. It was definitely time to pull rank. "I am trying to make allowances for the grief you must be suffering, but there are limits. I warn you not to overstep them." To the company in general I said, "We estimate that the murder took place between six and seven this morning. I must insist that each of you tell me where you were at that hour."

Pelham refused to be subdued. "When you say each of us, you mean Holdfast and me. We're the only suspects left. Well, I can tell you that I was in bed till gone seven—and I mean my own bed. The maid had to wake me up to give me my morning tea."

There was a stirring of petticoats across the room. "Pardon me," said Isabella Dundas, "but I will not be dismissed by Mr. Pelham as if I don't exist. I am as capable of wielding a poker as anyone else." This extraordinary claim secured everyone's attention, but the rest of her statement came as an anticlimax. "As it happened, I did not leave my bedroom all night, and I had breakfast served in my room at half past eight."

So all eyes turned to Holdfast, but it was Sweeney who spoke up. "I can vouch for Sir George, sir. I kept watch on his room all night. He didn't leave it until after the murder was discovered."

"Thank you, Inspector," said Holdfast.

Pelham said, "Well, I'm not satisfied. I'm entitled to an explanation. This is my sister who was brutally murdered by one of you. We all know Sir George wasn't in his room at the beginning of the night. I heard the Prince and the Inspector go in there after they woke me up. I heard the doors being opened as they searched the place." He turned to Miss Dundas. "Didn't you overhear it?"

"Actually, yes. I did."

"Where was he, then?" Pelham triumphantly demanded. "Why won't you tell us where you were, Holdfast?"

"Pelham, these insinuations are not only misconceived. They are deplorable," I reproached him. "Since the matter has been raised, I had better state that Inspector Sweeney and I traced Sir George to Lady Drummond's suite shortly after midnight. I cautioned him as to the danger I believed he was in, whereupon he left immediately."

To which Holdfast added, stressing every word, "And I returned directly to my own bedroom."

To my immense relief—and everyone's, I fancy—this squashed Pelham. He had been ready to convince us that Holdfast was the murderer, and now I had driven a coach and horses through his theory. George wasn't a murderer. He wasn't much of a philanderer, come to that.

For my part, I saw no purpose in regaling the company with an account of the way I spent the night. I wasn't under suspicion of murder. I was conducting the investigation. (And if you, the reader, harbor the slightest suspicion that I might somehow have committed the crimes, I would have you know that such thinking is not only preposterous, but tantamount to treason, even if you *are* expecting an ingenious solution.) Instead, I said, "It seems we shall get no further like this, so I shall be pursuing other lines of inquiry. I trust that nobody has thoughts of leaving, because I must insist that you remain at Desborough until further notice. We know enough about the methods of this murderer to be assured that no one else will be attacked today."

"What of tomorrow?" said Miss Dundas.

"I expect to have the case solved by then. But in any case tomorrow is Saturday, and according to that wretched verse, Saturday's victim works hard for a living, a description which can in no way apply to people of our class, with one obvious exception."

Sweeney crossed himself.

The Chaplain then asked if we still wished to proceed with Osgot-Edge's funeral on Saturday and I told him I saw no reason to alter the arrangement. Pelham not unreasonably announced that he wished to talk to the Chaplain about a funeral for Amelia, and I dismissed the meeting.

Sweeney was at my side in a twinkling. "Sir, I don't think we should wait. It's obvious who did it. Let me run the beggar in. He'll blow, I guarantee."

I said, "The only thing that's obvious to me, John Sweeney, is that you want an arrest before tomorrow. Who do you mean, by the way?"

He screwed up his face at my obtuseness. "Pelham."

"On what grounds?"

"It comes down to three people, sir, and didn't we just eliminate Sir George? He couldn't have killed Lady Drummond because I was watching his room when the murder occurred and he didn't so much as put his nose outside the door. That leaves Miss Dundas and Pelham. Why would Miss Dundas kill all those people, even if she's capable of it? She didn't know most of them from Adam before she was invited here."

"Very well, tell me Pelham's motive."

"The inheritance, sir. He's her nearest relative. She had no children and I don't suppose she made a will. He stands to inherit Desborough and all the Drummond estates."

"That has a certain cogency to it," I agreed, and then set him back on his heels with the comment, "but you have to explain why he murdered four others before he killed his sister."

I could almost hear the sound of dredging from his head as his brain labored. "Well, sir," he finally said, "he's a misanthrope."

"A *what*?" I was acquainted with the term, but I needed a moment to ponder its relevance to Pelham.

"A misanthrope. A despiser of mankind. I haven't heard a generous word from the man all week. He's as bitter as aloes."

"I'll grant you that."

"His sister married money and cold-shouldered him, that's about the size of it. He wasn't welcomed here until Lord Drummond died and Lady Amelia was stumped for a man to lead the shoot, with you being here and everything. She turned to Marcus for help and he agreed to come, but he was still eaten up with bitterness. And it wasn't just his sister who made him envious—it was the people the Drummonds had invited here in previous years. He hated them all and he wanted them to suffer, so after agreeing to come, he devised a plan. He would kill his sister and inherit the lot, but to disguise his motive he would make it one of a series of murders, one each day. He would knock off the people he despised most, the ones who had been preferred to him. And then he refined it some more by thinking of the verse, and the idea of the pieces of paper."

"To play cat and mouse with us, do you mean?"

"That's it in a nutshell, sir. He wanted to see you suffer."

"It sounds rather Irish to me, Sweeney," I told him. "How did he know that the people he wanted to murder would fit the verse?"

"They didn't, sir—not all of them. The very first one—fair of face—for example. Obviously that had to be a lady, but he didn't want to give himself away by killing his sister first, so he had to think of someone else. He picked Queenie Chimes. He'd met her in London, if you remember, so he knew she was pretty, and that was her death warrant—a pretty face."

"And the others?"

"Well, there were two that happened to fit the verse, the lines about Tuesday and Wednesday. He must have chosen it because they were so appropriate. Full of grace for a duke, and full of woe for a man whose initials happened to spell out the word."

"That's obvious."

"Indeed, sir. But Thursday, being far to go, tested his ingenuity somewhat, so he pushed Mr. Bullivant down the well. He could have done that to any of us, but he picked Mr. Bullivant because, like the Duke of Bournemouth and Mr. Osgot-Edge, that gentleman had been invited to previous shooting parties when he, Marcus, was *persona non grata*, if I have the expression right, sir. All three of those gentlemen fell foul of his envy."

"Continue."

"So we come to the fifth death, that of his sister, the one that would make his fortune. He claims to have been in his bed all night, but we only have his word for it."

I said, "Presumably the maid will confirm that she brought him tea at seven or thereabouts."

"But there's no certainty that he was in his own room at six or half-past. I think he murdered her and got back before the maid served the tea. And that isn't all, sir. Have you noticed how little grief he has shown since his sister's horrible death?"

"That was typical of the man," said I. "He lacks breeding. He has none of the finer feelings one expects of a gentleman. However, I don't think we can lay a murder at his door just because he doesn't know how to behave."

"As you wish, sir. But there's another thing I found indicative, and that was the liberty he took with his own poor dead sister's reputation when he said she was loving and giving—and left us in no doubt that he meant it in a most disagreeable sense."

"That *was* unnecessary," I agreed.

Sweeney became fearfully agitated at this. "Begging your pardon, sir, that isn't correct. The reverse is true. Pelham wanted to demonstrate that Lady Amelia's death was just one more in the series, so it *was* necessary, indeed it was vital, that he fitted her character to the verse. Then you and I wouldn't recognize this as the crucial murder, the one that provides the motive and gives him away. Have I made myself clear, sir?"

"My dear fellow," I said, "I'm mightily impressed. I didn't know you were capable of such a penetrating analysis of the case. It's a fine illustration of that saying of Dr. Johnson's, to the effect that when a man knows he is to be hanged in a fortnight, it concentrates his mind wonderfully."

"*Hanged*, sir?"

"Hanged in a fortnight or murdered tomorrow—the upshot is the same. As I said, you made a very persuasive case. However, it's mostly conjecture, isn't it? Inspired, I'm sure, but short of real evidence."

"That's why I want to run him through the mangle, sir. Squeeze out the facts."

"I'd rather you didn't."

His entire face drooped at the angle of his moustache, but I didn't relent. Proper detective work isn't a matter of putting people through mangles. Marcus Pelham might be the only suspect left, but we wanted cast-iron evidence, not a confession squeezed out under duress.

"Look at it this way," I said in a kindly tone. "If you and I are right about Pelham plotting all this to murder Amelia, then he has just accomplished his object, so there shouldn't be any more murders. Anyone such as yourself, who can be said to work hard for a living, need have no fears about Saturday. Isn't that so?"

"True."

"If, on the other hand, he feels that you are dangerously close to unraveling the truth, I wouldn't give twopence for your chances."

His eyes bulged for a moment and then glazed over with gratitude. "I didn't think of it like that, sir."

18

Now, a small confession from me.

Sweeney's theory had impressed me mightily—more than I cared to show. I would have been proud to have thought of it myself, which was awfully galling, considering that he was supposed to be a duffer fit for nothing more intelligent than bodyguarding duties. He had convinced me utterly that Pelham was our man, and if only I'd worked it out for myself I would have said by all means put the murderous blackguard through the mangle.

Instead, I sounded the cautious note that you heard at the end of the last chapter, because—here's the confession—I wanted to salvage some credit for myself. The grand unmasking of the culprit would have to be delayed. I had my growing reputation as a detective to consider. Now that we could pin the murders on Pelham, I reckoned I could put together some impressive evidence to show that my investigations had led triumphantly to the right conclusion.

Poor old Sweeney: you should have seen his stricken look when I said, "Well, have you finished? Don't you have something else to report?"

"I beg your pardon, sir?"

"The proof—the clincher. Out with it, man."

"I've told you all I know, sir."

"Come, come," I protested amiably. "You've saved it up for last, haven't you? You were keeping watch in the corridor all night. You must have seen Pelham come out of his bedroom and enter Amelia's room. And you must have seen him returning after the deed was done."

"No, sir."

"You didn't? But you were there."

"I was there, sir, and I wasn't," he said as only an Irishman could. "It's true that I kept watch on Sir George's room, but I wasn't in the corridor. That would have been too conspicuous. I spent the night in the linen cupboard opposite. I had the door ajar to keep an eye on Sir George's door, but I couldn't see along the corridor."

"That's a confounded nuisance. I thought you must have seen Pelham enter Amelia's room."

"I'm sorry."

"Are you telling me that your splendid theory is entirely supposition? We need a witness—at least one witness."

"There were no witnesses, sir," he said flatly.

"Sweeney, you are mistaken. Depend upon it, someone saw the murderer this morning."

He hesitated. "Was it you, sir?"

What neck! But it was no use denying where I had passed the night. I gave him my most frigid stare and said, "I was asleep at the time."

For that, I was subjected to a stare almost as frigid. In Sweeney's opinion if anyone had some questions to answer, it was me. All this must have added to his festering resentment, but I really preferred not to go into the story of how I had swallowed the chloral.

He said, "All the others were asleep as well, sir, or so they claimed."

"So they claimed."

We seemed to have reached an impasse, so I started thinking aloud, which is worth trying when all else seems to have failed. "Not everyone could have been in bed when the murder was committed. There must have been people up and about between the hours of six and seven: the servants, Sweeney, the servants!"

"True," he said without animation.

"How easy it is to overlook them!" I said, since the brilliance of my reasoning seemed to have passed him by.

He didn't so much as nod his head. His night in the linen cupboard had left him thoroughly out of humor.

I continued, "Why didn't we think of it before? The housemaids who brought the morning tea—let's have them up and hear what they have to say. I'll see them at once."

He lingered. "May I make a suggestion?"

"Well?"

"Leave the maids to me, sir. They'll be too scared of you to say a blessed word."

"My dear Sweeney, I can state without fear of contradiction that I have more experience of coaxing tongue-tied females to speak than any man in the kingdom. The secret is to put them at their ease. Sympathy and understanding do the trick—and my sympathy and understanding are unequaled. Now jump to it, blast you!"

I took his point, to a degree. Housemaids aren't used to being spoken to by anyone above the station of housekeeper. In certain houses they are expected to turn and face the wall if they happen to meet one of the family in the corridors. To be summoned upstairs to answer questions was daunting enough. To appear before me was another thing again. However, it couldn't be ducked. If there was a scrap of decent evidence to be unearthed, I wanted it.

The maid who was ushered in presently was no more than fifteen years of age by my estimate, a dumpy, black-haired child who curtseyed awkwardly and kept her head bowed. Her name, Sweeney announced, was Sarah.

"Step closer, Sarah. I won't eat you. How long have you worked here?"

She took a short step towards my chair, watching the carpet as if it were a cliff edge.

Sweeney said smugly, "She's nervous, sir."

"That is evident. Did you understand my question, Sarah?"

Sarah moved her head slightly and said nothing.

"Let's try something more simple. How old are you?"

"Fifteen."

"Sir," Sweeney prompted her at once, and her mouth clamped shut, not from insolence, but sheer panic.

I turned to Sweeney and asked whether he had succeeded in finding any other servants.

"I did, sir. There's another maid outside the door. Shall I ask her to step in?"

"No. Be so good as to join her, would you?"

There was a stunned pause. "As you wish, sir." He turned and made his way to the door, reddening noticeably around the back of the neck.

"So you are fifteen, my dear?" Without Sweeney's petrifying presence, Sarah the maid would soon respond to my charm.

She gripped the lace edge of her apron and managed to agree that she was, indeed, the age she had said.

"And at what hour did you rise this morning?"

"Half past five, sir."

"That's early. I expect it was quiet. Was anyone else up and about?"

"The kitchenmaids, sir. They get up at five, to clean and light the range."

At least a dozen words! "And what are you exactly—a chambermaid?"

"An under housemaid, sir."

"What is your first task each morning?"

"Cleaning grates."

"How many?"

"Twelve, sir."

"And when the grates are cleaned?"

"I make the morning tea."

"What time is that?"

"Quarter past six."

"So early?"

"Tea for the housekeeper, sir."

"Of course. Did you take tea to anyone else this morning?"

"Yes, sir. St. George."

"St. George, you say?" I didn't correct the girl. I rather enjoyed the notion of Holdfast as one of the company of saints. Lady Moira, I privately decided, was his dragon. "What time was that?"

"Seven o'clock."

"And did you take tea to anyone else?"

"Only Mr. Pelham, sir, just after."

"Mr. Pelham. Is that your daily duty, taking tea to Sir George Holdfast and Mr. Pelham?"

"And bread and butter, thinly sliced, sir."

"At the same time each day this week—about seven o'clock?"

"Yes, sir."

"Splendid. This isn't so agonizing, is it? Now, Sarah, I want you to think carefully about this morning. When you entered Mr. Pelham's room with the tray, did you knock first?"

"Oh, yes."

"And he called you to come in, I expect. Did he answer at once?"

"I think so."

"So you went in. Was he sitting up in bed?"

"No, sir. Lying down."

"Then what did you do with the tray?"

"I waited for him to sit up. Then I handed it to him."

"Was anything said?"

"I wished the gentleman good morning. He didn't speak, sir."

"Did you happen to notice anything irregular in the room?"

Creases of mystification appeared around the bridge of her nose.

"Things out of place," I explained. "Anything suggesting he might have got up in the night."

Just when the answers had been coming freely, she turned scarlet and stared at the floor again.

Reading her thoughts, I said, "I don't wish to know if he used his chamber pot. I want to know whether he had left the room, possibly only a short time before you entered. Is it light by seven these mornings?"

"Yes, sir. Sunrise is half past six."

"Did you notice whether the curtains were still drawn?"

"They was, sir."

"Was there, perhaps, the smell of a candle?"

"I can't remember."

"Did you happen to notice his dressing gown?"

"It was hanging on the back of the door, sir."

"Bedroom slippers?"

She shook her head.

It was evident that this avenue of inquiry was leading nowhere, so I tried another. "When you brought the tea to these gentlemen, you passed Lady Drummond's door, is that correct?"

"Yes, sir."

"Did you, by any chance, see anyone go in or out of that door?"

"No, sir."

"Did you meet anyone in the corridor?"

"Only servants, sir."

"No gentlemen or ladies?"

"No, sir."

"Did you hear anything from inside Lady Drummond's room—a shout or a scream or even the sound of people talking?"

"It's more than my job is worth, sir."

"What do you mean?"

"Listening at doors."

"Oh, indeed. I'm sure you wouldn't do such a thing. But you might have overheard something as you were passing."

She shook her head. But she made clear her wish to help by adding, "You could ask Singleton."

"Who is he?"

"It isn't a man, sir. She's waiting outside."

"Doesn't she have a Christian name?"

"I don't know, sir. She's the lady's maid."

The social distinctions below stairs are every bit as rigid as our own. "Then would you ask Singleton to step in here? You are dismissed. It goes without saying that none of what we have discussed should be repeated to a living soul. I mean that, Sarah. Do you know what will happen if you gossip?"

"The Lord will find out, sir, and I will surely burn in hell."

There was nothing I could profitably add. The interview had been pretty unproductive, but I suppose you can't expect a fifteen-year-old to supply the entire case for the prosecution.

I looked more hopefully at Singleton as she entered, a figure of more poise, at least twice the age of Sarah, with pleasingly mature proportions, and reddish-gold curls kept tidy by a white ribbon. She had a neatly proportioned face. A little powder over the shiny parts and she could well have passed for a lady.

Sweeney sidled up to me and asked stiltedly whether I wished him to remain.

"Provided that you don't interfere," I told him in confidence. "Simply observe. Leave this entirely to me and you will see how diplomatic one has to be in coaxing them to tell what they know." Then I bestowed a broad, disarming smile on Singleton. "Thank you for waiting. I believe you are the lady's maid."

She answered, "Yes," and immediately covered her face with her apron and burst into convulsive sobs.

"Oh, my hat!" I said. "What on earth is the matter?"

She didn't respond. I doubt if she heard me, the wailing was so terrific.

Now, if there's one thing I cannot cope with, it's a female who pipes her eyes. Having fathered three daughters I ought to be equal to the challenge by now, but I am still at a loss each time it happens. I sprang up to offer Singleton my handkerchief and she ignored it and howled even more loudly. I walked around her once and put my hand on her elbow and murmured what I thought were consoling words. As those didn't work, I told her sharply to pull herself together, whereupon she turned and fled.

Then I became aware of Sweeney's malignant eye on me. "Don't just stand there, damn you!" I thundered. "Go after her. Calm her down and bring her back in a better state of mind."

Fully fifteen minutes passed before he returned with the wretched woman. The tears had stopped, thank heaven, but her face was fearfully puffed up.

"What do you think?" I asked Sweeney.

"I think she can take it now, sir."

"All I did was mention her job."

"That was the trouble, sir. She's lost it."

"Really?"

"Well, she's the lady's maid and the Lady is no more."

"Ah." There was undeniable logic in what he said. I made a second start with Singleton. "I didn't ask you here to talk about your personal prospects, but I'm sure that every effort will be made to find you another position, if that is what distresses you."

For a moment I thought we were in for a repeat performance. The eyes glistened again. She said, "I'm dreadfully sorry, Your Royal Highness. I wasn't crying for myself. I was crying for my mistress, God rest her soul. It's horrible . . . so cruel. Lady Drummond treated me so kindly always. Three years, I've been her lady's maid."

"And you can render her a final service by helping me to discover exactly what happened," I said.

"I would if I could. I know nothing, sir."

"I'll be the judge of that. I have some simple questions. What time did you rise this morning?"

"Half past six, sir."

"And what are your duties in the morning?"

"I take tea on a tray to my Lady's room at half past seven, sir, and a jug of hot water for washing twenty minutes after. This week I have done the same for Miss Dundas."

"Do you mean that you go into their bedrooms?"

"No, sir. Not into my Lady's room. I was instructed to knock and leave the tray and the jug on the floor outside the door."

"That was the arrangement this morning?"

She modestly lowered her eyelids. "All the week, sir."

Poor Amelia—her secret hopes laid bare. "So you had no reason to enter the room this morning? Did you hear anything when you knocked?"

"There was no answer, sir."

"Did that strike you as peculiar?"

"No, sir. I supposed that it was not convenient for my Lady to respond at that minute."

Discreetly expressed. "Now tell me, did you happen to see any other person in the corridor?"

"Nobody except servants, sir."

Virtually identical to the answer I had got from Sarah the housemaid.

Singleton added, "The corridors are fairly swarming with servants at that time, delivering the tea and the jugs of water and clean shoes."

"People you know?"

"Not all of them, sir. We've had so many extra below stairs this week that we had to take our meals in sittings. Some of them have left, but there are still plenty who are strangers to me, such as Sir George's retinue and your own."

"I understand. So it would seem that nobody had any reason to enter Lady Drummond's rooms between six and seven this morning."

"No servant, anyway." She frowned thoughtfully and put her hand to her mouth.

"Is there something you wish to add?" I asked.

"I don't know if it's my place to mention it, but the chambermaid found a cigar butt under the bed when she swept my Lady's room this morning."

"No," I said rapidly, "it wouldn't be significant. Could have been there for days, you see."

She reddened. "The rooms are swept and dusted every morning, sir."

"So after you left the tray outside the room," I firmly resumed, "what did you do?"

"I returned to the kitchen and brought up the tray for Miss Dundas."

"Ah. And what was your arrangement with that good lady?"

"Miss Dundas comes to the door when I knock, sir."

"I know." Hastily I explained, "That is to say, I would expect it. She is an explorer, trained to react to the slightest sound. Did she have anything to say to you?"

"She ordered breakfast in her room, sir, for half past eight. I was to pass on the message that she wouldn't be down for breakfast."

Everything these servants had told me appeared to confirm the statements already made by the guests. I tried yet another tack. "As the lady's maid, you must have known Lady Drummond more intimately than any other person in this house."

That almost made her purr. "I dare say that is true, sir."

"You looked after her clothes and attended to her hair. You must have had many conversations."

"Oh, yes."

"I want to ask you about the things she may have said to you in the last few days. Did she admit to any fears?"

"Fears?" Singleton pondered the question. "I don't know about fears. She was extremely agitated about the dreadful things that happened, but I don't think she knew fear. She was the bravest lady I ever had the good fortune to serve, sir. She bore Lord Drummond's dreadful accident last year with wonderful fortitude."

"So I gathered, but I'm talking about this week. Did she pass on any suspicion she may have had about the person responsible for the tragic events?"

"No, sir."

"Did she speak of her brother at all?"

"Mr. Marcus?" She gave me a sudden guarded look. "I would rather not speak about him, if you will forgive me, sir."

"Why is that?"

Her mouth quivered. "If I am to seek a position in another household, I shall require a character, and I shall have to approach Mr. Marcus to see if he will supply me with one. There is no one else who can do it now. I wouldn't like to repeat anything to his discredit."

"*Is* there anything to his discredit?"

She lowered her face.

I said, "If there is, you must tell me. What did you hear from Lady Drummond?"

And much to my disappointment, she spoke as if she meant it, "My mistress was utterly loyal to her brother."

"Utterly—or blindly?"

"That is not for me to say, sir."

"But you have your private suspicions, I gather."

"They are not of any consequence."

"I shall ask you something else, then. You said just now—I'm quoting your own words—that the house is fairly swarming with servants early in the morning. Do you think it was possible for the murderer to have entered and left Lady Drummond's rooms without being seen by one of the servants?"

"It is most unlikely, sir."

"Did anyone in the servants' hall mention seeing anything suspicious this morning?"

"Not that I am aware of."

"Thank you, Singleton. I have no further questions at this juncture. I should think you will get the character reference you want, and if I were you, I would ask for it without delay."

"You see?" I said to Sweeney when we were alone again. "Perfectly amenable and extremely helpful."

Those black eyebrows of his reared up.

"What's the matter now?" I said.

"*Helpful*, sir?"

"Vitally so. We learned that Pelham wasn't seen going into the room or out of it. One of the servants would certainly have noticed him. What do you deduce from that?"

"He could have got in there sometime in the night, sir, before the servants were about."

"And when did he come out, do you suppose?"

"After he'd killed her."

"Which we estimate as sometime between six and seven, when the corridors were thick with servants. No, Sweeney, that won't wash."

He said without much conviction, "Then he must have remained hiding in the room until later."

I shook my head. "The housemaid found him tucked up harmlessly in his own bed when she brought the tea just after seven o'clock."

Sweeney was obviously stumped.

I put a hand on his shoulder. "Come upstairs and I shall demonstrate how it was done."

19

I led Sweeney briskly upstairs to Amelia's dressing room, which felt like the North Pole when we stepped inside, because the balcony windows still stood open. Sweeney hastened to close them.

"What on earth do you think you are doing?" I demanded with a frost of my own. "We're not here for the sake of our comfort, you know. We are about to reconstruct the crime. Pray leave them as you found them and step into the bedroom."

"I beg your pardon, sir."

"Right. I shall be the murderer, you the victim."

He did as instructed, while I remained in the dressing room.

"Close the door and lie on the bed as if you are asleep. Have you done that?"

A muffled, "Yes, sir."

"Good. Now listen for a disturbance. When you are convinced that you have heard something, enough to waken you from your slumbers, get up from the bed, cross the room and step in here to see what is the matter. Not yet. I am going outside." So saying, I moved to my position, not in the corridor, as he would suppose, but *on the balcony*, pulling the windows gently together.

I waited a few moments and then rapped on the glass. Through it, I presently saw the connecting door open and Sweeney emerge. Just as I had anticipated, he crossed to the dressing room door without a glance in my direction, and looked out into the corridor.

I tapped again and he spun on his heel, saw where I was, and gaped like a cuckoo.

"Look alive, man!" I shouted, for I was in danger of perishing from exposure out there. "Come over here and let me in."

He shook his great befuddled head as he admitted me.

"So," I said, "having gained entry, I take two strides to the fireplace like so, snatch up the poker like so, and strike you across the skull, which we shall have to leave to the imagination. You fall to the floor. Well, do it, man!"

He sank to his knees.

"I drop the poker, stoop and carry your unconscious, dead or dying body to the balcony. On your feet, Sweeney—I'm not going to risk a hernia for this." I took a firm grip on his arm. "Through the open window you go, out to the balcony and over the edge." As we advanced to the iron railing, Sweeney grabbed it like a drowning man and held on. I said, "You don't have to panic. This is only a demonstration. Do you see how it was done?"

"No, sir."

Reader, who could have blamed me if I had tipped him over? "What, then, is the difficulty?"

"How did the murderer get here, sir?"

"Get where?"

"Onto the balcony."

I said cuttingly, "Take a look to your right."

He did as instructed. "Well, I'll be jiggered!" He was looking, as you may have surmised, at the balcony of the room next door, a mere arm's length from where we stood. This wing of the building was so designed that pairs of balconies jutted from the facade at regular intervals. There was a long stretch of wall before the next pair, so Amelia's balcony was accessible from its neighbor to the right, but no other. Even Sweeney in his jittery state saw the significance. "Anyone could climb from there to here."

"And back," I said, "after committing murder."

"So that was why no one saw him in the corridor. He climbed over the balcony." He gave a whistle, which was rather *infra dig*, but gratifying in its way. "Smart of you to think of it, if I may say so, sir."

"You may."

"Such a thing would not have occurred to me in a million years."

"That I am willing to believe." I basked in his admiration for a short while, without troubling to mention how I had got the idea. You will recall that two nights before I had seen Claude Bullivant enter Isabella Dundas's room by way of the balcony.

"The next question is," Sweeney remarked with ponderous calculation, "whose balcony is that?"

"You ought to know. We looked into the room last night."

"Mr. Pelham's?"

"Correct."

He made a fist with his right hand and punched it into the palm of his left. "We've got him now, sir, thanks be to God!"

"Not yet," I cautioned. "We have merely established a possibility. We need proof that he entered the room this way. Clues, Sweeney, clues."

"Like a footprint on the balcony, sir?"

"A bloodstain is more likely. There was blood on the poker."

"But he dropped the poker, sir."

"There could have been blood on his hands, or his clothes. I propose that you climb over and see what you can find."

"Would you be asking me to climb onto Mr. Pelham's balcony, sir?"

"Precisely."

"Suppose he's in his room."

"He's downstairs. We saw him a minute or two ago."

"Sure and that's the truth," said Sweeney limply. He hoisted one leg awkwardly over the rail and reached for the other balcony. He had difficulty getting a foothold, and I didn't assist him. The point of the exercise was to demonstrate how easily a man could manage it alone.

He completed the maneuver eventually. A younger man such as Pelham could practically have vaulted the rails.

"No signs of blood here, sir."

"Examine the windows. Are they marked at all?"

"They are spotless, sir. Shall I come back?"

"Certainly not. See whether the windows open." When that suggestion came to nothing I said, "Very well. Remain where you are. I shall go into the room and open them from the inside."

I don't altogether approve of entering other people's bedrooms without invitation or permission, but this *was* a murder investigation. Who could say what damning discoveries I might make: a bloodstained garment possibly, or a copy of the *Times* with the name of the day cut out.

Not a soul was in the corridor when I stepped out of Amelia's room. I moved the few yards to Pelham's door, grasped the handle—and felt the horrid sensation of its turning independently. The door swung inwards and Marcus Pelham stood there, all teeth and charm.

"Do come in, Your Royal Highness."

I said on a high note of disbelief, "You were downstairs."

"And now I am here. As the only surviving member of the

family, I thought it proper to make myself available. Won't you come in, sir?"

Naturally I was wary, but he appeared not to have any murderous weapon to hand. "How did you know I was at your door?"

"I watched Inspector Sweeney climb onto my balcony. I cannot imagine why he should essay such an acrobatic feat except in the performance of his duty as a bodyguard. I therefore concluded that I was about to be graced by a Royal visit." He rounded off this sarcastic piece of insolence with a faint smile. He knew very well that I hadn't expected to find him in the room.

I said, "You wasted no time in coming upstairs."

"I followed you up," he admitted without turning a hair. "The obligations of host fall entirely to me now that my poor sister is no longer with us. I am at your service, sir, ready and willing to render assistance."

"Very well," I responded, treating his humbug as if I believed every word, "you can begin by opening your balcony window and inviting Inspector Sweeney to step inside. He's of more use as a bodyguard in here than out there."

"So I would have thought," said Pelham. "He's the one whose life is threatened."

"Why do you say that?" I asked at once.

"He'll catch pneumonia out there."

He approached the window and reached for the bolt. The wretched Sweeney saw his approach, dodged sideways and pressed himself against the railing in the corner, trying without success to escape from view, a mortifying spectacle. "I seem to have startled him," Pelham remarked.

I declined to comment. I was observing the attempt to open the window, which was in itself an action of overriding importance to the investigation. Sweeney's personal comfort was of no account compared with this. Pelham was having some difficulty, or so he wanted me to think.

"It's the devil to shift," he said.

I let him struggle a moment, and then told him to stand aside. I discovered that he had not been bluffing. The window *was* stuck fast. I had to put my shoulder to the frame to move it, and then I only succeeded at the fourth or fifth attempt. There was a rasp as it finally yielded and flakes of paint came away from the wood.

"No wonder," said Pelham. "It must have been given a coat of paint last summer and closed before it was dry, with the result that the surfaces stuck fast. Shoddy work. Step inside, Inspector, we're not discussing you."

Sweeney entered without a word. He didn't need to pass any comment. His look was eloquent enough. He had seen the efforts to open the windows. He could see the paint flakes on the floor. He knew, as I did, that those windows hadn't been opened in months. Our theory—no, let's be brutally honest—*my* theory had just been exposed as impossible.

20

So the hounds had bayed in vain. I was obliged to spend the rest of the day in the kennel, so to speak, gnawing at the bones of my theory and finding precious little meat. Reluctantly I was forced to conclude that my suspicions about Marcus Pelham had got the better of me. Try as I might, I was unable to fathom how he could have got into Amelia's room and out of it unseen when the corridor was swarming with servants. In fact, I couldn't fathom how anyone had managed it.

In bed that night (with a gundog and his handler on guard outside my bedroom door) I resolved to toss out all the suspicions and prejudices I had accumulated and adopt a more objective method. Emulating Scotland Yard, I would marshal the facts of the case and make a "wanted" portrait of the murderer.

Five deaths had to be accounted for. Five deaths in five days, and apart from the obvious fact that the victims were all members of our house party, the only thing they had in common was the piece of paper left beside or upon each of the bodies. Beyond doubt the murderer had left those clues for a purpose. The deaths were linked to a few lines of rhyming folklore. What could one deduce from that?

First, those lines of verse fitted the victims so aptly that the guest list must have been known to the murderer some time in advance. To put it in legal jargon, the crimes were premeditated.

Second, the daily killing was clearly presented as a challenge, or a taunt. We, the people under threat, were invited to guess who was to be next and we had been outwitted so far.

Third, this murderer was willing to take risks. The leaving of clues was a dangerous indulgence.

And fourth, it had taken exceptional foresight to calculate that the house party would not be abandoned and the police called in after one, two or three murders. The killer had banked on my personal refusal to embroil the office of Heir Apparent in a sensational case of murder. That stuck in my gullet.

Have a care, Bertie, I cautioned myself—the good detective strives to be impartial at all times.

With a firm eye on the facts, I characterized the murderer as a plotter of ingenuity and foresight, one for whom mere killing was insufficient satisfaction, who treated it as a macabre game, to baffle and taunt the victims. Unhappily, the description fell short of a physical picture. Age, height, build, hair, eyes, dress, marks or peculiarities. I wasn't even certain of the culprit's sex.

And this night was bringing us to Saturday. My thoughts became unscientific again and drifted back to my fellow guests, the remaining members of the house party, no doubt lying awake, like me, asking themselves the dread question, "Could I conceivably be described as one who works hard for a living?" George Holdfast, Marcus Pelham and Isabella Dundas. I did not seriously consider as possible victims Sweeney and all the servants; the killing had been confined to legitimate guests, and so I expected it to continue—unless and until I put a stop to it.

Holdfast, Pelham, Miss Dundas and myself. Survivors, thus far. You may wonder why any of us lingered any longer in that house of murder, and it is difficult to explain, but I will try. Two of the party had already chosen discretion as the better part of valor, of course, and who could blame them? But since Alix and Lady Moira had left, a sort of understanding had grown up. We who remained were all, in our different ways, dogged, self-reliant individuals with our own private reasons for refusing to leave. A sense of moral obligation played a part in my own case, and, I am sure, in others; there was an unspoken pact between us that no one else would quit until this monster was caught. Call us brave, if you must. The same dauntless spirit built the greatest Empire in history.

Besides, if anyone had packed his bags at this juncture we would all have smelled a rat.

SATURDAY

21

Have you ever gone to bed with a problem to resolve and found that when you woke up you had the answer? That was what happened to me that Saturday morning. But before you shout "Unfair" and protest that no self-respecting detective relies on dreams to resolve his cases, let me make myself clear. This wasn't a dream. I was roused by Wellard, one of my footmen, who brought me my usual glass of cold milk, and the sight of him prompted me to say, "What time is it?"

"Seven o'clock, sir."

"Seven, eh. Is it busy out there?"

"Busy, sir?"

"In the corridor. Servants going this way and that."

"Well, yes. Quite busy, sir."

"I dare say you're getting to know the other servants."

"Not to any noticeable degree, sir. Each retinue tends to keep to itself."

"So if you pass someone in the corridor, the chances are that you won't know who they are?"

"I'm afraid that is so, sir."

I sat bolt upright, alert to the importance of what my questions were revealing. "Now tell me this, Wellard. Would you recognize any of the guests if you passed them in the corridor?"

"The guests? Certainly, sir."

This wasn't the answer I wanted to hear. "How? How would you recognize them?"

"From their clothes, sir. They are not in uniform as the servants are."

"Never mind what they wear. Do you know any of the guests by sight—by face alone?"

"No, sir. My duties confine me to your suite and the servants' quarters."

"As I thought." I beamed at him with approval. "That is all I wanted to know, Wellard."

Thus, without fuss or fanfare, I finally grasped the key to the mystery. It was clear to me how the murderer had been able to pass through the house unremarked and unchallenged—*by posing as a servant*. This week Desborough was stuffed with visiting servants, and in most cases one flunky didn't know another from Adam—or from Pelham, or Holdfast, or Miss Dundas.

Breakfast found the four of us still alive and in pretty good spirits considering that the day held nothing more in prospect than a funeral. It was a fine day, too; the sort of sunny October morning when one ought to be off to Newmarket for the races, but the blinds were down and two mutes with crepe-covered wands were on duty at the front door. In the absence of the Chaplain, who had excused himself from leading the morning prayers, I said a brief grace and dismissed the servants. Then I enquired of Pelham what arrangements had been made.

He surprised me with an effusion of information, cheerily communicated. "The funeral service is at noon, sir, in the family chapel in the Hermit Wood, for reasons of privacy. It is not much used, but the Chaplain thought it more appropriate than the village church. The carriages are called for half past eleven. The hearse will lead the cortege, followed by your carriage, and then ours—Miss Dundas and Sir George riding with me. After a short service the burial will be in a plot to the rear of the chapel."

"It all sounds most appropriate, as you say. Apart from my presence, is anything required of me?"

"I think Wilfred will be sufficiently honored by your attendance at his funeral, sir."

I nodded. "Yes, it will be something of a departure for me—and much more of a departure for him, come to mention it." I thought this rather droll, and waited for the faces around the table to respond, which they eventually did. "True, I'm not often seen at the funeral of a commoner. I have to draw the line somewhere, or I could spend the whole of my time in graveyards. However, I'm pleased to pay my last respects to this fellow. Even more reason why we don't want any of today's doings reported in the press. You're quite sure we're the only mourners?"

"Yes, sir, except for the undertaker and his assistants."

"Don't forget the sky pilot," Holdfast jovially put in. Turning to Miss Dundas, he added, "The Chaplain, my dear—a term sailors use for the clergy."

She said evenly, "Thank you. I am not without experience of sea voyages."

The rebuke was lightly delivered, and Sir George gave a wry nod and smile. His avuncular presence had been a support to us all through this harrowing week. The amiable gleam had never left his eye. If anything, it had got brighter since Lady Moira's departure. In fact, looking about the table, I found it well nigh impossible to cast any of my companions as the scheming, stony-hearted assassin I had divined as responsible for the murders. Isabella Dundas looked perfectly demure in a simple black dress overlaid with jet beads that I suppose she would otherwise have worn for dinner one evening. She had her reddish-brown hair gathered to a chignon and fastened at the side with black combs. Women of her stamp are equal to every contingency. If we had all been transported to the moon she would still have found something correct to wear. As for Marcus Pelham, my opinion was mellowing. The tragic death of his sister seemed to have made a man of him. The adolescent scowl was less evident. He even showed commendable concern for someone other than himself by asking, "How is Inspector Sweeney this morning? No ill effects from yesterday, I trust?"

"Apparently not," I answered.

"Only I haven't seen him."

"I dare say he's about his business," said I.

Miss Dundas looked up and asked, "Did the Inspector have a bad experience yesterday?"

"A little time outside without an overcoat, that was all."

"He did look somewhat *distrait* towards the end of the day," she remarked. "I do hope nothing is amiss, sir."

None of us said any more about Sweeney until later.

Of necessity, the funeral of Wilfred Osgot-Edge was without much ostentation, even if it is imprinted on my memory forever. There were few of the trappings of these occasions. True, Hibbert the undertaker supplied us with hatbands and cloaks, but that was the extent of it. I had refused to have my pair of grays dyed black, so they weren't fitted with sable plumes, which would have looked silly. The hearse, of course, was drawn by plumed horses; Hibbert himself walked in front, which was heroic considering the state of the going, and the mutes and pallbearers also made the short journey on foot. We proceeded at the best gait they could manage along a sticky cart track through the wood, stopping at the lych-gate, where the Reverend Humphrey Paget stood waiting. As so often happens, the horses drawing the hearse marked our arrival with a mournful neighing—probably in protest at the tolling of the church bell.

While the pallbearers stepped forward to shoulder the coffin, I stood back with the others. The family chapel was a gloomy-looking, stone structure with a small belltower heavily encrusted with lichen. Although I doubt if it was more than a hundred years old, its location had exposed it critically to the depredations of nature. I didn't relish stepping inside. Pelham nudged my arm and offered me a hip flask. My first reaction was to take a nip, and then I thought better of it. After all, I told myself, there was a one in three chance that the funeral was Pelham's doing. A moment later, when I saw him put the flask to his lips, I wished I had been more trusting.

Hibbert nodded to the Chaplain and we followed the coffin through the lych-gate. The path was thick with moss and ivy, and one of the pallbearers stumbled slightly. But the dead and the living all got inside without serious mishap and the service commenced. The Padre had my backing when he steamed into his words like an express train, for the pews had no padding and the smell of mustiness was quite overpowering. None of us meant any disrespect to Osgot-Edge; I'm sure he wouldn't have wished any of us except his murderer to feel uncomfortable on his account.

In a strange way Osgot-Edge contrived to make his spiritual presence felt. When the Chaplain first said, "Let us pray," I was reminded of that poem about the obstinate boy and the lion that we'd heard recited on the first fateful evening. Curiously enough, on that occasion it had been the Chaplain who had read it to us. *"Let us prey."* When he spoke the words for the second or third time, my thoughts, shameful to relate, took a sacrilegious turn. I was prompted to ask myself whether I might have overlooked a possible suspect.

My skin prickled at the thought. *A man of the cloth?* Surely not. I tried to remember whether the Reverend Humphrey Paget had been present in the house each time a murder had been committed. Certainly he had been at dinner with us the first night, when

Queenie Chimes was poisoned. Moreover, he had joined us for lunch in the marquee on the day Jerry Gribble was shot.

"Amen," said the congregation.

On the night Osgot-Edge had been stabbed to death, the Chaplain had played with gusto in the parlor games.

"Psalm Ninety," announced the Reverend Humphrey Paget, "'Lord, thou hast been our refuge.'"

On the morning Bullivant was pushed down the well, who had led us in morning prayers? I particularly remembered, because everyone had been waiting when I arrived.

Could the Reverend Humphrey Paget possibly have entered the building secretly in the small hours of Friday morning disguised as a servant and murdered Amelia? Her own family chaplain?

As the words "Let us pray," were spoken yet again, I knelt and silently asked forgiveness for my unholy suspicions, and at such an ill-chosen time. I am sorry if this offends my more devout readers, but I fancy that a still, small, sporting voice said, "Hold your fire, Bertie, but keep your shooter loaded."

The service in the chapel came to an end and we shuffled silently from the pews and followed the coffin outside. The ground we traversed was fearfully overgrown with damp, rotting bracken. I did my best to beat a path with my stick while Miss Dundas, accustomed to the jungle, took a grip on her skirts and stepped in behind me.

I should explain that this wasn't in any sense a regular churchyard. There were no graves that one could see. I imagine that there was a family vault beneath the chapel where the Drummonds were interred, and where Amelia would be laid to rest in a day or two. Osgot-Edge, not being family, was accommodated outside, close to the dry-stone wall that enclosed the consecrated ground. We duly positioned ourselves around the grave and saw the coffin lowered. Four suspects and me. And I'm glad to say that the interment was completed with due reverence. We paid our respects and moved away. I told Pelham that I would now appreciate a nip from his flask.

He made the unnecessary remark, "So poor Wilfred is laid to rest."

"That was my understanding of what happened."

"A nicely conducted service, I thought, sir. It went well."

"Without a stutter," said I.

He missed the irony. "We can be grateful to the Chaplain."

"Yes, I intend to have a word with him." I handed back the flask.

"Why don't you and the others drive back to the Hall for lunch? I'll join you later."

"Just as you wish, sir." He hesitated as his features creased into a look of genuine concern. "Is it safe?"

"What exactly do you mean by that?"

"I mean out here in the open, without your bodyguard. No one has seen hide nor hair of Inspector Sweeney."

I assured Pelham that I would take care of myself and he went back to Holdfast and Miss Dundas. I raised my hat to the lady and made clear my intention to be independent by picking my way through the bracken towards the far side of the chapel. They were soon out of sight. Presently I heard their carriage move off. Soon after, the hearse left as well. I had noticed the Reverend Humphrey Paget re-enter the chapel by a back door, presumably the vestry, so I was alone apart from an estate worker who had started the work of filling in the grave. The man was soon lost to view as I made my way around the building.

I was in no hurry to question the Chaplain. If possible, I wanted to remove a lingering doubt from my mind, only I hadn't reckoned with the bracken, which was knee-high, even after the recent frost had brought it down some feet from its full summer glory. Hacking with my stick and looking to right and left, I progressed methodically towards the lych-gate until I spotted what I was seeking, surprisingly close to the path that the cortege had used as we entered the chapel.

I had discovered a gravestone, a plain, rectangular slab of granite jutting up from the ground and almost obscured by the bracken. A few swings of my stick enabled me to read the inscription, which was recent in origin:

ROBERT BELL
Died October 20, 1889, aged 17
Gone, but not forgotten

Not forgotten, but almost lost to view, I reflected wryly. This was, of course, the resting place of the youth accidentally shot a year ago by Claude Bullivant. Decent of the Drummonds to have had a stone put up for him. *Gone, but not forgotten*. Only a couple of days ago I had been inspired to concoct an entire theory out of the fate of this boy and Bullivant's consequent difficulties. A misfounded theory, as events had proved beyond doubt, but I had wanted to see the grave for myself. I still had a strange intimation that it had a bearing on our present difficulties.

And now, with a thrill of discovery, I understood why. I understood almost everything about the Desborough Hall murders.

22

I didn't have long to savour the moment. I flung myself to the ground at the sound of gunfire.

I lay still and waited, flat to the ground. I knew the identity of the murderer now, knew it for certain. This was no empty boast, as you will discover, reader. If you flatter yourself that you could have matched my success as a sleuth, then you had better name your suspect at once, without sneaking a look at the last pages of the book.

For the benefit of those who prefer to remain mystified until the last possible moment, I shall continue to unfold the events as they happened. Obviously this was not the time to step forward and unmask the murderer.

Two shots had been discharged. If thirty years' experience of shooting counted for anything, I knew they had been fired from a double-barreled shotgun, in which case the firer was probably reloading at this minute—or already taking aim. One can never be certain about the effects of echo in the vicinity of a building, but it seemed to me that the shots had come from somewhere close to the chapel. Nor could I be entirely sure that I was the intended target. Now that I considered the matter, I hadn't noticed shot being sprayed in my vicinity.

I wasn't comforted. I remained motionless, praying that my black clothes were not conspicuous. The sensation of helplessness made me shake with rage. If I *was* the target, the contest was so uneven. Even a wretched game bird has a sporting chance. What chance had a burly middle-aged man out there in the open equipped with nothing more effective in defense than a walking stick?

The boundary wall was twenty yards or more behind me. If I could run that far without being shot, I would still have the devil's own job to get out of the firing line. Scrambling over walls isn't the sort of exercise I am accustomed to taking. And the lych-gate was at least forty yards away. So I settled for discretion and a faceful of damp foliage.

The extra shots I expected were not discharged. There followed a long, tense time when nothing happened except for a colony of rooks returning to occupy the chapel roof and tower which they had noisily abandoned. I wished I had their confidence.

Finally I risked raising my head sufficiently to peer around the gravestone. A patch of taller and more verdant bracken was to my left. I considered whether it was worth scrambling on my stomach for ten yards to get some better cover. I stared in the direction of the chapel and saw no sign of life. Yes, I would risk it.

First I removed the mourning cloak, made a bundle of it with the silk hat and walking stick and pushed them under some fronds. Then I started a passable imitation of an Indian scout, leaving the shelter of the gravestone to drag myself forward on elbows, hips and knees. No shot came. I crossed the divide and collapsed breathlessly into the denser foliage. Sanctuary.

I lay on my stomach for a few minutes recovering my breath. I reckoned that I could stay there in reasonable safety for an indefinite interval. Until dark, in fact. There was no point in taking unnecessary risks. It wasn't just a matter of saving my hide; the future of the realm had to be safeguarded.

I was tempted to light up a cigar, but smoke signals would be taking the scouting to excess, so I rolled onto my side.

To my absolute horror, I saw the mistake I had made. I stared back at the way I had come. My route through the bracken was flattened into a track so obvious that I might as well have unrolled a red carpet and stood a guard of honor on either side. Any fool could tell where I was. All the subterfuge had been useless. I would have done better to have stood up and walked. In fact, I would have to move somewhere on foot, and fast.

Someone was approaching. I could hear steps on the gravel by the chapel door.

A dash for the lych-gate was out of the question now. It would make more sense to look for a sheltered place behind the chapel, or, better still, inside. Gingerly I raised my eyes above the level of the foliage. Ahead was another oasis of tall bracken. I got up and bolted towards it. Out of the corner of my eye I had a blurred impression of the figure by the chapel door. I ducked down. In one more gallop I could get out of range on the far side of the building. I took a deep breath and was off like a rabbit.

I tripped, staggered, put a hand to the ground and kept my footing by the sheer force of my onward rush. I didn't mean to stop until I reached the chapel wall. Suddenly a pheasant rose up screeching and brushed my face with its tail feathers. It didn't stop my charge. Nothing but a cartridge would do that.

So when I glimpsed something red and white below me, I leapt over it and ran on. It wasn't as startling as the pheasant because it didn't move. Not startling in that sense, but in another. It was a glimpse of death.

The white object was the Reverend Humphrey Paget's surplice. Do I need to say what the red was? The Chaplain had been shot through the head. It wasn't a sight that a susceptible reader would wish me to describe, or that I should care to. Anyone who knows the power of a twelve-bore will have an idea of its effect at close range.

I lurched on until I flattened my hands on the chapel wall. I felt ready to vomit, but I dared not stop. Somehow I had to stay in control, get inside the vestry and lock the door behind me. I groped my way to the door, grasped the handle, turned it and let myself in. As it slammed shut, I leaned against it and breathed a great, shuddering sigh. That sigh stopped prematurely.

I was looking into the twin barrels of a shotgun.

The shock was profound. I failed to understand how it was possible. I was not capable of understanding. My brain had not fully absorbed the horror of the Chaplain's death, and now I faced my own destruction. I am not at all proud of the spectacle I presented. I wanted to plead for my life. I merely gibbered.

I was at the mercy of the murderer, and she had now revealed herself. She was Miss Queenie Chimes.

The lady should have been dead, but she was not. She was standing with the shotgun leveled, her finger against the trigger. She was not an apparition. She had not, after all, been killed. You must take my word for it that I wasn't in the least surprised. I had deduced that she was the murderer the moment I had seen that gravestone.

She *did* succeed in taking my breath away when she said, "You can sit down, Your Royal Highness. I shall not shoot unless you make it necessary. But I shall continue to aim the gun at you. There is a chair to your left."

I wanted to protest about poor Paget, but the words would not leave my lips. I sank onto the chair. Queenie Chimes remained standing in the center of the vestry, which was furnished with a row of empty clothes hooks and a cupboard. She was dressed in a riding habit and silk hat. Appropriately she favored the color of mourning. I could recall the black velvet dress she had worn when I had seen her last. The signs of strain showed more strikingly in her face than they had that Monday evening, but she was well in control of herself.

She lowered the gun to the level of my chest. "You *do* remember who I am?"

I nodded.

She said, "Are you unable or unwilling to speak?"

I succeeded in saying, "Miss Chimes, or do you prefer Miss Bell?"

"I don't mind very much how you address me. So you found the grave? I saw you searching for it."

"The grave, yes. Am I correct in deducing that Robert Bell was your brother?"

"My dear brother Bob." A glaze of moisture came over her eyes. "My family. All the family I had in this world until he was murdered."

I said as gently as I could, "If you are speaking of what happened a year ago, that was an accident, surely."

The mouth twitched and she said with bitterness, "Yes, call it an accident. Dismiss it. Just an orphan boy who happened to stray into the line of fire. An unfortunate incident, not worth canceling the shoot for. They didn't. My brother wasn't killed outright, you know. He was hit by scores of pellets, and in terrible pain, but it was inconvenient to call a doctor or take him to a hospital while the shoot was in progress, so they had him carried to the nearest cottage and left in the care of an old woman of eighty who tried to comfort him with hot milk. The shooting party went back to slaughtering pheasants. Three hours after the shoot was over a footman was sent to the cottage with a flask of brandy. That was all the interest that any of them took. Sometime after midnight my poor brother died of his wounds. Do you know what they were doing in the Hall that evening? Singing around the piano."

"Such insensitivity!" I said, trying to show sympathy without sounding insincere. "I'm profoundly sorry. One can only assume that nobody realized how serious the injuries were."

She let out a harsh, indignant breath. "If he had been one of theirs—a brother or a son—do you suppose they would have abandoned him like that? Bob's death need not have happened. They were responsible. And they knew it. They buried him in secret without an inquest. The servants were instructed never to mention it, or they would be dismissed. He wasn't even buried in a proper coffin. One of the estate woodmen was given the task of making a box from unseasoned timber." She pressed her lips together. "I can't bear to think of it."

I said in a futile attempt to assuage the bitterness, "They provided a decent stone for him."

"Pardon me, they did not. I paid for the stone when I learned how my brother had died and been left in an unmarked grave. I had it delivered here without any indication of who had sent it. Each of them assumed that one of the others had ordered it in a fit of conscience. So it was erected as a headstone, and touched nobody's conscience at all. You saw how the grave was overgrown."

Still trying not to antagonize her, I remarked, "Then the words on the stone were your choice. *Gone, but not forgotten.*"

She gave a laugh bereft of any amusement. "What restraint I showed! My first thought was to have the truth engraved there. '*Cruelly struck down and allowed to die.*' But my plan was already made, you see. I couldn't put it at risk."

"Your plan?"

"The Drummonds and their friends made the mistake of believing that Bob was alone in the world. They thought he could be buried and forgotten."

"So the words on the stone are not without point," I commented.

"They didn't know of my existence. Bob wasn't one to talk about his past—it was too painful." She sighed. "You see, as children we were separated after both our parents were called to God. On top of the grief, we had to endure loneliness. Sometimes cruelty. Yet we kept in touch. Don't ask me how—it was God's work. We were only young children, but we refused to be cut off from each other. The tie of blood was too strong. As the elder child, I felt responsible, even after we had both grown up. So I knew that Bob had gone to work on the Desborough estate, and when my birthday came and I heard nothing from him, I was worried. I came here to see him and no one would tell me what had happened to him. Their lips were sealed, but I could see in their faces that a tragedy had happened. Finally by sheer persistence I found the old woman in whose cottage he died. She was brave enough to tell me the dreadful truth. It was almost a relief to know for certain. Yes, I traveled back to London feeling gratified. Can you understand that?"

I nodded.

She said, "Later it turned to grief, of course, and self-pity. Then anger. Outrage. Blind fury at those monsters who had conspired to cover up their crime. It was a crime, you know, failure to report a death."

"I'm sure that is so."

"The greater crime was letting him die. The law might not hold them responsible for that, but I did. I blamed them. The outrage didn't diminish. If anything it grew as I learned what it truly means to be alone in the world. I lived with my anger for a time. I tried to subdue it, I really did, and eventually I succeeded. I achieved a sort of calm by planning vengeance. I vowed to kill everyone who had conspired in Robert's death, every member of that house party including the chaplain who buried him." She paused, I suppose to see the effect of this statement.

The effect upon me was that I remained outwardly impassive whilst privately thanking my stars that all my shooting last year had been done at Sandringham and Balmoral.

She continued in the same toneless voice, "I was saved the trouble of disposing of Lord Frederick Drummond. He was gored by a bull."

"That much I know," said I.

"Five others remained. I set myself the task of finding out everything I could about them. As a first step, I contrived to meet Marcus Pelham and gain his confidence. He had not been one of the party, but he was worth cultivating because he took particular interest in his sister's social attachments."

"Indeed he did."

"I learned from Marcus what I hoped to hear—that another shooting party was to be held at Desborough."

I gave a nod. "And did he tell you that I was to be the principal guest?"

"That was a mishap I had not foreseen," she said without realizing how tactless a remark it was. "Alarming at first, I confess, but the more I thought about it, the more I saw the opportunity it presented."

"In what way?"

"Well, an unexplained death in the house would put Lady Drummond and her brother into an appalling quandary. They would want to avoid the matter becoming public knowledge."

"For reasons which you need not go into," said I.

She gave me an unsympathetic glance. "I contrived a mysterious death with shocking possibilities of scandal—an actress who collapses at the dinner table in front of the Prince of Wales. Everyone's instinct would be to conceal it from the police and the press, to behave as if nothing had happened."

"Which everyone did," said I. "And now I discover that there was no dying actress, unless you have a twin sister."

"I don't. There was no dying actress. There was an actress pretending to die."

"Extraordinary behavior!"

"It was necessary. It enabled me to test the water, so to speak, and discover how everyone would react. And it removed me from all suspicion."

"This is all very cunning and ingenious," said I, "but I fail to see how it was done."

"With a convincing performance," she said with just a hint of self-congratulation.

"I'll grant you that—but we had Jerry Gribble's word later that you died in his arms. Collapsing is one thing, dying is quite another. There must be limits to what an actress can achieve. Jerry was no fool. I can't believe that he was taken in by this performance of yours. And what of the hospital? They know a corpse when they see one."

She said with an air of contempt, "We didn't go near the hospital. You're perfectly right about Jerry. He wasn't taken in. So far as he was concerned, we were playing a very artful practical joke on the rest of you."

"A joke?"

"You must understand that I had planned this for months. I first met Jerry at a cricket match."

"I know."

"Yes, but it wasn't a chance meeting. I contrived it. I set out to win his affections, which was all too easy."

"If I may say so, you're extremely single-minded."

She let out a short, audible breath. "He didn't inflame me with passion, I assure you. I yielded to him simply to get myself invited to Desborough Hall. Before we arrived I persuaded Jerry to conspire with me in the practical joke I mentioned. He knew how much you enjoyed a good hoax. The idea was that I would pretend to collapse at dinner on that first evening. Jerry would take me off supposedly to the doctor. Later he would return and say that I had died in his arms."

"Strange sort of joke," I commented.

"Yes, but the next night I would start my haunting. I would come back as a ghost. Don't you remember the talk of ghosts that first evening? We would have no end of fun scaring the living daylights out of all of you—or so Jerry believed. Of course I had no intention of dressing up as a ghost, but I gather that Jerry succeeded in convincing you that I was dead. I arranged to meet him the next morning at one of the stands where you were due to shoot later on. He told me proudly that everyone was taken in. I resisted the temptation to say that the joke was on him. I simply shot him and put the gun in his hand."

"And left a piece of newspaper in his pocket."

"Yes."

"Why?"

"Why did I shoot him? I've explained. He was one of that group who allowed my brother to die."

"I meant why the piece of paper?"

"Ah. The verse. It was something I thought of at an early stage to embroider the plan. I once heard somebody address Jerry as "Your Grace" and that inspired the idea. It happened that Wilfred Osgot-Edge had initials that fitted the line for Wednesday, so I arranged to kill him on Wednesday. It wasn't difficult to fit in the others."

"You were taking a risk by leaving clues."

"Not much of a risk. If anything, it was a diversion from my real motive. Anyone could cut out words from the *Times*. That gave nothing away. I did it to mystify you all, and you in particular, Your Royal Highness."

"Me?"

"It's well known that you relish a challenge, whether it's racing your yacht or shooting with the best guns in Europe."

"Granted."

"You've never been known to walk away. I was confident that you would see out the week in hopes of outwitting me. And if you were willing to remain at the house, so would my victims."

I said, "I hope you're not implicating me in this plot."

She ignored me and asked, "What time is it?"

I felt for my watch and incidentally became aware of the disgraceful state my clothes were in. "Just after two o'clock."

"I can't remain much longer. I've told you what drove me to do these things."

"What do you propose to do now?"

"I shall dispose of you first—"

"What?"

"Lock you up whilst I make my escape. There's a room at the top of the tower that I have used from time to time this week. No doubt someone will find you there before the day is out."

"You don't intend to injure me?"

She said as if such a treasonous thought had never crossed her mind, "Why should I wish to do you any harm? My brother's death isn't on your conscience, is it?"

"Emphatically not," I said, then sensed that I ought to add something. "And I deplore the way he was treated. My dear lady, I can assure you, if I had been one of the party—"

She raised the shotgun a fraction. "Let us go upstairs, then."

"Is that all you're proposing to tell me?"

"On your feet, please. I'll tell you about the others as we go. I want you to open the door behind me and walk down the aisle to the main door. Just to the left of it you'll see the steps."

I obeyed, hoping fervently that there wasn't anyone left in the chapel. When there's a gun at your back you don't want unexpected things to happen. The place appeared to be deserted, thank the Lord. I started down the aisle with Queenie Chimes in close attendance. "Am I right in supposing that you masqueraded as a servant?" I asked.

"Yes. I'm well accustomed to acting the role of housemaid. I could come and go as I pleased. Very few of the servants knew each other. I meant to kill Mr. Osgot-Edge in his bedroom, but an opportunity came earlier, when you all played Sardines."

"How did you know that Osgot-Edge was to be the hider?"

"I was one of the maids who served the punch."

"And nobody recognized you?"

"Of course not. Nobody gives a servant a second look. I was in apron and cap and that was disguise enough. When the game started and the lights were out, I pursued Mr. Osgot-Edge and stabbed him with a kitchen knife." The dreadful statement defiled our surroundings, although she had spoken it in a voice as commonplace as if she were reading the liturgy.

I asked about Bullivant's murder.

She said, "That was simple. I wrote him a note supposedly from Miss Dundas suggesting a dawn assignation at the well. He was so dumbfounded when he saw me that he quite failed to notice the poker I had concealed behind my back."

"You attacked a man of his strength with a poker?"

"He had no opportunity to use his strength. I said, 'Look behind you!' He turned his head and I swung the poker. He fell without a sound. Then I heaved him into the well."

"*Thursday's corpse has far to go.*"

I stopped. We had reached the spiral stairs that led up the tower. "And Amelia—Lady Drummond? You posed as a servant to enter her dressing room and attack her?"

"Yes, that was more dangerous than I anticipated. Move on, Your Royal Highness. Up the stairs, and not too quickly. I had been led to believe by the servants that Lady Drummond took chloral and would be lethargic, to say the least. I intended to use the poker again. It had proved so effective against Mr. Bullivant. However, she was out of bed when I entered the room and she put up no end of a fight. I don't believe she was drugged. Finally I struck her with the poker and tipped her over the balcony."

"Why did you kill her? Surely she wasn't one of the guns?"

"Neither was the Chaplain, but I killed him. They condoned it, you see. They conspired with the others to cover up what they had done. And surely a woman with a spark of compassion would have gone to visit the wounded boy."

"Yet you characterized her as loving and giving."

"She was, where men were concerned. Didn't you know?"

Her remark was so far beneath contempt that I declined to answer it. Instead I said, "So Saturday's corpse was the Chaplain. How inconvenient that he didn't fit the epithet by being a wage-earning man."

She had an answer to that. "As a clergyman he had a benefice, or a living, as it is commonly known. I don't know how hard he worked, but he did it for a living."

We had reached the top of the stairs. Ahead was a door. I hesitated. "And is the killing complete? What of the corpse who was killed on the Sabbath day?"

She said, "After all, you are not quite so perceptive as I supposed. Didn't you take note of the date on the gravestone? My brother was shot on Saturday and died on Sunday. He was the one who died on the Sabbath Day. *Bonny and blithe and good and gay.* Every word was true of Robert. Yes, it's all over now."

But it was not.

23

I stood facing the door. "Do you wish me to open it?"

"If you please." Her tone as she fairly barked out the words belied the suggestion that I had any choice in the matter.

As I reached for the handle I told her, "You must make allowances—I'm not accustomed to opening doors." This was true, but I *am* conversant with the principle of turning a door handle. I made the remark—in a carrying voice—to announce our presence, and my predicament. It was not impossible that someone was listening nearby. "It's jammed, I think," I added.

"It can't be."

"You didn't lock it, perhaps?"

"No."

"You are welcome to try it yourself," I offered. "The handle turns, but the door is stuck fast. Do you wish to try?"

"Put your shoulder to it."

"Not with a shotgun against my back. If you stand clear, I'll do the best I can."

"Very well." The pressure in the small of my back eased. She said, "I won't hesitate to shoot if necessary."

I told myself that if a certain party *had* overheard us, at least he could be trusted not to put my life at risk. Heroics weren't in order here. I stepped up to the door and made a show of resting my shoulder against it while glancing back at Miss Chimes. She had the twelve-bore trained on me. She had backed against the curve of the wall two steps from the top and she was totally in shadow except for a pale menacing glint from her eyes.

You will have gathered that the door was not jammed at all. I offered up a short, silent prayer and pushed it open.

The speed of what happened next is impossible to convey. In one sense it was instantaneous and in another terrifyingly slow. The door swung inwards. The room was unoccupied. I stepped inside and to the right in an endeavor to put the wall between me and the shotgun. Then my blood ran cold as shots were fired. How many, I could not say, for the echoes in that small space hammered at my eardrums. I flung myself to the floor and covered my face. Bits of shot, stone and plaster spattered about the room.

If anything, the silence that followed was harder to endure than the shooting. I lay hunched and trembling, a trapped beast awaiting the *coup de grâce*.

I heard no footsteps approach, yet they did. My shoulder was gripped. I opened an eye and saw two feet a short distance from my face. Large feet, wearing black socks. The voice of Inspector Sweeney asked, "Are you hurt, sir?"

I opened the other eye.

"It's impossible to say. I am numb, completely numb." I pushed myself up to a kneeling position. "Is she . . . ?"

"Two shots through the heart, sir." He proudly held out his hand. A revolver lay across it.

"You weren't in the room?"

"No, sir, I was on the stairs below her. I took off my boots and followed you up, staying just out of sight around the curve of the stairs. As you stepped into the room, I crept into a firing position and pulled the trigger twice."

"I suppose I had better congratulate you."

"Bodyguarding is my job, sir."

"You have made the point several times this week, Sweeney. There's no need to harp on it."

"I beg your pardon, sir."

I got to my feet and brushed myself down. "Was it unavoidable to shoot the lady?"

"She was pointing a shotgun at you, sir, and after what she did to the Father . . ."

"Whose father was that?"

"The priest."

"Oh, the Chaplain. Ghastly. Did you actually see him shot?"

"Yes, sir. I was too far off to do anything about it. I was guarding you, as my duty requires."

"I didn't notice you."

"I try not to be too obvious about it, sir."

I frowned. "If you were guarding me, Sweeney, how was it that you allowed me to be taken prisoner?"

He ran his tongue guiltily along his upper lip. "I lost sight of you after the Father was shot, sir."

"I was facedown in the bracken." I paused as a possibility occurred to me. "A short while afterwards I spotted a figure by the lych-gate. Was that you?"

"Yes, sir—making a search for you."

"You put the fear of death into me. So it was you I ran away from, blast it, straight into the vestry where Queenie Chimes was lying in wait. A fine bodyguard you are!"

Presently we made our way downstairs, and not without difficulty, for we had to step over Miss Chimes's body. She still had the shotgun cradled in her arms. She had squeezed the trigger at the moment she was hit, and the pellets of shot were everywhere, making Sweeney wince as he stepped on them with his stockinged feet. He collected his boots and we returned on foot to the house.

I left Desborough Hall within the hour and I have not returned since. There was time only to inform young Pelham what had happened and to make my farewells to Isabella Dundas and Sir George Holdfast. Sir George decently agreed to remain behind and impress upon the police the need for discretion. As I informed you more than once in these pages, he was a stalwart. He was also a personal friend of the Chief Constable of Buckinghamshire.

24

When the inquests into the deaths of the Reverend Humphrey Paget and Victoria Bell, also known as Queenie Chimes, were held, a letter that Miss Chimes had penned to Mr. Henry Irving was read out. It had been found in a pocket of her riding jacket and it made clear her intention to resign from the Lyceum company. It went on to state that she intended to justify her actions to the press before surrendering herself to the law, and that she was sorry for any unwanted publicity that might come the way of Irving and her friends at the Lyceum. From that, I gather that if she had not been shot she would have made her way to some newspaper office to give them what would have been a sensational story, unthinkably damaging in its consequences. As it transpired, the inquest found that Queenie murdered the Chaplain and was herself shot by some person unknown. On instructions from the Chief Constable of Buckinghamshire, no more inquiries were made into the matter.

Upon my return to Sandringham, I found Alix in a strange mood. I had rather relished giving her an account of my investigation, but she disappointed me by professing some sympathy for the murderess. Admittedly, Queenie Chimes had a genuine grievance against her victims, but her revenge was out of all proportion to the original offense. I said as much to Alix and cautioned her not to permit her heart to rule her head.

She said, "Well, I can only hope that the whole sorry episode has been instructive for you, Bertie."

"Instructive—certainly," said I.

"Will you now admit that you ought not to have interfered?"

"*Interfered.* Alix, my dear, if you remember, I was sent an invitation."

"Which you accepted with alacrity."

"It was a perfectly proper invitation to a shoot. I wasn't to know that it would result in wholesale carnage—not of the human sort, anyway. What am I to do—cut myself off from society in case of a repetition? If you have your way, I shall end up like Mama, a fusty old recluse."

"I think the Queen is not so cut off from the world as you suppose."

"She's blinkered."

"Not necessarily, Bertie."

I heard a warning note. "What has happened?"

"A message arrived from Windsor this morning. The Queen commands you to visit her urgently." She sat back in her chair and paused before mildly asking, with maddening irony, "What do you deduce from that, my dear?"